IN ROSEWOOD, FANTASIES about reversing fate are as common as girls receiving Tiffany heart pendants for their thirteenth birthdays. And four former best friends would do anything to travel back in time and make things right. But what if they really could go back? Would they be able to keep their fifth best friend alive . . . or is her tragedy part of their destiny?

Sometimes the past holds more questions than answers. And in Rosewood, nothing is *ever* what it seems.

UNBELIEVABLE

PRETTY LITTLE LIARS

Sara Shepard

HARPER TEEN
An Imprint of HarperCollins Publishers

HarperTeen is an imprint of HarperCollins Publishers.

Unbelievable
Copyright © 2008 by Alloy Entertainment and Sara Shepard
All rights reserved. Printed in the United States of America. No part
of this book may be used or reproduced in any manner whatsoever
without written permission except in the case of brief quotations
embodied in critical articles and reviews. For information address
HarperCollins Children's Books, a division of HarperCollins
Publishers, 195 Broadway, New York, NY 10007.
www.epicreads.com

Library of Congress Cataloging-in-Publication Data
Shepard, Sara, 1977–
  Unbelievable : a pretty little liars novel / [by Sara Shepard]. – 1st ed.
    p. cm.
  "Produced by Alloy Entertainment"—Copyright p.
  Summary: Four girls living in a wealthy suburb discover the identity of a
stalker who has been sending them shocking text messages, and uncover the
mystery of who killed their childhood friend.
  ISBN 978-0-06-314462-0
  [1. Friendship–Fiction. 2. Mystery and detective stories.] I. Title.
PZ7.S54324Un 2008   2008010288
[Fic]–dc22   CIP
            AC
                    Typography by Amy Trombat
        22 23 24 25 26   PC/LSCH   10 9 8 7 6 5 4 3 2 1
                            ❖
                Revised paperback edition, 2022

To Lanie, Les, Josh, and Sara

No one can wear a mask for very long.

—LUCIUS ANNAEUS SENECA

UNBELIEVABLE

HOW TO SAVE A LIFE

Ever wish you could go back in time and undo your mistakes? If only you hadn't drawn that clown face on the doll your best friend got for her eighth birthday, she wouldn't have dropped you for the new girl from Boston. And back in ninth grade, you would never have skipped soccer practice to hit the beach if you'd known Coach would bench you for the rest of the season. If only you hadn't made those bad choices, maybe your ex-BFF would have given you that extra front-row ticket to Marc Jacobs's fashion show. Or maybe you'd be playing goalie for the women's national soccer team by now, with a Nike modeling contract and a beach house in Nice. You could be jet-setting around the Mediterranean instead of sitting in geography class, trying to find it on a map.

In Rosewood, fantasies about reversing fate are as common as girls receiving Tiffany heart pendants for their thirteenth birthdays. And four former best friends would do anything to travel back in time and make things right. But what if they really could go back? Would they be able to keep their fifth best friend alive . . . or is her tragedy part of their destiny?

Sometimes the past holds more questions than answers. And in Rosewood, nothing is *ever* what it seems.

"She's going to be so psyched when I tell her," Spencer Hastings said to her best friends Hanna Marin, Emily Fields, and Aria Montgomery. She straightened her sea-green eyelet T-shirt and pressed Alison DiLaurentis's doorbell.

"Why do *you* get to tell her?" Hanna asked as she hopped from the porch step to the sidewalk and back again. Ever since Alison, their fifth best friend, had told Hanna that only fidgety girls stayed thin, Hanna had been making a lot of extra movements.

"Maybe we should all tell her at the same time," Aria suggested, scratching the temporary dragonfly tattoo she'd pasted on her collarbone.

"That would be fun." Emily pushed her blunt-cut, reddish-blond hair behind her ears. "We could do a choreographed dance and say, 'Ta-da!' at the end."

"No way." Spencer squared her shoulders. "It's my barn—*I* get to tell her." She rang the DiLaurentises' door-bell again.

As they waited, the girls listened to the buzz of the landscapers pruning Spencer's hedges next door and the *thwock-thwock* of the Fairfield twins playing tennis on their backyard court two houses down. The air smelled like lilacs, mown grass, and Neutrogena sunscreen. It was a typical idyllic Rosewood moment—everything about the town was pretty, and that included its sounds, smells, *and* inhabitants. The girls had lived in Rosewood nearly all their lives, and they felt lucky to be part of such a special place.

They loved Rosewood summers best of all. Tomorrow morning, after they completed their last seventh-grade final at Rosewood Day, the school they all attended, they would take part in the school's annual graduation-pin ceremony. One by one Principal Appleton would call each student's name, from kindergarten through eleventh grade, and each student would receive a twenty-four-karat gold pin. After that, they would be released for ten glorious weeks of tanning, cookouts, boating trips, and shopping excursions to Philly and New York. They couldn't *wait*.

But the graduation ceremony wasn't the true rite of passage for Ali, Aria, Spencer, Emily, and Hanna. Summer wouldn't really start for them until tomorrow night, at their end-of-seventh-grade slumber party. And the girls had a surprise for Ali that was going to make this summer's kickoff extra special.

When the DiLaurentises' front door was finally flung open, Mrs. DiLaurentis stood before them, wearing a short pale pink wrap dress that showed off her long, muscular, tanned calves. "Hello, girls," she said coolly.

"Is Ali here?" Spencer asked.

"She's upstairs, I think." Mrs. DiLaurentis stepped out of the way. "Go on up."

Spencer led the group through the hall, her white pleated field hockey skirt swinging, her dirty-blond braid bouncing against the middle of her back. The girls loved Ali's house—it smelled like vanilla and fabric softener, just like Ali. Lush photographs of past DiLaurentis trips to Paris, Lisbon, and Lake Como lined the walls. There were plenty of photos of Ali and her brother, Jason, from grade school on. The girls especially loved Ali's second-grade school picture. Ali's vibrant pink cardigan made her whole face glow. Back then, Ali's family had lived in Connecticut, and Ali's old private school hadn't required her to wear stuffy blue blazers for yearbook pictures like Rosewood Day did. Even as an eight-year-old, Ali was irresistibly cute—she had clear blue eyes, a heart-shaped face, adorable dimples, and a naughty-yet-charming expression, which made it impossible to stay mad at her.

Spencer touched the bottom-right corner of their favorite photo, the one of the five of them camping in the Poconos the previous July. They were all standing next to a giant canoe, drenched in murky lake water, grinning from ear to ear, as happy as five twelve-year-old best friends could be. Aria put her hand on top of Spencer's, Emily put her hand on top of Aria's, and Hanna piled her hand on last. They closed their eyes for a split second, hummed, and broke away. The girls had started the photo-touching habit when the picture first went up, a memento of their first summer of best-friendship. They couldn't believe that Ali, *the* girl of Rosewood Day, had chosen the four of them as her inner circle. It was a little like being joined at the hip with an A-list celebrity.

But admitting that would be . . . well, lame. Especially now.

As they passed the living room, they noticed two graduation robes hanging on the knob of a French door. The white one was Ali's, and the more official-looking navy one was Jason's, who would be going on to Yale in the fall. The girls clasped their hands, excited to put on their own graduation gowns and berets, which Rosewood Day graduates had worn ever since the school had opened in 1897. Just then, they noticed a movement in the living room. Jason was sitting in the leather love seat, staring blankly at CNN.

"Heeyyy, Jason," Spencer called, waving. "Are you *so* psyched for tomorrow?"

Jason glanced at them. He was the hot boy version of Ali, with buttery blond hair and stunning blue eyes. He smirked and went back to the TV without saying a word.

"Oh-kaay," the girls all murmured in unison. Jason had his hilarious side—he was the one who had invented the "not it" game with his friends. The girls had borrowed and reinvented the game for their own uses, which mostly meant making fun of nerdier girls in their presence. But Jason definitely got into funks, too. Ali called them his Elliott Smith moods, after the morose singer-songwriter he liked. Only, Jason certainly didn't have any reason to be upset now—by this time tomorrow, he'd be on a plane to Costa Rica to teach adventure kayaking all summer. Boo-hoo.

"Whatever." Aria shrugged. The four girls turned and bounced up the stairs to Ali's room. As they reached the landing, they noticed that Ali's door was closed. Spencer frowned. Emily cocked her head. Inside the room, Ali let out a giggle.

Hanna gently pushed the door open. Ali had her back to them. Her hair was up in a high ponytail, and she'd tied her striped silk halter top in a perfect bow at her neck. She stared down at the open notebook in her lap, completely entranced.

Spencer cleared her throat, and Ali whirled around, startled. "Guys, hi!" she cried. "What's up?"

"Not much." Hanna pointed at the notebook in Ali's lap. "What's that?"

Ali closed the notebook fast. "Oh. Nothing."

The girls felt a presence behind them. Mrs. DiLaurentis pushed past, waltzing into Ali's bedroom. "We need to talk," she said to Ali, her voice clipped and taut.

"But, Mom . . ." Ali protested.

"*Now.*"

The girls glanced at one another. That was Mrs.

DiLaurentis's you're-in-trouble voice. They didn't hear it often.

Ali's mother faced the girls. "Why don't you girls wait on the deck?"

"It'll just take a second," Ali said quickly, shooting them an apologetic smile. "I'll be right down."

Hanna paused, confused. Spencer squinted, trying to see which notebook Ali was holding. Mrs. DiLaurentis raised an eyebrow. "C'mon, girls. Go."

The four of them swallowed hard and filed back down the stairs. Once on Ali's wraparound porch, they arranged themselves in their usual places around the family's enormous square patio table—Spencer at one end, and Aria, Emily, and Hanna at the sides. Ali would sit at the table's head, next to her father's deck-mounted stone birdbath. For a moment, the four girls watched as a couple of cardinals frolicked in the bath's cold, clear water. When a blue jay tried to join them, the cardinals squawked and quickly sent him away. Birds, it seemed, were just as cliquey as girls.

"That was weird upstairs," Aria whispered.

"Do you think Ali's in trouble?" Hanna whispered. "What if she's grounded and can't come to the sleepover?"

"Why would she be in trouble? She hasn't done anything wrong," whispered Emily, who always stuck up for Ali—the girls called her Killer, as in Ali's personal guard dog.

"Not that *we* know of," Spencer muttered under her breath.

Just then, Mrs. DiLaurentis burst out of the French patio doors and across the lawn. "I want to make sure you have the dimensions right," she screamed to the workers who were perched lazily on an enormous bulldozer at the back of the property. The DiLaurentises were building a twenty-person gazebo for summer parties, and Ali had mentioned that her mom was being very type A about the whole process, even though they were only at the hole-digging stage. Mrs. DiLaurentis marched up to the workers and started chastising them. Her diamond wedding ring glinted in the sun as she waved her arms around frenetically. The girls exchanged glances—it looked like Ali's lecture hadn't taken very long.

"Guys?"

Ali stood at the edge of the porch. She had changed out of her halter into a faded navy blue Abercrombie tee. There was a baffled look on her face. "Uh . . . hi?"

Spencer stood up. "What did she bust you for?"

Ali blinked. Her eyes darted back and forth.

"Were you getting in trouble *without* us?" Aria cried, trying to make it sound like she was teasing. "And why'd you change? That halter you had on was so cute."

Ali still looked flustered . . . and kind of upset. Emily stood up halfway. "Do you want us to . . . go?" Her voice dripped with uncertainty. All the others looked at Ali nervously—was *that* what she wanted?

Ali twisted her blue string bracelet around her wrist three full rotations. She stepped onto the patio and sat down in her rightful seat. "Of course I don't want you to go. My mom was mad at me because I . . . I threw my hockey clothes in with her delicates again." She gave them a sheepish shrug and rolled her eyes.

Emily stuck out her bottom lip. A small beat went by. "She got mad at you for *that*?"

Ali raised her eyebrows. "You know my mom, Em. She's more anal than Spencer." She snickered.

Spencer faux-glared at Ali while Emily ran her thumb along one of the grooves in the teak patio table.

"But don't worry, girls, I'm not grounded or anything." Ali pressed her palms together. "Our sleepover extravaganza can proceed as planned!"

The four of them sighed with relief, and the odd, uneasy mood began to evaporate. Only, each of them had a weird feeling Ali wasn't telling them everything—it certainly wouldn't be the first time. One minute, Ali would be their best friend, and the next, she'd drift away from them, making covert phone calls and sending secret texts. Weren't they supposed to share everything? The other girls had certainly shared enough of themselves— they'd slipped secrets to Ali that no one, absolutely *no one* else, knew. And, of course, there was the big secret that they all shared about Jenna Cavanaugh—the one they'd sworn to take to the grave.

"Speaking of our sleepover extravaganza, I have huge

news," Spencer said, breaking them out of their thoughts. "Guess where we're having it?"

"Where?" Ali leaned forward on her elbows, slowly morphing back into her old self.

"Melissa's barn!" Spencer cried. Melissa was Spencer's older sister, and Mr. and Mrs. Hastings had renovated the family's backyard barn and allowed Melissa to use it as her own personal pied-à-terre during her junior and senior years of high school. Spencer would get the same privilege, once she was old enough.

"Sweet!" Ali whooped. "How?"

"She's flying out to Prague tomorrow night after graduation," Spencer answered. "My parents said we could use it, so long as we clean it up before she gets back."

"Nice." Ali leaned back and laced her hands together. Suddenly, her eyes focused on something a bit to the left of the workers. Melissa herself was traipsing through the Hastingses' bordering yard, her posture rigid and proper. Her white graduation gown swung from a hanger in her hand, and she'd slung the school's royal blue valedictorian mantle over her shoulders.

Spencer let out a groan. "She's being so obnoxious about the whole valedictorian thing," she whispered. "She even told me I should feel grateful that Andrew Campbell will probably be valedictorian instead of me when we're all seniors—the honor is '*such* a huge responsibility.'" Spencer and her sister hated each other, and

Spencer had a new story about Melissa's bitchiness nearly every day.

Ali stood up. "Hey! Melissa!" She started waving.

Melissa stopped and turned around. "Oh. Hey, guys." She smiled cautiously.

"Excited to go to Prague?" Ali singsonged, giving Melissa her brightest smile.

Melissa tilted her head slightly. "Of course."

"Is *Ian* going?" Ian was Melissa's gorgeous boyfriend. Just thinking about him made the girls swoon.

Spencer dug her nails into Ali's arm. *"Ali."* But Ali pulled her arm away.

Melissa shaded her eyes in the harsh sunlight. The royal blue mantle flapped in the wind. "No. He's not."

"Oh!" Ali simpered. "Are you sure that's a good idea—leaving him alone for two weeks? He might get another girlfriend!"

"Alison," Spencer said through her teeth. "Stop it. *Now.*"

"Spencer?" Emily whispered. "What's going on?"

"Nothing," Spencer said quickly. Aria, Emily, and Hanna looked at one another again. This had been happening lately—Ali would say something, one of them would freak, and the rest of them would have no clue what was going on.

But this clearly wasn't nothing. Melissa straightened the mantle around her neck, squared her shoulders, and turned. She looked long and hard at the giant hole at the edge of the DiLaurentises' yard, then walked into the barn, slamming the door behind her so hard that it made the twig-braided wreath on the back of the door thump up and down.

"Something's certainly up *her* butt," Ali said. "I was just kidding, after all." Spencer made a little whimpering noise at the back of her throat, and Ali started giggling. She had a faint smile on her face. It was the same smile Ali gave them whenever she dangled a secret over one of their heads, taunting that she could tell the others if she wanted to.

"Anyway, who cares?" Ali gazed at each of them, her eyes bright. "You know what, girls?" She drummed her fingers excitedly on the table. "I think this is going to be the Summer of Ali. The Summer of *All* of Us. I can just feel it. Can't you?"

A stunned moment passed. It seemed like a humid cloud hung above them, fogging up their thoughts. But slowly, the clouds faded and an idea formed in each of their minds. Maybe Ali was right. This *could* be the best summer of their lives. They could turn their friendship around and make it as strong as it had been last summer. They could forget all the scary, scandalous things that had happened and just start over.

"I can feel it, too," Hanna said loudly.

"Definitely," Aria and Emily said at the same time.

"Sure," Spencer said softly.

They all grabbed hands and squeezed hard.

✦ ✦ ✦

It rained that night, a hard, pounding rain that made puddles in driveways, watered gardens, and created little mini pools on top of the Hastingses' swimming pool cover. When the rain stopped in the middle of the night, Aria, Emily, Spencer, and Hanna awakened and sat up in bed at almost the exact same moment. A foreboding feeling had settled over each of them. They didn't know if it was from something they'd just dreamed about, or excitement about the next day. Or maybe it was due to something else entirely . . . something far deeper.

They each looked out their windows onto Rosewood's tranquil, empty streets. The clouds had shifted and all the stars had come out. The pavement shone from the rain. Hanna stared at her driveway—only her mother's car was there now. Her father had moved out. Emily looked at her backyard and the forest beyond it. She'd never braved those woods—she'd heard ghosts lived in them. Aria listened to the sounds emanating from her parents' bedroom, wondering if they'd woken up, too—or perhaps they were fighting again and hadn't fallen asleep yet. Spencer gazed at the DiLaurentises' back porch, then across their yard to the huge hole the workers had dug for the gazebo's foundation. The rain had turned some of the dug-up dirt to mud. Spencer thought about all the things in her life that made her angry. Then she thought about all the things in her life she wanted to have—and all the things she wanted to change.

Spencer reached under her bed, found her red flash-light, and shone it into Ali's window. One flash, two flashes, three flashes. This was her secret code to Ali that she wanted to sneak out and talk in person. She thought she saw Ali's blond head sitting up in bed, too, but Ali didn't flash back.

All four of them fell back onto their pillows, telling themselves that the feeling was nothing and they needed their sleep. In twenty-four short hours, they'd be at the end of their seventh-grade sleepover, the first night of summer. The summer that would change everything.

How right they were.

1

THE ZEN IS MIGHTIER
THAN THE SWORD

Aria Montgomery woke up mid-snore. It was Sunday morning, and she was curled up on a blue vinyl chair in the Rosewood Memorial Hospital waiting room. Everyone—Hanna Marin's parents, Officer Wilden, Hanna's best friend Mona Vanderwaal, and Lucas Beattie, a boy in her class at Rosewood Day who looked like he'd just arrived—was staring at her.

"Did I miss something?" Aria croaked. Her head felt like it was stuffed with marshmallow Peeps. When she checked the Zoloft clock hanging over the waiting room entrance, she saw it was only eight thirty. She'd been out for just fifteen minutes.

Lucas sat down next to her and picked up a copy of *Medical Supplies Today* magazine. According to the cover, the issue featured all the latest colostomy bag models. Who puts a medical supplies magazine in a hospital *waiting room*? "I just got here," he answered. "I heard about the accident on the morning news. Have you seen Hanna yet?"

Aria shook her head. "They still won't let us."

The two of them fell gravely silent. Aria surveyed the others. Ms. Marin wore a rumpled gray cashmere sweater and a pair of great-fitting distressed jeans. She was barking into her AirPods, even though the nurses had said they couldn't use cell phones in here. Officer Wilden sat next to her, his Rosewood PD jacket unbuttoned to his mid-chest and showing a frayed white T-shirt beneath it. Hanna's father was slumped in the chair closest to the intensive care unit's two giant double doors, jiggling his left foot. In a pale pink Juicy sweat suit and flip-flops, Mona Vanderwaal looked uncharacteristically disheveled, her face puffy from crying. When Mona looked up and saw Lucas, she gave him an annoyed stare, as if to say, *This is for close friends and family only. What are you doing here?* Aria couldn't blame everyone for feeling testy. She had been here since 3 a.m., after the ambulance came to the Rosewood Day Elementary School parking lot and swept Hanna off to the hospital. Mona and the others had arrived at various points in the morning, when the news had begun to circulate. The last update the doctors had given them was that Hanna had been moved to intensive care. But that was three hours ago.

Aria reviewed the previous night's horrific details. Hanna had called to tell her that she knew the identity of A, the diabolical messenger who had been taunting

Hanna, Aria, Emily, and Spencer for the past month. Hanna hadn't wanted to reveal any details over the phone, so she'd asked Aria and Emily to meet her at the Rosewood Day swings, their old special spot. Emily and Aria had arrived just in time to see a black SUV mow Hanna down and speed away. As the paramedics rushed to the scene, put a cervical collar around Hanna's neck, and carefully lifted her onto a stretcher and into the ambulance, Aria had felt numb. When she pinched herself hard, it didn't hurt.

Hanna was still alive . . . but barely. She had internal injuries, a broken arm, and bruises everywhere. The accident had caused head trauma, and now she was in a coma.

Aria shut her eyes, ready to burst into tears again. The most inconceivable thing about all of this was the text Aria and Emily had received after Hanna's accident. *She knew too much*. It was from A. Which meant . . . A *knew* what Hanna knew. Just like A knew everything else—all their secrets, the fact that it had been Ali, Aria, Spencer, Emily, and Hanna who'd blinded Jenna Cavanaugh, not Jenna's stepbrother, Toby. A probably even knew the truth about who killed Ali.

Lucas tapped Aria on the arm. "You were there when that car hit Hanna, right? Did you get a look at the person who did it?"

Aria didn't know Lucas very well. He was one of those kids who *loved* school activities and clubs, whereas Aria was the type to stay far, far away from all things involving her Rosewood Day peers. She didn't know what connection he had to Hanna, but it seemed sweet that he was here. "It was too dark," she mumbled.

"And you have no idea who it could have been?"

Aria bit down hard on her bottom lip. Wilden and a couple other Rosewood cops had shown up the night before just after the girls received their note from A. When Wilden asked the girls what happened, they all insisted that they hadn't seen the driver's face or the make of the SUV. And they swore over and over that this must have been an accident—they didn't know why anyone would do this on purpose. Maybe it was wrong to withhold this information from the police, but they were all terrified of what A had in store for the rest of them if they told the truth.

A had threatened them about not telling before, and Aria and Emily both had been punished once already for ignoring those threats. A had sent Aria's mother, Ella, a letter telling her that Aria's father was having an affair with one of his university students, and revealed that Aria had kept her dad's secret. Then A had told the entire school that Emily was dating Maya, the girl who had moved into Ali's old house. Aria glanced at Lucas and silently shook her head no.

The door to the ICU swept open, and Dr. Geist strode into the waiting room. With his piercing gray eyes, sloped nose, and shock of white hair, he looked a little like Helmut, the German landlord of the old row house

Aria's family had rented in Reykjavík, Iceland. Dr. Geist gave everyone the same judging stare Helmut had given Aria's brother, Mike, when he discovered that Mike had been keeping Diddy, his pet tarantula, in an empty terra-cotta pot Helmut used to grow tulips.

Hanna's parents nervously stood up and walked over to the doctor.

"Your daughter is still unconscious," Dr. Geist said quietly. "Not much has changed. We've set her broken arm and are checking the extent of her internal injuries."

"When can we see her?" Mr. Marin asked.

"Soon," Dr. Geist said. "But she's still in very critical condition."

He turned to go, but Mr. Marin caught his arm. "When will she wake up?"

Dr. Geist fiddled with his clipboard. "She has a lot of swelling in her brain, so it's hard for us to predict the extent of the damage at this point. She might wake up just fine, or there might be complications."

"Complications?" Ms. Marin went pale.

"I've heard that people who are in comas have less of a chance of recovering from them after a certain amount of time," Mr. Marin said nervously. "Is that true?"

Dr. Geist rubbed his hands on his blue scrubs. "That is true, yes, but let's not get ahead of ourselves, okay?"

A murmur went through the room. Mona burst into tears again. Aria wished she could call Emily . . . but Emily was on a plane to Des Moines, Iowa, for reasons she hadn't explained—only that A had done something to send her there. Then there was Spencer. Before Hanna had called with her news, Aria had pieced together something terrifying about Spencer . . . and when Aria had seen her cowering in the woods, twitching like a feral animal just after the SUV hit Hanna, it had only confirmed her worst fears.

Ms. Marin picked up her oversize brown leather tote from the floor, breaking Aria out of her thoughts. "I'm going to go get some coffee," Hanna's mom said softly to her ex-husband. Then, she gave Officer Wilden a kiss on the cheek—before tonight Aria hadn't known there was something going on between them—and disappeared toward the elevator bank.

Officer Wilden slumped back down in his chair. The week before, Wilden had visited Aria, Hanna, and the others, asking them questions about the details surrounding Ali's disappearance and death. In the middle of that interview, A had sent each of them a note saying that if they *dared* tattle about the notes A had been sending them, they'd be sorry. But just because Aria couldn't tell Wilden what A had potentially done to Hanna, that didn't mean she couldn't share the horrible thing she'd realized about Spencer.

Can I talk to you? she mouthed to Wilden across the room. Wilden nodded and stood. They walked out of the waiting room and into a little alcove marked VEND-ING. Inside were six glowing vending machines, offering a range from sodas to full-on meals, unidentifiable sand-wiches, and shepherd's pie, which reminded Aria of the glop her father, Byron, used to make for dinner when her mother, Ella, was working late.

"So listen, if this is about your teacher friend, we let him go." Wilden sat down on the bench next to the microwave and gave Aria a coy little smile. "We couldn't hold him. And just so you know, we've kept it quiet. We won't punish him unless you want to press charges. But I should probably tell your parents."

The blood drained from Aria's face. Of course Wilden knew about what had happened the night before with her and Ezra Fitz, the love of her life *and* her AP English teacher. It was probably the talk of the Rosewood Police Department that a twenty-two-year-old English teacher had been canoodling with a minor—and that it was the minor's *boyfriend* who'd ratted them out. They'd proba-bly gossiped about it at the Hooters that was next to the police station, among Buffalo wings and cheese fries and girls with big boobs.

"I don't want to press charges," Aria sputtered. "And please, *please* don't tell my parents." The last thing she needed was some sort of big, dysfunctional family dis-cussion.

Aria shifted her weight. "But anyway, that's not why I want to talk to you. I . . . I think I might know who killed Alison."

Wilden raised an eyebrow. "I'm listening."

Aria took a deep breath. "First off, Ali was seeing Ian Thomas."

"Ian Thomas," Wilden repeated, his eyes widening. "Melissa Hastings's boyfriend?"

Aria nodded. "I noticed something in the video that was leaked to the press last week. If you watch it closely, you can see Ian and Ali touching hands." She cleared her throat. "Spencer Hastings had a crush on Ian, too. Ali and Spencer were competitive, and they got into this awful fight the night Ali disappeared. Spencer ran out of the barn after Ali, and she didn't come back for at least ten minutes."

Wilden looked incredulous.

Aria took a deep breath. A had sent Aria various clues about Ali's killer—that it was someone close by, someone who wanted something Ali had, and someone who knew every inch of Ali's backyard. With those clues in place, and once Aria had realized Ian and Ali were together, Spencer was the logical suspect. "After a while, I went outside to look for them," she said. "They weren't anywhere . . . and I just have this horrible feeling that Spencer . . ."

Wilden sat back. "Spencer and Alison weighed about the same, right?"

Aria nodded. "Sure. I guess."

"Could *you* drag someone your size over to a hole and push her in?"

"I–I don't know," Aria stammered. "Maybe? If I was mad enough?"

Wilden shook his head. Aria's eyes filled with tears. She recalled how eerily silent it had been that night. Ali had been just a few hundred yards away from them, and they hadn't heard a sound.

"Spencer also would've had to calm down enough so she didn't seem suspicious when she returned to you guys," Wilden added. "It takes a pretty damn good actor to pull that off–not a seventh-grade girl. I think who-ever did this was obviously nearby, but the whole thing took more time." He raised his eyebrows. "Is this what you Rosewood Day girls do these days? Blame your old friends for murder?"

Aria's mouth dropped open, surprised at Wilden's scolding tone. "It's just–"

"Spencer Hastings is a competitive, high-strung girl, but she doesn't strike me as a killer," Wilden interrupted. Then, he smiled at Aria sadly. "I get it. This must be tough for you–you just want to figure out what happened to your friend. I didn't know that Alison was secretly with Melissa Hastings's boyfriend, though. *That's* interesting."

Wilden gave Aria a terse nod, stood up, and turned back to the hallway. Aria remained by the vending machines, her eyes on the mint-green linoleum floor. She felt overheated and disoriented, as if she'd spent too much time in a sauna. Maybe she should be ashamed of herself, blaming an old best friend. And the holes Wilden had poked in her theory made a lot of sense. Maybe she'd been foolish to trust A's clues at all.

A chill went up Aria's spine. Perhaps A had sent Aria those clues to deliberately throw her off track—and take the heat off the true murderer. And maybe, just maybe, the true murderer was . . . *A*.

Aria was lost in her thoughts when suddenly she felt a hand on her shoulder. She flinched and turned, her heart racing. Standing behind her, wearing a ratty Hollis College sweatshirt and a pair of jeans with a hole through the left front pocket, was Aria's father, Byron. She crossed her arms over her chest, feeling awkward. She hadn't really spoken to her father in a few weeks.

"Jesus, Aria. Are you all right?" Byron blurted out. "I saw you on the news."

"I'm okay," Aria said stiffly. "It was Hanna who was hurt, not me."

As her father pulled her in for a hug, Aria wasn't sure whether to squeeze him tight or let her arms go limp. She'd missed him since he'd moved out of their house a month ago. But Aria was also furious that it had taken a life-threatening accident and a TV appearance to motivate Byron to leave Meredith's side and reach out to his own daughter.

"I called your mother this morning, asking how you were, but she said you weren't living there anymore." Byron's voice quivered with concern. He ran his hand over the top of his head, mussing up his hair even more. "Where *are* you living?"

Aria stared blearily at the brightly printed Heimlich maneuver poster tucked behind the Coke machine. Someone had drawn a pair of boobs on the choking victim's chest, and it looked like the person giving the Heimlich was feeling her up. Aria had been staying at her boyfriend Sean Ackard's house, but Sean had made it clear she wasn't welcome there anymore when he'd ordered a raid on Ezra's apartment and dumped Aria's crap on Ezra's doorstep. Who had tipped Sean off about Aria's affair with Ezra? *Ding ding ding!* A.

She hadn't given a new living situation much thought. "The Olde Hollis Inn?" Aria suggested.

"The Olde Hollis Inn has rats. Why don't you stay with me?"

Aria vigorously shook her head. "You're living with—"

"Meredith," Byron stated firmly. "I want you to get to know her."

"But . . ." Aria protested. Her father, however, was giving her his classic Buddhist monk look. Aria knew the look well—she'd seen it after he'd refused to let Aria go to an arty summer camp in the Berkshires instead of Hollis Happy Hooray day camp for the fourth summer in a row, which meant ten long weeks of making paper-bag puppets and competing in the egg-and-spoon race. Byron had donned the look again when Aria asked if she could finish school at the American Academy in Reykjavík instead of coming back to Rosewood with the rest of the family. The look was often followed by a saying Byron had learned from a monk he'd met during his graduate work in Japan: *The obstacle is the path*. Meaning what wouldn't kill Aria would just make her stronger.

But when she imagined moving in with Meredith, a more appropriate quote came to mind: *There are some remedies worse than the disease*.

2

ABRACADABRA, NOW WE LOVE EACH OTHER AGAIN

Ali sank onto one hip and glared at Spencer Hastings, who stood across from her on the back path that led from the Hastingses' barn to the woods. "You try to steal everything from me," she hissed. "But you can't have this."

Spencer shivered in the cold evening air. "Can't have what?"

"*You* know," Ali said. "You read it in my diary." She pushed her honey-blond hair over her shoulder. "You think you're so special, but you're so lame, acting like you didn't know Ian was with me. Of course you knew, Spence. That's why you liked him in the first place, isn't it? Because *I'm* with him? Because your sister's with him?"

Spencer's eyes boggled. The night air turned sharp, almost acrid-smelling. Ali stuck out her bottom lip. "Oh, Spence. Did you really believe he *liked* you?"

Suddenly, Spencer felt a burst of anger, and her

arms shot out in front of her, pushing Ali in the chest. Ali teetered backward, stumbling against the slippery rocks. Only, it wasn't Ali anymore—it was Hanna Marin. Hanna's body flew up in the air, and she hit the ground with a sharp crack. Instead of all her makeup and iPhone bursting out of her purse as from a smashed-open piñata, Hanna's internal organs spewed out of her body, raining down on the concrete like hail.

Spencer shot up, her blond hair damp with sweat. It was Sunday morning, and she was lying in her bed, still in the black satin dress and uncomfortable thong under-wear she'd meant to wear to Mona Vanderwaal's birthday party the night before. Soft gold light slanted across her desk, and starlings chirped innocently in the giant oak next to her window. She'd been awake nearly all night, waiting for her phone to ring with news about Hanna. But no one had called. Spencer had no idea if the silence was good . . . or terrible.

Hanna. She'd called Spencer late last night, just after Spencer had recalled her long-suppressed memory of shoving Ali in the woods the night Ali disappeared. Hanna had told Spencer she'd found out something important, and that they had to meet at the Rosewood Day swings. Spencer had pulled up to the parking lot just as Hanna's body flew into the air. She'd maneuvered her car to the side of the road, then run out on foot into the trees, shocked by what she saw. "Call an ambulance!" Aria was shrieking. Emily was sobbing with fear. Hanna remained immobile. Spencer had never witnessed any-thing so terrifying in her entire life.

Seconds later, Spencer's phone had pinged with a text from A. Still shrouded in the woods, Spencer saw Emily and Aria pull out their phones as well, and her stomach flipped as she realized they must have all received the same creepy message: *She knew too much.* Had A fig-ured out whatever it was that Hanna had discovered—something that A must have been trying to hide—and hit Hanna to shut her up? That had to be it, but it was hard for Spencer to truly believe it had actually happened. It was just so diabolical.

But maybe *Spencer* was just as diabolical. Just hours before Hanna's accident, she'd shoved her sister, Melissa, down the stairs. And she'd finally remembered what had happened the night Ali went missing, recovered those lost ten minutes she'd suppressed for so long. She'd pushed Ali to the ground—maybe even hard enough to kill her. Spencer didn't know what had happened next, but it seemed like A did. A had sent Spencer a text only a couple days ago, hinting that Ali's murderer was right in front of her. Spencer had received the text just as she was looking in the mirror . . . at *herself.*

Spencer hadn't run into the parking lot to join her friends. Instead, she'd sped home, in desperate need to think all this through. *Could* she have killed Ali? Did she have it in her? But after an entire sleepless night, she just couldn't compare what she had done to Melissa and Ali to what A had done to Hanna. Yes, Spencer lost her temper, yes, Spencer could be pushed to the limit, but deep down, she just didn't think she could kill.

Why, then, was A so convinced Spencer was the culprit? Was it possible A was wrong . . . or lying? But A knew about Spencer's seventh-grade kiss with Ian Thomas, her illicit affair with Wren, Melissa's college boyfriend, and that the five of them had blinded Jenna Cavanaugh—all things that were true. A had so much ammo on them, it was hardly necessary to start making stuff up.

Suddenly, as Spencer wiped the sweat off her face, something hit her, sending her heart sinking to her feet. She could think of a very good reason why A might have lied and suggested that Spencer killed Ali. Perhaps A had secrets, too. Perhaps A needed a scapegoat.

"Spencer?" Her mother's voice floated up. "Can you come downstairs?"

Spencer jumped and peeked at her reflection in her vanity mirror. Her eyes looked puffy and bloodshot, her lips were chapped, and her hair had leaves stuck in it from hiding in the woods last night. She couldn't handle a family meeting right now.

The first floor smelled of fresh-brewed Nicaraguan Segovia coffee, Fresh Fields Danishes, and the fresh-cut calla lilies their housekeeper, Candace, bought every morning. Spencer's father stood at the granite-topped island, decked out in his black spandex bike pants and US Postal Service bike jersey. Perhaps that was a good sign—they couldn't be too angry if her dad had gone for his regular 5 a.m. bike ride.

On the kitchen table was a copy of the Sunday *Philadelphia Sentinel.* At first Spencer thought it was there because it had news of Hanna's accident. But then she saw her own face staring back at her from the paper's front page. She wore a sleek black suit and was giving the camera a confident smirk. *Future Chairwoman of the Board!* the headline said. *Golden Orchid Essay Contest Nominee Spencer Hastings Is Coming!*

Spencer's stomach heaved. She'd forgotten. The paper was on everyone's doorsteps right now.

A figure emerged from the pantry. Spencer stepped back in fear. There was Melissa, glaring at her, clutching a box of Raisin Bran so tightly Spencer thought she might crush it. There was a tiny scratch on her sister's left cheek, a Band-Aid over her right eyebrow, a yellow hospital bracelet still around her left wrist, and a pink cast on her right wrist, clearly a souvenir of yesterday's fight with Spencer.

Spencer lowered her eyes, feeling a whole mess of guilty feelings. Yesterday, A had sent Melissa the first few sentences of her old AP Economics paper, the very one Spencer had pilfered from Melissa's computer hard drive and disguised as her own AP Economics homework. The same essay Spencer's econ teacher, Mr. McAdam, had nominated for a Golden Orchid essay award, the most prestigious high school–level award in the country.

Melissa had figured out what Spencer had done, and although Spencer had begged for forgiveness, Melissa had said horrible things to her—things way worse than Spencer thought she deserved. The fight had ended when Spencer, enraged by Melissa's words, had accidentally shoved her sister down the stairs.

"So, girls." Mrs. Hastings set her coffee cup on the table and gestured for Melissa to sit. "Your father and I have made some big decisions."

Spencer braced for what was coming. They were going to turn Spencer in for plagiarizing. She wouldn't get into college. She'd have to go to trade school. She'd end up working as a telemarketer at QVC, taking orders for ab rollers and fake diamonds, and Melissa would get off scot-free, just like she always did. Somehow, her sister always found a way to come out on top.

"First off, we don't want you girls to see Dr. Evans anymore." Mrs. Hastings laced her fingers together. "She's done more harm than good. Understood?"

Melissa nodded silently, but Spencer scrunched up her nose in confusion. Dr. Evans, Spencer and Melissa's shrink, was one of the few people who didn't try to kiss Melissa's ass. Spencer began to protest but noticed the warning looks on both her parents' faces. "Okay," she mumbled, feeling a bit hopeless.

"Second of all." Mr. Hastings tapped the *Sentinel,* squashing his thumb over Spencer's face. "Plagiarizing Melissa's paper was very wrong, Spencer."

"I know," Spencer said quickly, terrified to look anywhere in Melissa's direction.

"But after some careful thought, we've decided that we don't want to go public with it. This family's been through too much already. So, Spencer, you'll continue to compete for the Golden Orchid. We will tell no one about this."

"*What?*" Melissa slammed her coffee cup down on the table.

"That's what we've decided," Mrs. Hastings said tightly, dabbing the corner of her mouth with a napkin. "And we also expect Spencer to win."

"To win?" Spencer repeated, shocked.

"You're *rewarding* her?" Melissa shrieked.

"*Enough.*" Mr. Hastings used the tone of voice he typically reserved for underlings at his law practice when they dared call him at home.

"Third thing," Mrs. Hastings said. "You girls are going to bond."

Her mother pulled two snapshots out of her cardigan pocket. The first was of Spencer and Melissa at four and nine years old, respectively, lying on a hammock at their grandmother's beach house in Stone Harbor, New Jersey. The second photo was of them in the same beach house's playroom, a few years later. Melissa wore a magician's hat and cape, and Spencer had on her Tommy Hilfiger stars-and-stripes ruffled bikini. On her feet were the black motorcycle boots she'd worn until they'd gotten so small that they cut off all the circulation to her toes. The sisters were performing a magic show for their parents; Melissa was the magician, and Spencer was her lovely assistant.

"I found these this morning." Mrs. Hastings passed the photos to Melissa, who glanced at them quickly and passed them back. "Remember how you girls used to be such good friends? You were always babbling in the back-seat of the car. You never wanted to go anywhere without each other."

"That was ten years ago, Mom," Melissa said wearily.

Mrs. Hastings stared at the photo of Spencer and Melissa on the hammock. "You used to love Nana's beach house. You used to be *friends* at Nana's beach house. So we've decided to take a trip to Stone Harbor today. Nana isn't there, but we have keys. So pack up your things."

Spencer's parents were nodding feverishly, their faces hopeful.

"That's just stupid," Spencer and Melissa said together. Spencer glanced at her sister, astounded they'd thought the same thing.

Mrs. Hastings left the photo on the counter and carried her mug to the sink. "We're doing it, and that's final."

Melissa rose from the table, holding her wrist at an awkward angle. She glanced at Spencer, and for a moment, her eyes softened. Spencer gave her a tiny smile. Perhaps they'd connected just then, finding common ground in hating their parents' naïve plan. Perhaps

Melissa could forgive Spencer for shoving her down the stairs and stealing her paper. If she did, Spencer would forgive Melissa for saying their parents didn't love her.

Spencer looked down at the photo and thought of the magic shows she and Melissa used to perform. After their friendship had splintered, Spencer had thought that if she muttered some of her and Melissa's old magic words, they'd be best friends again. If only it were that easy.

When she looked up again, Melissa's expression had shifted. She narrowed her eyes and turned away. "Bitch," she said over her shoulder as she sashayed down the hall.

Spencer curled her hands into fists, all of her anger gushing back in. It would take a whole lot more than magic for them to get along. It would take a miracle.

3

EMILY'S OWN AMERICAN GOTHIC

Late Sunday afternoon, Emily Fields followed an old lady with a walker onto the moving sidewalk of the Des Moines International Airport, dragging her ratty blue swim duffel behind her. The bag was stuffed with all her worldly goods—her clothes, shoes, her two favorite stuffed walruses, her journal, her phone, and various carefully folded notes from Alison DiLaurentis that she couldn't bear to part with. When the plane was over Chicago, she realized she'd forgotten underwear. But then, that was what she got for packing frantically this morning. She'd only gotten three hours of sleep, shell-shocked from seeing Hanna's body fly up into the air when that SUV hit her.

Emily arrived in the main terminal and ducked into the first bathroom she could find, squeezing around a very large woman in too-tight jeans. She stared at her bleary-eyed reflection in the mirror over the sink. Her parents had really done it. They'd really sent her here, to Addams, Iowa, to live with her aunt Helene and her uncle Allen. It was all because A had outed Emily to the entire school, and all because Emily's mother had caught her hugging Maya St. Germain, the girl she loved, at Mona Vanderwaal's party last night. Emily had known the deal—she'd promised to do the "gay-away" Tree Tops program to rid herself of her feelings for Maya or it was goodbye, Rosewood. But when she discovered that even her Tree Tops counselor, Becka, couldn't resist her true urges, all bets were off.

The Des Moines airport was small, boasting only a couple of restaurants, a bookshop, and a store that sold colorful Vera Bradley bags. When Emily reached the baggage claim area, she looked around uncertainly. All she remembered about her aunt and uncle was their super-strictness. They avoided anything that might trigger sexual impulses—even certain *foods*. As she scanned the crowd, Emily half-expected to see the stern, long-faced farmer and his plain, bitter wife from the *American Gothic* painting standing near the baggage carousel.

"Emily."

She whirled around. Helene and Allen Weaver were leaning against a Smarte Carte machine, their hands clasped at their waists. Allen's tucked-in mustard-yellow golf shirt prominently displayed his massive gut. Helene's short gray hair looked shellacked. Neither was smiling.

"Did you check any luggage?" Allen asked gruffly.

"Uh, no," Emily said politely, wondering if she should go in for a hug. Weren't aunts and uncles usually happy to see their nieces? Allen and Helene just looked annoyed.

"Well, then, let's go," Helene said. "It's about two hours to Addams."

Their car was an old, wood-paneled station wagon. The inside smelled like fake pine-tree air freshener, a smell that always made Emily think of long, cross-country drives with her grumpy grandparents. Allen drove at least fifteen miles under the speed limit—even a frail old woman squinting over her steering wheel passed them. Neither her aunt nor her uncle said a word the whole drive—not to Emily, and not to each other. It was so quiet, Emily could hear the sound of her heart breaking into seven million tiny pieces.

"Iowa sure is pretty," Emily commented loudly, gesturing to the endless flat land all around her. She'd never seen a place so desolate—there weren't even any rest stops. Allen made a small grunt. Helene pursed her lips even tighter. If she'd pursed any harder, she'd have swallowed her lips altogether.

Emily's cell phone, cool and smooth in her jacket pocket, felt like one of the last bridges to civilization. She brought it out and stared at the screen. No new messages, not even from Maya. She'd sent Aria a text before she left, asking how Hanna was doing, but Aria hadn't responded. The newest text in her inbox was the one A had sent last night—*She knew too much*. Had A really hit Hanna? And what about the things Aria had told her before Hanna's accident—could Spencer be Ali's killer? Tears dotted Emily's eyes. This was definitely the wrong time to be so far from Rosewood.

Suddenly, Allen took a sharp right off the road, veering onto a bumpy dirt path. The car wobbled over the uneven ground, crossing over several cattle guards and passing a few rickety-looking houses. Dogs ran up and down the length of the path, barking viciously at the vehicle. Finally, they pulled onto yet another dirt road and came to a gate. Helene got out and unlocked it, and Allen drove the car through. A two-story, white-shingled house loomed ahead. It was spare and modest, sort of reminiscent of the Amish houses in Lancaster, Pennsylvania, that Emily and her parents used to stop at to buy authentic shoofly pie.

"Here we are," Helene said blandly.

"It's beautiful," Emily said, trying to sound upbeat as she got out of the car.

Like the other houses they'd passed, the Weavers' property was surrounded by a chain-link fence, and there were dogs, chickens, ducks, and goats everywhere. One brave goat attached to the cattle guard by a long chain trotted right up to Emily. He butted her with his dirty-looking horns, and she screamed.

Helene looked at her sternly as the goat waddled away. "Don't scream like that. The chickens don't like it."

Perfect. The chickens' needs took precedence to Emily's. She pointed to the goat. "Why is he chained like that?"

"She," Helene corrected her. "She's been a bad girl, that's why."

Emily bit her lip nervously as Helene led her into a tiny kitchen that looked like it hadn't been updated since the fifties. Emily immediately missed her mom's cheery kitchen, with its chicken collectibles, year-round Christmas towels, and refrigerator magnets shaped like Philadelphia monuments. Helene's fridge was bare and magnet-free and smelled like rotting vegetables. When they walked into a small living room, Helene pointed to a girl about Emily's age sitting on a vomit-colored chair and reading *Jane Eyre.* "You remember Abby?"

Emily's cousin Abby wore a pale khaki jumper that came to her knees and a demure eyelet blouse. She'd pulled her hair back at the nape of her neck, and she wore no makeup. In her tight LOVE AN ANIMAL, HUG A SWIMMER tee, ripped Abercrombie jeans, tinted moisturizer, and cherry-flavored lip gloss, Emily felt like a whore.

"Hello, Emily," Abby said primly.

"Abby was nice enough to offer to share her room with you," Helene said. "It's just up the stairs. We'll show you."

There were four bedrooms upstairs. The first was Helene and Allen's, and the second was for John and Matt, the seventeen-year-old twins. "And that one's for Sarah, Elizabeth, and baby Karen," Helene said, gesturing to a room that Emily had mistaken for a broom closet.

Emily gaped. She hadn't heard of any of those cousins. "How old are they?"

"Well, Karen's six months, Sarah is two, and Elizabeth is four. They're at their grandmother's right now."

Emily tried to hide a smile. For people who shunned sex, they certainly had a lot of offspring.

Helene led Emily into an almost-empty room and pointed to a twin cot in the corner. Abby settled down on her own bed, folding her hands in her lap. Emily couldn't believe the room had been lived in—the only furniture was the two beds, a plain dresser, a small round rug, and a bookshelf with hardly any books on it. At home, her room was plastered with posters and pictures; her desk was strewn with perfume bottles, cutouts from magazines, and books. Then again, the last time Emily was here, Abby had told her she was planning to become a nun, so perhaps no-frills living was part of her nunnish training. Emily glanced out the big picture window at the end of the room and saw the Weavers' enormous field, which included a large stable and a silo. Her two older boy cousins, John and Matt, were lugging bales of hay out of the stable and onto the bed of a pickup truck. There was nothing on the horizon. At all.

"So, how far away is your school?" Emily asked Abby.

Abby's face lit up. "My mom didn't tell you? We're homeschooled."

"Ohh . . ." Emily's will to live slowly seeped out the

sweat glands in her feet.

"I'll give you the class schedule tomorrow." Helene plunked a few grayish towels onto Emily's bed. "You'll have to take some exams to see where I place you."

"I'm a junior in high school," Emily offered. "I'm in some AP classes."

"We'll see where I place you." Helene gave her a hard look.

Abby got up from her bed and disappeared into the hall. Emily gazed desperately out the window. *If a bird flies by in the next five seconds, I'll be back to Rosewood by next week.* Just as a delicate sparrow fluttered past, Emily remembered she wasn't playing her little superstitious games anymore. The events of the last few months—the workers finding Ali's body in the gazebo hole, Toby's suicide, A's . . . everything—had made her lose all faith in things happening for a reason.

Her cell phone chimed. Emily pulled it out and saw that Maya had sent her a text. Are you really in Iowa? Pls call me when you can.

Help me, Emily began to type, when Helene snatched the phone from her hands.

"We don't allow cell phones in this house." Helene switched the phone off.

"But . . ." Emily protested. "What if I want to call my parents?"

"I can do that for you," Helene sang. She came close to

Emily's face. "Your mother has told me a few things about you. I don't know how they do things in Rosewood, but around here, we live by my rules. Is that clear?"

Emily flinched. Helene spat when she spoke, and Emily's cheek felt moist. "It's clear," she said shakily.

"Good." Helene walked out into the hallway and dropped the phone into a large, empty jar on a wooden end table. "We'll just put this here for safekeeping." Someone had printed the words SWEAR JAR on the lid, but the jar was completely empty except for Emily's phone.

Emily's phone looked lonely in the swear jar, but she didn't dare unscrew the lid—Helene probably had it wired with an alarm. She walked back into the empty bedroom and threw herself onto the cot. There was a sharp bar in the middle of the mattress, and the pillow felt like a slab of cement. As the Iowa sky turned from russet to purple to midnight blue to black, Emily felt hot tears stream down her face. If this was the first day of the rest of her life, she'd much rather be dead.

The door opened a few hours later with a slow *creeeeaaak*. A shadow lengthened across the floor. Emily sat up on her cot, her heart pounding. She thought of A's note. *She knew too much.* And of Hanna's body, crashing down to the pavement.

But it was only Abby. She snapped on a small bedside table lamp and dropped down on her stomach next to her bed. Emily bit the inside of her cheek and pretended not to notice. Was this some freaky Iowan form of praying?

Abby sat up again, a jumble of fabric in her hands. She pulled her khaki jumper over her head, unhooked her beige bra, stepped into a denim miniskirt, and wriggled into a red tube top. Then she reached under her bed again, located a pink-and-white makeup bag, and brushed mascara over her lashes and red gloss on her lips. Finally, she pulled her hair out of its ponytail, turned her head upside down, and ran her hands through her scalp. When she flipped back up, her hair was wild and thick around her face.

Abby met Emily's eyes. She grinned broadly, as if to say, *Close your mouth. You're letting flies in.* "You're coming with us, right?"

"Wh-Where?" Emily sputtered, once she found her voice.

"You'll see." Abby walked over to Emily and took her hand. "Emily Fields, your first night in Iowa has just begun."

4

IF YOU BELIEVE IT,
THEN IT'S TRUE

When Hanna Marin opened her eyes, she was alone in a long, white tunnel. Behind her, there was only darkness, and ahead of her, only light. Physically, she felt fantastic—not bloated from eating too many white cheddar Cheez-Its, not dry-skinned and frizzy-haired, not groggy from lack of sleep or stressed from social maneuvering. In fact, she wasn't sure when she'd last felt this . . . perfect.

This didn't feel like an ordinary dream, but something way more important. Suddenly, a pixel of light flitted in front of her eyes. And then another, and another. Her surroundings eased into view like a photo slowly loading on a web page.

She found herself sitting with her three best friends on Alison DiLaurentis's back porch. Spencer's dirty-blond hair was in a high ponytail, and Aria wore her wavy, blue-black mane in braids. Emily wore an aqua-colored T-shirt and boxers with ROSEWOOD

SWIMMING written across the butt. A feeling of dread swept over Hanna, and when she looked at her reflection in the window, her seventh-grade self stared back. Her braces had green and pink rubber bands. Her poop-brown hair was twisted into a bun. Her arms looked like ham hocks and her legs were pale, flabby loaves of bread. So much for feeling wonderful.

"Uh, guys?"

Hanna turned. Ali was *here*. Right in front of her, staring at them as if they'd sprouted out of the ground. As Ali came closer, Hanna could smell her minty gum and Ralph Lauren Blue perfume. There were Ali's purple Puma flip-flops—Hanna had forgotten about them. And there were Ali's feet—she could cross her crooked second toe over her big toe, and said it was good luck. Hanna wished Ali would cross her toes right now, and do all of the other uniquely Ali things Hanna wanted so desperately to remember.

Spencer stood up. "What did she bust you for?"

"Were you getting in trouble without us?" Aria cried. "And why'd you change? That halter you had on was so cute."

"Do you want us to go?" Emily asked fearfully.

Hanna remembered this exact day. She still had some of the notes from her seventh-grade history final scribbled on the heel of her hand. She reached into her Manhattan Portage canvas messenger bag, feeling the edge of her white cotton Rosewood Day graduation beret. She had picked it up in the gym during lunch period, in preparation for tomorrow's graduation ceremony.

Graduation wasn't the only thing that would happen tomorrow, though.

"Ali," Hanna said, standing up so abruptly that she knocked over one of the patio table's citronella candles. "I need to talk to you."

But Ali ignored her, almost as if Hanna hadn't spoken at all. "I threw my hockey clothes in with my mom's delicates again," she said to the others.

"She got mad at you for *that*?" Emily looked incredulous.

"*Ali.*" Hanna waved her hands in front of Ali's face. "You have to listen to me. Something awful is going to happen to you. And we have to stop it!"

Ali's eyes flickered over to Hanna. She shrugged and shook her hair out of its polka-dotted headband. She looked at Emily again. "You know my mom, Em. She's more anal than Spencer!"

"Who cares about your mom?" Hanna shrieked. Her skin felt hot and tingly, like a zillion bees had stung her.

"Guess where we're having our end-of-seventh-grade sleepover tomorrow night?" Spencer was saying.

"Where?" Ali leaned forward on her elbows.

"Melissa's barn!" Spencer cried.

"Sweet!" Ali whooped.

"No!" Hanna cried. She climbed onto the middle of the table, to make them see her. How did they *not* see her? She was as fat as a manatee. "Guys, we *can't*. We have to have our sleepover somewhere else. Somewhere where there are people. Where it's safe."

Her mind started churning. Perhaps the universe had a kink in it, and she was really, truly back in seventh grade, right before Ali died, with knowledge of the future. She had the chance to change things. She could call the Rosewood PD and tell them she had a horrible feeling that something was going to happen to her best friend tomorrow. She could build a barbed-wire fence around the hole in the DiLaurentises' yard.

"Maybe we shouldn't have a sleepover at all," Hanna said frantically. "Maybe we should do it another night."

Finally, Ali grabbed Hanna's wrists and dragged her off the table. "Stop it," she whispered. "You're making a big deal over nothing."

"A big deal over *nothing*?" Hanna protested. "Ali, you're going to *die* tomorrow. You're going to run out of the barn during our sleepover and just . . . disappear."

"No, Hanna, listen. I'm not."

A clammy feeling washed over Hanna. Ali was staring right into her eyes. "You're . . . not?" she stammered.

Ali touched Hanna's hand. It was a comforting caress, the kind of gesture Hanna's father used to make when she was sick. "Don't worry," Ali said softly in Hanna's ear. "I'm okay."

Her voice sounded so close. So real. Hanna blinked and opened her eyes, but she wasn't in Ali's yard anymore. She was in a white room, flat on her back. Harsh fluorescent lights hung over her. She heard beeping somewhere to her left, and the steady hiss of a machine, in and out, in and out.

A blurry figure swam over her. The girl had a heart-shaped face, bright blue eyes, and brilliant white teeth. She slowly caressed Hanna's hand. Hanna struggled to focus. It looked like . . .

"I'm okay," Ali's voice said again, her breath hot against Hanna's cheek. Hanna gasped. Her fists opened and closed. She struggled to hold on to this moment, to this realization, but then everything faded out—all sound, all smells, the feeling of Ali's hand touching hers. Then there was only darkness.

5

THIS MEANS WAR

Late Sunday afternoon, after Aria left the hospital—Hanna's condition hadn't changed—she walked up the uneven porch steps of the Old Hollis house where Ezra lived. Ezra's bottom-floor apartment was just two blocks away from the house Byron now shared with Meredith, and Aria wasn't quite ready to go there yet. She didn't expect Ezra to be home, but she'd written him a letter, telling him where she'd be living, and that she hoped they could talk. As she struggled to fit the note through Ezra's mailbox slot, she heard a creak behind her.

"Aria." Ezra emerged in the foyer, wearing faded jeans and a tomato-colored Gap T-shirt. "What are you doing?"

"I was . . ." Aria's voice was taut with emotion. She held up the note, which had crumpled a little during her attempt to shove it in the mailbox. "I was going to give this to you. It just said to call me." She took a tentative step toward Ezra, afraid to touch him. He smelled exactly as he had last night, when Aria was last here—a little like Scotch, a little like moisturizer. "I didn't think you'd be here," Aria sputtered. "Are you okay?"

"Well, I didn't have to spend the night in jail, which was good." Ezra laughed, then frowned. "But . . . I'm fired. Your boyfriend told the school staff everything—he had pictures of us to prove it. Everyone would rather keep it quiet, so unless *you* press charges, it's not going to go on my record." He hooked his thumb around one of his belt loops. "I'm supposed to go there tomorrow and clean out my office. I guess you guys are going to have a new teacher for the rest of the year."

Aria pressed her hands to her face. "I am so, *so* sorry." She grabbed Ezra's hand. At first, Ezra resisted her touch, but he slowly sighed and gave in. He brought her close to him and kissed her hard, and Aria kissed back like she'd never kissed before. Ezra slid his arms under the clasp of her bra. Aria grabbed at his shirt, tearing it off. It didn't matter that they were outside or that a group of bong-smoking college kids were staring at them from the porch next door. Aria kissed Ezra's bare neck, and Ezra circled his arms around her waist.

But when they heard a police car siren *whoop*, they shot apart, startled.

Aria ducked behind the basket-weave porch wall. Ezra crouched beside her, his face flushed. Slowly, a police car rolled past Ezra's house. The cop was on his cell phone, not paying any attention to them.

When Aria turned back to Ezra, the sexy mood had fizzled. "Come on in," Ezra said, pulling his shirt back on and walking into his apartment. Aria followed him, stepping around his front door, which still hung off its hinges from when the cops had knocked it down yesterday. The apartment smelled as it usually did, like dust and Kraft macaroni and cheese.

"I could try and find you another job," Aria suggested. "Maybe my father needs an assistant. Or he could pull some strings at Hollis."

"Aria . . ." There was a surrendering look on Ezra's face. And then, Aria noticed the U-Haul boxes behind him. The bathtub that sat in the middle of the living room had been emptied of all its books. The blobby blue candles on the mantel were gone. And Bertha, the French maid blow-up doll some friends had bought for Ezra as a joke back in college, was no longer perched on one of the kitchen chairs. In fact, most of Ezra's personal artifacts were missing. Only a few lonely, junky pieces of furniture remained.

A cold, clammy feeling washed over her. "You're leaving."

"I have a cousin who lives in Providence," Ezra mumbled into his chest. "I'm going to go up there for a while. Clear my head. Take some pottery classes at Rhode Island School of Design. I don't know."

"Take me with you," Aria blurted out. She walked up to Ezra and pulled on the hem of his shirt. "I've always wanted to go to RISD. It's my first-choice school. Maybe I could apply early." She raised her eyes to Ezra again. "I'm moving in with my father and Meredith—which is pretty much a fate worse than death. And . . . and I've never felt like I do when I'm around you. I'm not sure I ever will again."

Ezra squeezed his eyes shut, swinging Aria's hands back and forth. "I think you should look me up in a couple years. Because, I mean, I feel that way about you, too. But I have to get out of here. You know it, and I know it."

Aria dropped his hands. She felt like someone had opened up her chest and removed her heart. Just last night, for a few hours, everything had been perfect. And then Sean—and A—had ripped it all apart again.

"Hey," Ezra said, noting the tears spilling down Aria's cheeks. He pulled her into him and held her tight. "It's okay." He peered into one of his boxes, then handed her his William Shakespeare bobblehead. "I want you to have this."

Aria gave him a tiny smile. "Seriously?" The first time she'd come here, after Noel Kahn's party back in the beginning of September, Ezra had told her the bobble-head was one of his favorite possessions.

Ezra traced the line of Aria's jaw with the tip of his

pointer finger, starting at her chin and ending at her earlobe. Shivers went up her spine. "Really," he whispered.

She could feel his eyes on her as she turned for the door. "Aria," he called, just as she was stepping over a big pile of old phone books to get out into the hall.

She stopped, her heart lifting. There was a wise, calm look on Ezra's face. "You're the strongest girl I've ever met," he said. "So just . . . screw 'em, you know? You'll be fine."

Ezra leaned down, sealing up boxes with clear packing tape. Aria backed out of the apartment in a daze, wondering why he'd suddenly turned all guidance counselor on her. It was like he was saying that he was the adult, with responsibilities and consequences, and she was just a kid, her whole life in front of her.

Which was *exactly* what she didn't want to hear right then.

"Aria! Welcome!" Meredith cried. She stood at the edge of the kitchen, wearing a black-and-white striped apron—which Aria was trying to imagine as a prison uniform—and a cow-shaped oven mitt covered her right hand. She was grinning like a shark about to swallow a minnow.

Aria dragged in the last of the bags Sean had dumped at her feet last night and looked around. She knew Meredith had quirky taste—she was an artist, and taught classes at Hollis College, the same place where Byron was tenured—but Meredith's living room looked like a psychopath had decorated it. There was a dentist's chair in the corner, complete with a tray for all the instruments of torture. Meredith had covered a whole wall with pictures of eyeballs. She branded messages into wood as a form of artistic expression, and there was a big wood chunk across the mantel that said, BEAUTY IS ONLY SKIN DEEP, BUT UGLY GOES CLEAN TO THE BONE. There was a large cutout of the Wicked Witch of the West pasted over the kitchen table. Aria was half tempted to point to it and say she hadn't known Meredith's mother was from Oz. Then she saw a raccoon in the corner and screamed.

"Don't worry, don't worry," Meredith said quickly. "He's stuffed. I bought him at a taxidermy store in Philly."

Aria wrinkled her nose. This place rivaled the Mütter Museum of medical oddities in Philadelphia, which Aria's brother loved almost as much as the sex museums he'd visited in Europe.

"Aria!" Byron appeared from behind a corner, wiping his hands on his jeans. Aria noted that he was wearing dark denim jeans *with a belt* and a soft gray sweater—maybe his usual uniform of a sweat-stained Sixers T-shirt and frayed plaid boxers wasn't good enough for Meredith. "Welcome!"

Aria grunted, hefting up her duffel again. When she

sniffed the air, it smelled like a combination of burnt wood and Cream of Wheat. She eyed the pot on the stove suspiciously. Perhaps Meredith was cooking gruel, like an evil headmistress in a Dickens novel.

"So let me show you your room." Byron grabbed Aria's hand. He led her down the hall to a large, square room that contained a few big chunks of wood, some branding irons, an enormous band saw, and welding tools. Aria assumed this was Meredith's studio—or the room where she finished off her victims.

"This way," Byron said. He led her to a space in the corner of the studio that was separated from the rest of the room by a floral curtain. When he pushed the curtain back, he crowed, "Taa-*daaa*!"

A twin bed and a dresser missing three of its drawers occupied a space only slightly larger than a shower stall. Byron had carried in her other suitcases earlier, but because there was no room on the floor, he'd piled them on the bed. There was one flat, yellowed pillow propped up against the headboard, and someone had balanced a tiny portable TV in the windowsill. There was a sticker on the top of it that said in old, faded, seventies lettering, SAVE A HORSE, RIDE A WELDER.

Aria turned to Byron, feeling nauseated. "I have to sleep in Meredith's studio?"

"She doesn't work at night," Byron said quickly. "And look! You have your own TV and your own fireplace!" He pointed to a huge brick monstrosity that took up most of the far wall. Most Old Hollis houses had fireplaces in every room because their central heating systems sucked. "You can make it cozy in here at night!"

"Dad, I have no idea how to *light* a fireplace." Then Aria noticed a trail of cockroaches going from one corner of the ceiling to another. "Jesus!" she screamed, pointing at them and cowering behind Byron.

"They're not real," Byron reassured her. "Meredith painted them. She's really personalized this place with an artistic touch."

Aria felt like she was going to hyperventilate. "They look real to me!"

Byron looked honestly surprised. "I thought you'd like this place. It was the best we could put together on such short notice."

Aria shut her eyes. She missed Ezra's shabby little apartment, with its bathtub and thousands of books and map of the New York City subway system shower curtain. There were no roaches there, either—real *or* fake.

"Honey?" Meredith's voice rang out from the kitchen. "Dinner's ready."

Byron gave Aria a tight smile and turned for the kitchen. Aria figured she should follow. In the kitchen, Meredith was setting bowls at each of their plates. Thankfully, dinner wasn't gruel, but innocent-looking chicken soup. "I thought this would be best for my stomach," she admitted.

"Meredith's been having some stomach issues," Byron explained. Aria turned to the window and smiled. Maybe she'd get lucky and Meredith would have somehow contracted the bubonic plague.

"It's low-salt." Meredith punched Byron in the arm. "So it's good for you, too."

Aria looked at her father curiously. Byron used to salt every single bite while it was on the fork. "Since when do you eat low-salt stuff?"

"I have high blood pressure," Byron said, pointing to his heart.

Aria wrinkled her nose. "No, you don't."

"Yes, I do." Byron tucked his napkin into his collar. "I have for a while now."

"But . . . but you've never eaten low-salt stuff before."

"I know, I'm no fun," Meredith insisted, scraping back a seat and sitting down. Meredith had positioned Aria at the head of the Wicked Witch cutout. Aria slid her bowl over to cover the witch's pea-green visage. "I keep him on a regimen," Meredith went on. "I make him take vitamins, too."

Aria slumped, dread welling in her stomach. Meredith was already acting like Byron's wife, and he'd only lived with her for a month.

Meredith pointed to Aria's hand. "Whatcha got there?"

Aria stared down at her lap, realizing she was still

holding the Shakespeare bobblehead Ezra had given her. "Oh. It's just . . . something from a friend."

"A friend who likes *literature*, I guess." Meredith reached out and made Shakespeare's head bob up and down. There was a tiny glint in her eye.

Aria froze. Could Meredith *know* about Ezra? She glanced at Byron. Her father slurped his soup, oblivious. He wasn't reading at the table, something he constantly did at home. Had Byron seriously been unhappy at home? Did he honestly enjoy bug-painting, taxidermy-loving Meredith more than he loved Aria's sweet, kind, loving mother, Ella? And what made Byron think Aria could just sit idly by and accept this?

"Oh, Meredith has a surprise for you," Byron piped up. "Every semester, she gets to take a class at Hollis for free. She says you can use this semester's credit to take a class instead."

"That's right." Meredith passed the Hollis College continuing education course book to Aria. "Maybe you'd like to take one of the art classes I'm teaching?"

Aria bit down hard on the inside of her cheek. She'd rather have shards of glass permanently lodged in her throat than spend a single additional moment with Meredith.

"Come on, pick a class," Byron urged. "You know you want to."

So they were forcing her to do this? Aria whipped

open the book. Maybe she could take something in German filmmaking, or microbiology, or Special Topics in Neglected Children and Maladjusted Family Behavior.

Then something caught her eye. *Mindless Art: Create uniquely crafted masterpieces in tune with your soul's needs, wants, and desires. Through sculpture and touch, students learn to depend less on their eyes and more on their inner selves.*

Aria circled the class with the gray ROCKS ROCK! Hollis geology department pencil she'd found wedged in the course book. The class definitely sounded kooky. It might even end up being like one of those Icelandic yoga classes where instead of stretching, Aria and the rest of the students danced with their eyes closed, making hawk noises. But she needed a little mindlessness right now. Plus, it was one of the few art classes that Meredith wasn't teaching. Which pretty much made it perfect.

Byron excused himself from the table and bounded off to Meredith's minuscule bathroom. After he turned on the bathroom's overhead fan, Meredith laid down her fork and looked squarely at Aria. "I know what you're thinking," she said evenly, rubbing her thumb along the pink spiderweb tattoo on her wrist. "You hate that your father's with me. But you'd better get used to it, Aria. Byron and I are going to be married as soon as your parents' divorce goes through."

Aria accidentally swallowed an unchewed bite of noodles. She coughed up the broth, sputtering it all over the table. Meredith jumped back, her eyes wide. "Something you ate not agreeing with you?" she simpered.

Aria looked away sharply, her throat burning. Something hadn't agreed with her, all right, but it wasn't the Wicked Witch's soup.

EMILY'S JUST A SWEET, INNOCENT MIDWESTERN GAL

"Come on!" Abby urged, pulling Emily across the farmyard. The sun was sinking over the flat Iowa horizon, and all sorts of long-legged midwestern bugs were coming out to play. Apparently, Emily, Abby, and Emily's two eldest boy cousins, Matt and John, were also going out to play.

The four of them stopped at the edge of the road. John and Matt had both changed out of their plain white T-shirts and work pants into baggy jeans and T-shirts with beer slogans. Abby pulled at the bodice of her tube top and checked her lipstick in her little compact mirror. Emily, in the same jeans and swimming T-shirt she'd worn when she arrived, felt plain and underdressed—which was pretty much how she always felt back in Rosewood.

Emily gazed over her shoulder at the farmhouse. All of its lights were off, but the dogs were still running crazily around the property, and the bad goat was still chained to the cattle guard, the bell around her neck clanging back and forth. It was a wonder Helene and Allen didn't put bells on their children. "Are you sure this is a good idea?" she wondered aloud.

"It's fine," Abby answered, her hoop earrings swinging. "Mom and Dad go to bed at eight p.m. like clockwork. That's what happens when you wake up at four."

"We've been doing this for months and haven't gotten caught once," Matt assured her.

Suddenly, a silver pickup truck appeared on the horizon, dust kicking up in its wake. The truck rolled slowly up to the four of them and stopped. A hip-hop song Emily couldn't place wafted out, along with the strong smell of menthol cigarettes. A dark-haired, Noel Kahn look-alike waved to the cousins, then smiled at Emily. "Soooo . . . this is your cousin, huh?"

"That's right," Abby said. "She's from Pennsylvania. Emily, this is Dyson."

"Get in." Dyson patted the seat. Abby and Emily climbed in the front, and John and Matt climbed into the pickup bed. As they rolled off, Emily glanced once more at the farmhouse receding in the distance, an uneasy feeling gnawing at her.

"So, what brings you to glamorous Addams?" Dyson clunkily shifted gears.

Emily glanced at Abby. "My parents sent me."

"They sent you away?"

"Totally," Abby interrupted. "I heard you're a real

badass, Emily." She looked at Dyson. "Emily lives on the edge."

Emily stifled a laugh. The only rebellious thing she'd ever done in front of Abby was sneak an extra Oreo for dessert. She wondered if her cousins knew the truth of why her parents had banished her here. Probably not—*lesbian* was most likely a swear-jar word.

Within minutes, they drove up an uneven path to a large, burnt-orange silo, and parked on the grass next to a car with a bumper sticker that read, I BRAKE FOR HOOTERS. Two pale boys rolled out of a red pickup and bumped fists with a couple beefy, towheaded boys climbing out of a black Dodge Ram. Emily smirked. She'd always thought using the word *corn-fed* to describe someone from Iowa was a cliché, but right now, it was the only description that came to mind.

Abby squeezed Emily's arm. "The ratio of guys to girls here is four to one," she whispered. "So you'll totally hook up tonight. I always do."

So Abby didn't know about Emily. "Oh. Great." Emily tried to smile. Abby winked and jumped out of the truck. Emily followed the others toward the silo. The air smelled like Jo Malone perfume; hoppy, soapy beer; and dried grass. When she walked inside, she expected to see bales of hay, a farm animal or two, and maybe a portal to another dimension, like in a sci-fi movie. Instead, the silo had been cleared out and Christmas lights hung from the ceiling. Plush, plum-colored couches lined the walls, and Emily saw a turntable in the corner and a bunch of enormous kegs near the back.

Abby, who'd already grabbed a beer, pulled a couple of guys toward Emily. Even in Rosewood, they would've been popular—they all had floppy hair, angular faces, and brilliant white teeth. "Brett, Todd, Xavi ... *this* is my cousin Emily. She's from Pennsylvania."

"Hi," Emily said, shaking the boys' hands.

"Pennsyl*va*nia." The boys nodded appreciatively, as if Abby had said Emily was from Naughty Dirty Sex Land.

As Abby wandered off with one of the boys, Emily made her way to the keg. She stood in line behind a blond couple who were grinding against each other. The DJ morphed into a hip-hop song that seemed to play in the background of every popular TikTok meme at the moment. Really, people in Iowa didn't seem that different from people at her school. The girls all wore short skirts and cute sneakers, and the guys wore oversize hoodies and ripped jeans, and seemed to be experimenting with facial hair. Emily wondered where all of them went to school, or if their parents homeschooled them as well.

"Are you the new girl?"

A tall, white-blond girl in a striped tunic and dark jeans stood behind her. She had the broad shoulders and powerful stance of a professional volleyball player, and four small earrings snaked up her left ear. But there was something very sweet and open about her round face, light blue eyes, and small, pretty lips. And unlike practically every other girl in the silo, she didn't have a guy's hands draped over her boobs. "Uh, yeah," Emily replied. "I just got here today."

"And you're from Pennsylvania, right?" The girl pivoted back on her hips and appraised Emily carefully. "I was there once. We went to Harvard Square."

"I think you mean Boston, in Massachusetts," Emily corrected her. "That's where Harvard is. Pennsylvania has Philadelphia. The Liberty Bell, Ben Franklin stuff, all that."

"Oh." The girl's face fell. "I haven't been to Pennsylvania, then." She lowered her chin at Emily. "So. If you were candy, what kind would you be?"

"Sorry?" Emily blinked.

"Come on." The girl poked her. "Me, I'd be an M&M."

"Why?" Emily asked.

The girl lowered her eyes seductively. "Because I melt in your mouth, obviously." She poked Emily. "So how about you?"

Emily shrugged. This was the strangest getting-to-know-you question anyone had ever asked her, but she kind of liked it. "I've never thought about it. A Tootsie Roll?"

The girl violently shook her head. "You wouldn't be a Tootsie Roll. That looks like a big long poop. You'd be something *way* sexier than that."

Emily breathed in very, very slowly. Was this girl *flirting* with her? "Um, I think I need to know your name before we talk about . . . sexy candy."

The girl stuck out her hand. "I'm Trista."

"Emily." As they shook, Trista spiraled her thumb around the inside of Emily's palm. She never took her eyes off Emily's face.

Maybe this was just some sort of cultural Iowan way of saying hello.

"Do you want a beer?" Emily sputtered, turning back for the keg.

"Absolutely," Trista said. "But let *me* pour it for you, Pennsylvania. You probably don't even know how to pump a keg." Emily watched as Trista pumped the keg handle a few times and let the beer filter slowly into her cup, producing almost no foam.

"Thanks," Emily answered, taking a sip.

Trista poured herself a beer and led Emily away from the line to one of the couches that lined the walls of the silo. "So, did your family just move here?"

"I'm staying with my cousins for a little while." Emily pointed to Abby, who was dancing with a tall blond boy, and to Matt and John, who were smoking cigarettes with a petite redhead wearing a skintight pink sweater and skinny jeans.

"You on a little vacation?" Trista asked, fluttering her eyelashes.

Emily couldn't be sure, but it seemed like Trista was moving closer and closer to her on the couch. She was doing everything in her power not to touch Trista's long legs, which were dangling inches from her own. "Not exactly," she blurted out. "My parents kicked me out of the house because I couldn't live by their rules."

Trista fiddled with the strap of her tan boots. "My mom's like that. She thinks I'm at a choir concert right now. Otherwise she never would've let me out."

"I used to have to lie to my parents about going to parties too," Emily said, suddenly afraid she was going to start crying again. She tried to imagine what was happening at her house right now. Her family had probably gathered around the TV after dinner. Just her mom, her dad, and Carolyn, happily chatting among themselves, *glad* that Emily, the heathen, was gone. It hurt so much it made her feel nauseated.

Trista glanced at Emily sympathetically, as if she sensed something was wrong. "So hey. Here's another one. If you were a party, what kind of party would you be?"

"A surprise party," Emily blurted out. That seemed like the story of her life lately—one big surprise after another.

"Good one." Trista smiled. "I'd be a toga party."

They smiled at each other for a long moment. There was something about Trista's heart-shaped face and wide, blue eyes that made Emily feel really . . . safe. Trista leaned forward, and so did Emily. It was almost like they were going to kiss, but then Trista bent down very slowly and fixed the strap on her shoe.

"So why'd they send you here, anyway?" Trista asked when she sat back up.

Emily took a huge swallow of beer. "Because they caught me kissing a girl," she blurted out.

When Trista leaned back, her eyes wide, Emily thought she'd made a horrible mistake. Perhaps Trista *was* just being midwestern friendly, and Emily had misinterpreted. But then, Trista broke into a coy smile. She moved her lips close to Emily's ear. "You *totally* wouldn't be a Tootsie Roll. If it were up to me, you'd be a red-hot candy heart."

Emily's heart did three somersaults. Trista stood up and offered Emily her hand. Emily took it, and without a word, Trista led her to the dance floor and started dancing sexily to the music. The song changed to a fast one, and Trista squealed and started to jump around as if she were on a trampoline. Her energy was intoxicating. Emily felt like she could be goofy with Trista—not constantly poised and cool, as she always felt she had to behave around Maya.

Maya. Emily stopped, breathing in the rank, humid silo air. Last night, she and Maya had said they loved each other. Were they still together, now that Emily was possibly permanently stuck here, amid all this corn and cow manure? Did this qualify as cheating? And what did it mean that Emily hadn't thought of her once tonight, until now?

Trista's cell phone beeped. She stepped out of the

circle of dancers and pulled it out of her pocket. "My stupid mom's texting me for like the gazillionth time tonight," she yelled over the music, shaking her head.

A shock vibrated through Emily—any minute now, she'd probably be getting a text of her own. A always seemed to know when she was having naughty thoughts. Only, her cell phone . . . was in the swear jar.

Emily let out a thrilled bleat of laughter. Her phone was in the *swear jar*. She was at a party in Iowa, thousands of miles from Rosewood. Unless A was supernatural, there was no way A could know what Emily was doing.

Suddenly, Iowa wasn't quite so bad. Not. At. All.

7

BARBIE DOLL . . . OR VOODOO DOLL?

Sunday evening, Spencer swung gently on the hammock on the wraparound porch of her grandmother's vacation house. As she watched yet another hot, muscular surfer boy catch a wave at Nun's, the surfing beach just down the road that bordered a convent, a shadow fell over her.

"Your father and I are going to the yacht club for a while," her mother said, shoving her hands into her beige linen trousers.

"Oh." Spencer struggled to get out of the hammock without getting her feet tangled in the netting. The Stone Harbor yacht club was in an old sea shack that smelled a little like brine in a moldy basement. Spencer suspected her parents liked going there solely because it was a members-only establishment. "Can I come?"

Her mother caught her arm. "You and Melissa are staying here."

A breeze that smelled of surf wax and fish smacked

Spencer in the face. She tried to see things from her mother's perspective—it must have sucked to see her two children fighting so bloodthirstily. But Spencer wished her mom could understand *her* perspective, too. Melissa was an evil superbitch, and Spencer didn't want to speak to her for the rest of her life.

"Fine," Spencer said dramatically. She pulled open the sliding glass door and stalked into the grand family room. Even though Nana Hastings's Craftsman-style house had eight bedrooms, seven bathrooms, a private path to the beach, a deluxe playroom, a home theater, a gourmet chef's kitchen, and Stickley furniture through-out, Spencer's family had always affectionately called it the "taco shack." Perhaps it was because Nana's mansion in Longboat Key, Florida, had wall frescoes, marble floors, three tennis courts, and a temperature-controlled wine cellar.

Spencer haughtily passed Melissa, who was lounging on one of the tan leather couches, murmuring on her iPhone. She was probably talking to Ian Thomas. "I'll be in my room," Spencer yelled dramatically at the base of the stairs. "All. Night."

She flopped down on her sleigh bed, pleased to see that her bedroom was exactly as she'd left it five years ago. Alison had come with her the last time she visited, and the two of them had spent hours gazing at the surfers through her late grandpa Hastings's antique mahogany spyglass on the crow's-nest deck. That had been in the early fall, when Ali and Spencer were just starting seventh grade. Things were still pretty normal between them—maybe Ali hadn't started seeing Ian yet.

Spencer shuddered. Ali had been seeing *Ian*. Did A know about that? Did A know about Spencer's argument with Ali the night Ali disappeared, too—had A *been* there? Spencer wished she could tell the police about A, but A seemed above the law. She looked around haltingly, suddenly frightened. The sun had sunk below the trees, filling the room with eerie darkness.

Her phone rang, and Spencer jumped. She pulled it out of her robe pocket and squinted at the number. Not recognizing it, she put the phone to her ear and tentatively said hello.

"Spencer?" said a girl's smooth, lilting voice. "It's Mona Vanderwaal."

"Oh." Spencer sat up too fast, and her head started to spin. There was only one reason why Mona would be calling her. "Is . . . Hanna . . . okay?"

"Well . . . no." Mona sounded surprised. "You haven't heard? She's in a coma. I'm at the hospital."

"Oh my God," Spencer whispered. "Is she going to get better?"

"The doctors don't know." Mona's voice wobbled. "She might not wake up."

Spencer began to pace around the room. "I'm in New Jersey right now with my parents, but I'll be back tomorrow morning, so–"

"I'm not calling to make you feel guilty," Mona interrupted. She sighed. "I'm sorry. I'm stressed. I called because I heard you were good at planning events."

It was cold in the bedroom and smelled a little like sand. Spencer touched the edge of the enormous conch shell that sat on top of her bureau. "Well, sure."

"Good," Mona said. "I want to plan a candlelight vigil for Hanna. I think it would be great to get everyone to, you know, band together for Hanna."

"That sounds great," Spencer said softly. "My dad was just talking about a party he was at a couple of weeks ago in this gorgeous tent on the fifteenth green. Maybe we could hold it there."

"Perfect. Let's plan for Friday—that'll give us five days to get everything ready."

"Friday it is." After Mona said she'd write out the invitations if Spencer could secure the location and the catering, Spencer hung up. She flopped back on the bed, staring at its lacy canopy. Hanna might *die*? Spencer pictured Hanna lying alone and unconscious in a hospital room. Her throat felt tight and hot.

Tap . . . tap . . . tap . . .

The wind grew still, and even the ocean was quiet. Spencer pricked up her ears. Was someone out there?

Tap . . . tap . . . tap . . .

She sat up fast. "Who's there?" The bedroom window offered a sandy view. The sun had set so quickly that all she could see was the weathered wooden lifeguard stand in the distance. She crept into the hall. Empty. She ran into one of the guest bedrooms and looked below to the front porch. No one.

Spencer slid her hands down her face. *Calm down*, she told herself. *It's not like A is here.* She stumbled out of the room and down the staircase, nearly tripping over a stack of beach towels. Melissa was still on the couch, holding a copy of *Architectural Digest* with her good hand and propping up her broken wrist on an oversize velvet pillow.

"Melissa," Spencer said, breathing hard. "I think there's someone outside."

Her sister turned around, her face pinched. "Huh?"

Tap . . . tap . . . tap . . .

"Listen!" Spencer pointed to the door. "Don't you hear that?"

Melissa stood up, frowning. "I hear *something*." She looked at Spencer worriedly. "Let's go to the playroom. There's a good view all around the house from there."

The sisters checked and double-checked the locks before bolting up the stairs to the second-floor playroom. The room smelled closed-up and dusty, and looked as if a much-younger Melissa and Spencer had just run out for dinner and would be back at any second to resume playing. There was the Lego village that had taken them three weeks to complete. There was the make-your-own-jewelry kit, the beads and clasps still strewn all over the table. The indoor mini golf holes were still set up around the room, and the enormous chest of dolls was still open.

Melissa reached the window first. She pushed back the sailboat-printed curtain and peered into the front yard, which was landscaped with sea glass pebbles and tropical flowers. Her pink cast made a hollow sound as it tapped against the windowpane. "I don't see anyone."

"I already looked out front. Maybe they're around the side."

Suddenly, they heard it again. *Tap . . . tap*. It was growing louder. Spencer grabbed Melissa's arm. They both peered out the window again.

Then a drainpipe at the bottom of the house rattled a bit, and finally something scuttled out. It was a *seagull*. The thing had somehow gotten stuck in the pipe; the tapping sounds had probably been caused by its wings and beak as it struggled to break free. The bird waddled away, shaking its feathers.

Spencer sank down on the antique FAO Schwarz rocking horse. At first, Melissa looked angry, but then the corners of her mouth wobbled. She snorted with laughter.

Spencer laughed as well. "Stupid bird."

"Yeah." Melissa let out a huge sigh. She looked around the room, first at the Legos and then at the six oversize My Little Pony mannequin heads set up on the far table. She pointed at them. "Remember how we used to do the ponies' makeup?"

"Sure." Mrs. Hastings would give them all of last season's Chanel eye shadows and lipsticks, and they'd spend hours giving the ponies smoky eyes and plumped-up lips.

"You used to put eye shadow on their nostrils," Melissa teased.

Spencer giggled, petting the blue-and-purple mane of a pink pony. "I wanted their noses to be as pretty as the rest of their faces."

"And remember these?" Melissa walked to the over-size chest and peered inside. "I can't believe we had so many dolls."

Not only were there more than a hundred dolls, ranging from Barbies to German antiques that probably shouldn't have been carelessly tossed into a toy chest, but also tons of coordinating outfits, shoes, purses, cars, horses, and lapdogs. Spencer pulled out a Barbie in a serious-looking blue blazer and pencil skirt. "Remember how we used to make them be CEOs? Mine was the CEO of a cotton-candy factory, and yours was the CEO of a makeup company."

"We made this one president." Melissa pulled out a doll whose dirty-blond hair was cut bluntly to her chin, just like her own.

"And this one had lots of boyfriends." Spencer held up a pretty doll with long, blond hair and a heart-shaped face.

The sisters sighed. Spencer felt a lump in her throat. Back in the day, they used to play for hours. Half the time they didn't even want to go down to the beach, and when it was time for bed, Spencer always sobbed and begged her parents to let her sleep in Melissa's bedroom.

"I'm sorry about the Golden Orchid thing," Spencer blurted out. "I wish it had never happened."

Melissa picked up the pretty doll Spencer had been holding—the one with lots of boyfriends. "They're going to want you to go to New York, you know. And talk about your paper in front of a panel of judges. You'll have to know the material inside out."

Spencer squeezed CEO Barbie tightly around her impossibly disproportionate waist. Even if her parents wouldn't punish her for cheating, the Golden Orchid committee would.

Melissa strolled to the back of the room. "You'll do fine, though. You'll probably win. And you know Mom and Dad will get you something amazing if you do."

Spencer blinked. "And you'd be okay with that? Even though it's . . . your paper?"

Melissa shrugged. "I'm over it." She paused for a moment, then reached into a high cabinet Spencer hadn't noticed before. Her hand emerged with a tall bottle of Grey Goose vodka. She shook it, the clear liquid swishing inside the glass. "Want some?"

"S-Sure," Spencer sputtered.

Melissa walked to the cabinet above the room's mini fridge and pulled out two cups from the minia-ture china tea set. Using only her good hand, Melissa awkwardly poured vodka into two teacups. With a nos-talgic smile, she handed Spencer her old favorite pale blue teacup—Spencer used to pitch a fit if she had to drink out of any of the others. She was astounded that Melissa remembered.

Spencer sipped, feeling the vodka burn down her throat. "How did you know that bottle was here?"

"Ian and I snuck here for Senior Week years ago," Melissa explained. She sat down in a purple-and-pink striped child-size chair, her knees piked up to her chin. "Cops were all over the roads, and we were terrified to bring it back with us, so we hid it here. We thought we'd come back for it later . . . only, we didn't."

Melissa got a faraway look on her face. She and Ian had unexpectedly broken up shortly after Senior Week—that same summer Ali had gone missing. Melissa had been extra-industrious that summer, working two part-time jobs and volunteering at the Brandywine River Museum. Even though she never would have admitted it, Spencer suspected she'd been trying to keep herself busy because the breakup with Ian had really devastated her. Maybe it was the hurt look on Melissa's face, or maybe it was that she'd just told Spencer she'd probably win the Golden Orchid after all, but suddenly, Spencer wanted to tell Melissa the truth.

"There's something you should know," Spencer blurted out. "I kissed Ian when I was in seventh grade, when you guys were dating." She swallowed hard. "It was only one kiss, and it didn't mean anything. I swear." Now that that was out, Spencer couldn't stop herself. "It wasn't like the thing Ian had with Ali."

"The thing Ian had with Ali," Melissa repeated, staring down at the Barbie she was holding.

"Yeah." Spencer's insides felt like a molten lava–filled volcano–rumbling, about to overflow. "Ali told me right before she disappeared, but I must've blocked it out."

Melissa began to brush the popular blond Barbie's hair, her lips twitching slightly.

"I blocked out some other stuff, too," Spencer continued shakily, feeling a little uneasy. "That night, Ali really teased me–she said that I liked Ian, that I was trying to steal him away. It was like she *wanted* me to get mad. And then I shoved her. I didn't mean to hurt her, but I'm afraid I . . ."

Spencer covered her hands with her face. Repeating the story to Melissa revived that awful night all over again. *Earthworms from the previous night's rain wriggled across the path. Ali's pink bra strap slid down her shoulder, and her toe ring glimmered in the moonlight.* It was *real.* It had happened.

Melissa put the Barbie down on her lap and took a slow drink of her vodka. "Actually, I knew Ian kissed you. And I knew that Ali and Ian were together."

Spencer gaped. "Ian *told* you?"

Melissa shrugged. "I guessed. Ian wasn't very good at keeping that kind of stuff a secret. Not from me."

Spencer stared at her sister, a shudder snaking down her spine. Melissa's voice was singsongy, almost like she was suppressing a giggle. Then Melissa turned to face

Spencer head-on. She smiled widely, weirdly. "As for being worried that *you* were the one who killed Ali, I don't think you have it in you."

"You . . . *don't?*"

Melissa shook her head slowly, and then made the doll in her lap shake her head, too. "It takes a very unique person to kill, and that's not you."

She tipped her teacup of vodka to the ceiling, draining it. Then, with her good hand, Melissa picked the Barbie up by its neck and popped its plastic head clean off. She handed the dismembered head to Spencer, her eyes open wide. "That's not you at all."

The doll's head fit perfectly in the pit of Spencer's palm, the lips pursed in a flirtatious smile, the eyes a brilliant sapphire blue. A wave of nausea went through Spencer. She'd never noticed before, but the doll looked exactly like . . . Ali.

8

DOESN'T EVERYONE TALK ABOUT THIS STUFF IN A HOSPITAL ROOM?

Monday morning, instead of rushing to English class before the bell rang, Aria was running toward the Rosewood Day exit. She'd just received a text message on her phone from Lucas. Aria, come to the hospital if you can, it said. They're finally letting people in to see Hanna.

She was so engrossed and focused, she didn't see her brother, Mike, until he was standing right in front of her. He wore a Playboy bunny–icon T-shirt underneath his Rosewood Day jacket and a blue Rosewood Day varsity lacrosse bracelet. Engraved in the bracelet's rubber was his team nickname, which, for whatever reason, was Buffalo. Aria didn't dare ask why—it was probably an inside joke about his penis or something. The lacrosse team was becoming more and more of a frat every day.

"Hey," Aria said, a bit distracted. "How are you?"

Mike's hands seemed welded to his hips. The sneer on his face indicated he wasn't up for small talk. "I hear you're living with Dad now."

"As a last resort," Aria said quickly. "Sean and I broke up."

Mike narrowed his ice-blue eyes. "I know. I heard that too."

Aria stepped back, surprised. Mike didn't know about Ezra, did he? "I just wanted to tell you that you and Dad deserve each other," Mike snapped, whipping around and nearly colliding with a girl in a cheerleading uniform. "See ya later."

"Mike, wait!" Aria cried. "I'm going to fix this, I promise!"

But he just kept going. Last week, Mike had found out that Aria had known about their dad's affair for three years. On the surface, he'd acted all tough and cool about their parents' dissolving marriage. He played varsity lacrosse, made lewd comments to girls, and tried to give his teammates titty twisters in the hallways. But Mike was like an ABBA song—all happy and giddy and fun on the surface, but bubbling with turmoil and pain underneath. She couldn't imagine what Mike would think if he found out Byron and Meredith were planning to get married.

As she heaved a huge sigh and continued toward the side door, she noticed a figure in a three-piece suit staring at her from across the hall.

"Going somewhere, Ms. Montgomery?" Principal Appleton asked.

Aria flinched, her face growing hot. She hadn't seen Appleton since Sean had told the Rosewood staff about Ezra. But Appleton didn't exactly look pissed—more like . . . nervous. Almost as if Aria was someone he had to treat very, very delicately. Aria tried to hide a smirk. Appleton probably didn't want Aria to press charges against Ezra or talk about the incident ever again. It would draw indecent attention to the school, and Rosewood Day could never have *that*.

Aria turned, fueled with power. "There's somewhere I have to be," she insisted.

It was against Rosewood Day policy to walk out of a class, but Appleton did nothing to stop her. Perhaps the Ezra mess was good for something, after all.

She reached the hospital quickly and sprinted up to the third-floor intensive care unit. Inside, patients were sprawled out in a circle, separated only by curtains. A long, U-shaped nurse's desk sat in the middle of the room. Aria passed an old Black woman who looked dead, a silver-haired man in a neck brace, and a groggy-looking fortysomething who was muttering to herself. Hanna's partitioned-off area was along one of the walls. With her long, healthy auburn hair, unlined skin, and taut, young body, Hanna was definitely the thing in the ICU that didn't belong. Her cordoned-off area was full of flowers, boxes of candy, stacks of magazines, and stuffed animals. Someone had bought her a large, white teddy bear that wore a patterned wrap dress. When Aria flipped open the tag on the bear's plushy arm, she saw that the bear's name was Diane von FurstenBEAR. There was a brand-new white cast on Hanna's arm. Lucas Beattie, Mona Vanderwaal, and Hanna's parents had already signed it.

Lucas was sitting in the yellow plastic chair by Hanna's bed, a *Vogue* on his lap. "'Even the pastiest legs will benefit from Lancôme Soleil Flash Bronzer tinted mousse, which gives skin a subtle sheen,'" he read, licking his finger to turn the page. When he noticed Aria, he stopped, a sheepish look crossing his face. "The doctors say it's good to talk to Hanna—that she can hear. But maybe fall is a stupid time to talk about self-tanners? Maybe I should read her the article on Coco Chanel instead? Or the one about the TikTok designer who's taken fashion by storm?"

Aria glanced at Hanna, a lump growing in her throat. Metal guards lined the sides of her bed, as if she was a toddler at risk of rolling out. There were green bruises on her face, and her eyes seemed sealed closed. This was the first time Aria had seen a coma patient up close. A monitor recording Hanna's heartbeat and blood pressure let out a constant *beep, beep, beep* noise. It made Aria uneasy. She couldn't help but anticipate that the beeping would abruptly flatline, like it always did in the movies before someone died. "So, have the doctors said anything about her prognosis?" Aria asked shakily.

"Well, her hand's fluttering. Like that, see?" Lucas gestured to Hanna's right hand, the one with the cast on it. Her fingernails looked like someone had recently painted them a brilliant coral. "Which seems promising. But the doctors say it might not mean anything—they still aren't sure if she has any brain damage."

Aria's stomach dropped.

"But I'm trying to think positive. The fluttering means she's about to wake up." Lucas closed the magazine and set it on Hanna's bedside table. "And apparently, some of her brain activity readouts show that she might've been awake last night . . . but nobody saw it." He sighed. "I'm going to go get a soda. Want anything?"

Aria shook her head. Lucas stood up from his chair and Aria took his place. Before Lucas left, he drummed his fingers against the doorframe. "Did you hear there's going to be a candlelight vigil for Hanna on Friday?"

Aria shrugged. "Don't you think it's sort of bizarre that it's at a country club?"

"Sort of," Lucas whispered. "Or fitting."

He gave Aria a smirk and padded away. As he smacked the automatic door button and walked out of the ICU ward, Aria smiled. She liked Lucas. He seemed as jaded about pretentious Rosewood bullshit as she was. And he certainly was a good friend. Aria had no idea how he was able to miss so much school to stay with Hanna, but it was nice that someone was with her.

Aria reached out and touched Hanna's hand, and Hanna's fingers curled around hers. Aria pulled away, startled, then chastised herself. It wasn't like Hanna was *dead*. It wasn't like Aria had squeezed a corpse's hand and the corpse had squeezed back.

"Okay, I can be there this afternoon, and we can go through the candids together," a voice said behind her. "Is that doable?"

Aria whirled around, nearly falling off her chair. Spencer hit the off button on her phone and gave Aria an apologetic smile. "Sorry." She rolled her eyes. "Yearbook can't do anything without me." She looked at Hanna, paling a bit. "I came here as soon as my free period started. How's she doing?"

Aria cracked her knuckles so hard, her thumb joint made a disconcerting *pop*. It was amazing that in the middle of all this, Spencer still ran eight thousand committees and had even found time to be on the front page of yesterday's *Philadelphia Sentinel*. Even though Wilden had more or less exonerated Spencer, there was still something about her that gave Aria pause.

"Where have you been?" Aria asked sharply.

Spencer took a step back, as if Aria had shoved her. "I had to go away with my parents. To New Jersey. I came as soon as I could."

"Did you get A's note on Saturday?" Aria demanded. "*She knew too much?*"

Spencer nodded but didn't speak. She flicked the tassels of her tweed Kate Spade bag and looked warily at all of Hanna's electronic medical devices.

"Did Hanna tell you who it is?" Aria goaded.

Spencer frowned. "Who *who* is?"

"A." Spencer still looked confused, and an edgy feeling gnawed at Aria's gut. "Hanna knew who A was, Spencer." She looked at Spencer carefully. "Hanna didn't tell you why she wanted to meet?"

"No." Spencer's voice cracked. "She just said she had something important to tell me." She let out a long breath.

Aria thought of Spencer's cagey, crazy eyes peeping out from the woods behind Rosewood Day. "I saw you, you know," she blurted out. "I saw you in the woods on Saturday. You were just . . . standing there. What were you doing?"

The pigment disappeared from Spencer's face. "I was scared," she whispered. "I'd never seen anything so scary in my whole life. I couldn't believe that someone would actually *do* that to Hanna."

Spencer looked terrified. All of a sudden, Aria felt her suspicion seep out of her. She wondered what Spencer would think if she knew Aria had thought Spencer was Ali's killer, and had even shared that theory with Wilden. She recalled Wilden's judging words: *Is this what you girls do? Blame your old friends for murder?* Maybe Wilden was right: Spencer might have starred in some of the school plays, but she wasn't a good enough actress to have killed Ali, traipsed back to the barn, and convinced her remaining best friends that she was as innocent, clueless, and scared as they all were.

"I can't believe anyone would do that to Hanna either," Aria said quietly. She sighed. "So, I figured something out Saturday night. I think . . . I think Ali and Ian Thomas were dating, back when we were in seventh grade."

Spencer's mouth fell open. "I figured that out Saturday, too."

"You didn't already know?" Aria scratched her head, thrown off guard.

Spencer took another step into the room. She kept her eyes fixed on the clear liquid that filled Hanna's IV bag. "No."

"Do you think anyone else knew?"

An indescribable expression crossed Spencer's face. Talking about all this seemed to make her really uncomfortable. "I think my sister did."

"Melissa knew all this time but never said anything?" Aria ran her hands along the edge of her chin. "That's weird." She thought of A's three clues about Ali's killer: that she was close by, that she wanted something Ali had, and that she knew every inch of the DiLaurentises' yard. All three clues together only applied to a handful of people. If Melissa knew about Ali and Ian, then maybe she was one of them.

"Should we tell the cops about Ian and Ali?" Spencer suggested.

Aria wrung her hands together. "I mentioned it to Wilden."

A flush of surprise passed over Spencer's face. "Oh," she said in a small voice.

"Is that okay?" Aria asked, raising an eyebrow.

"Of course," Spencer said briskly, regaining composure. "So . . . do you think we should tell him about A?"

Aria widened her eyes. "If we do, A might . . ." She trailed off, feeling nauseated.

Spencer stared at Aria for a long time. "A's completely running our lives," she whispered.

Hanna was still immobile in her bed. Aria wondered if she really could hear them, just like Lucas said. Perhaps she'd heard everything they'd just said about A and wanted to tell them what she knew, only she was trapped inside her coma. Or maybe she'd heard everything they'd said and was disgusted that they were talking about this instead of fretting over whether Hanna would ever wake up.

Aria smoothed the sheets over Hanna's chest, tucking them up to her chin like Ella used to do when Aria had the flu. Then, a flickering reflection in the little window behind Hanna's bed caught her eye. Aria straightened, her nerves jangling. It looked like someone outside

Hanna's partition was lurking next to an empty wheel-chair, trying not to be seen.

She whipped around, her heart racing, and pulled back the curtain.

"What?" Spencer cried, turning around too.

Aria took a deep breath. "Nothing." Whoever it was had vanished.

9

IT'S NO FUN BEING THE SCAPEGOAT

Light streamed into Emily's eyes. She hugged her pillow and sank back into sleep. Rosewood's morning sounds were as predictable as the sunrise—the barking of the Kloses' dog as they set off on their walk around the block, the rumbling of the garbage truck, the sounds of the *Today* show, which her mother watched every morning, and the crowing of the rooster.

Her eyes sprang open. A *rooster*?

The room smelled like hay and vodka. Abby's bed was empty. Since the cousins had wanted to stay longer at last night's party than Emily did, Trista had dropped her off at the Weavers' gate. Maybe Abby hadn't come home yet—the last she'd seen of Abby at the party, she'd been all over a guy who wore a University of Iowa T-shirt that featured a big, scowling Herky the Hawk mascot on the back.

When she turned her head, she saw her aunt Helene standing in the doorway. Emily screamed and pulled the sheets around her. Helene was already dressed in a long patchwork jumper and a ruffle-edged T-shirt. Her glasses teetered precariously on the end of her nose. "I see you're up," she said. "Please come downstairs."

Emily rolled out of bed slowly, pulling on a shirt, a pair of Rosewood Day Swim Team pajama pants, and argyle socks. The rest of the previous night rushed back to her, as comforting as sinking into a long, hot bath. Emily and Trista had spent the rest of the night making up a crazy square dance, and a bunch of the boys had joined in. They'd talked nonstop on the drive back to the Weavers' house, even though both of them were exhausted. Before Emily got out of the car, Trista had touched the inside of Emily's wrist. "I'm glad I met you," Trista whispered. And Emily was glad too.

John, Matt, and Abby were at the kitchen table, staring sleepily at their bowls of Cheerios. A plate of pancakes sat in the middle of the table. "Hey, guys," Emily said cheerfully. "Is there anything for breakfast other than Cheerios or pancakes?"

"I don't think breakfast should be your main concern right now, Emily."

Emily turned, her blood running cold. Uncle Allen stood at the counter, his posture stiff, a look of disappointment on his lined, weathered face. Helene leaned against the stove, equally stern. Emily looked nervously from Matt to John to Abby, but not one of them returned her gaze.

"So." Helene started pacing around the room, her square-toed shoes clacking against the plank floor. "We know what the four of you did last night."

Emily sank into a chair, heat creeping into her cheeks. Her heart began to pound.

"I want to know whose idea this was." Helene circled the table like a hawk zeroing in on her prey. "Who wanted to hang out with those public school kids? Who thought it was okay to drink alcohol?"

Abby poked at a lone Cheerio in her bowl. John scratched his chin. Emily kept her lips pasted together. *She* certainly wasn't going to say anything. She and her cousins would form a bond of solidarity, keeping quiet for the benefit of all. It was how Emily, Ali, and the others had operated years ago, on the rare occasion that someone actually caught them doing something.

"Well?" Helene said sharply.

Abby's chin shook. "It was Emily," she exploded. "She threatened me, Mom. She knew about the public school party and demanded that I take her to it. I took John and Matt along so we'd be safe."

"*What?*" Emily gasped. She felt like Abby had smacked her in the chest with the large wooden cross that hung over the doorway. "That's not true! How would I have known about some party? I don't know anyone but you!"

Helene looked disgusted. "Boys? Was it Emily?"

Matt and John stared at their cereal bowls and nodded slowly.

Emily looked around the table, too angry and betrayed to breathe. She wanted to shout out what had really happened. Matt had done body shots from a girl's navel. John had danced to "We Don't Talk About Bruno" in his boxers. Abby had made out with five guys and possibly a cow. Her limbs began to shake. Why were they doing this? Weren't they her *friends*? "None of you seemed very upset to be there!"

"That's a lie!" Abby shrieked. "We were all *very* upset!"

Allen pulled at Emily's shoulder, jolting her back to her feet in a forceful, manhandling way Emily had never felt in her life. "This isn't going to work," he said in a low voice, bringing his face close to hers. He smelled like coffee and something organic, perhaps soil. "You're no longer welcome here."

Emily took a step back, her heart sinking to her feet. "What?"

"We did your parents a big favor," Helene growled. "They said you were a handful, but we never expected *this*." She pushed the on button of the cordless phone. "I'm calling them now. We'll drive you back to the airport, but they'll have to figure out a way to pay for you to get home. And they'll have to decide what to do with you."

Emily felt all five pairs of Weaver eyes on her. She willed herself not to cry, taking big, gulping breaths of the stale farmhouse air. Her cousins had betrayed her. None of them were on her side. *No one* was.

She turned around and fled up to the little bedroom.

Once there, she threw her clothes back into her swim bag. Most of her clothes still smelled like home—a mix of Snuggle fabric softener and her mom's homey cooking spices. She was glad they would never smell like this horrible place.

Just before zipping the duffel closed, she paused. Helene was probably calling her parents, telling them everything. She pictured her mother standing in her kitchen in Rosewood, holding the phone to her ear and saying, "*Please* don't send Emily back here. Our life is perfect without her."

Emily's vision blurred with tears, and her heart literally hurt. No one wanted her. And what would Helene's next option be? Would she try to ship Emily off somewhere else? Military school? A *convent*? Did those still exist?

"I have to get out of here," Emily whispered to the cold, spare room. Her cell phone was still lying at the bottom of the swear jar in the hall. The lid came off easily, and no alarm sounded. She dropped the phone into her pocket, grabbed her bags, and crept down the stairs. If she could just get off the Weaver property, she was pretty sure there was a minuscule grocery store about a mile down the road. She could plan her next move from there.

When she burst out onto the front porch, she almost didn't notice Abby curled up on the chain-link porch swing. Emily was so startled she dropped her duffel on her feet.

Abby's mouth settled into an upside-down U. "She never catches us. So *you* must have done something to get her attention."

"I didn't do anything," Emily said helplessly. "I swear."

"And now, because of you, we're going to be stuck in lockdown for months." Abby rolled her eyes. "And for the record, Trista Taylor is a huge slut. She tries to hump anything that moves—guy *or* girl."

Emily backed up, at a loss for words. She grabbed her bag and sprinted down the front walk. When she came to the cattle gate, that same goat was still tethered to the metal post, the bell clanging softly around her neck. The rope didn't offer enough slack for her to lie down, and it looked like Helene hadn't even put out water for her. When Emily looked into the goat's yellow eyes and odd, square pupils, she felt a connection—scapegoat to "bad" goat. She knew what it was like to be cruelly, unjustly punished.

Emily took a deep breath and slid the rope off the goat's neck, then opened the cattle guard and waved her arms. "Go, girl," she whispered. "Shoo." The goat glanced at Emily, her lips pursed. She took one step forward, then another. Once she crossed the cattle guard, she broke into a trot, waddling down the road. She seemed happy to be free.

Emily slammed the cattle guard shut behind her. She was pretty damn happy to be free of this place, too.

10

ABOUT AS FAR FROM MINDLESS AS ARIA COULD GET

The clouds rolled in on Monday afternoon, darkening the sky and bringing winds that ripped through Rosewood's yellow-leafed sugar maples. Aria pulled her strawberry-colored merino wool beret down over her ears and scampered into the Frank Lloyd Wright Memorial Visual Arts Building at Hollis College for her very first Mindless Art class. The lobby walls were full of student exhibits, announcements for art sales, and want ads for housemates. Aria noticed a flyer that said, HAVE YOU SEEN THE ROSEWOOD STALKER? There was a xeroxed photograph of a figure looming in the woods, as blurry and cryptic as the murky shots of the Loch Ness Monster. Last week, there had been all sorts of news reports on the Rosewood Stalker, who was following people around, spying on their every move. But Aria hadn't heard any stalker news for a few days now . . . about the same amount of time that A had been silent.

The elevator was out of service, so Aria climbed the cold, gray concrete stairs to the second floor. She located her Mindless Art classroom and was surprised to find it silent and dark. A jagged shape flickered against the window on the far side of the room, and as Aria's eyes adjusted, she realized the room was full.

"Come in," called a woman's husky voice.

Aria felt her way to the back wall. The old Hollis building creaked and groaned. Someone near her smelled like menthol and garlic. Someone else smelled like cigarettes. She heard a giggle.

"I believe we're all here," the voice called out. "My name is Sabrina. Welcome to Mindless Art. Now, you're all probably wondering why we're standing here with the lights off. Art is about seeing, right? Well, guess what? It isn't, not entirely. Art is also touching and smelling . . . and most definitely feeling. But mostly, it's about letting go. It's about taking everything you thought was true and throwing it out the window. It's about embracing life's unpredictability, letting go of boundaries, and starting over."

Aria stifled a yawn. Sabrina had a slow, soporific voice that made her want to curl up and close her eyes.

"The lights are off for a little exercise," Sabrina said. "We all form an image of someone in our heads, based on certain easy clues. The way one's voice sounds, maybe. The type of music someone likes. The things you know about a person's past, perhaps. But sometimes, our judgments aren't right; in fact, sometimes they're quite wrong."

Years ago, Aria and Ali used to go to Saturday art classes together. If Ali were in this class with her now, she'd roll her eyes and say that Sabrina was a flaky granola-head with hairy armpits. But Aria thought what Sabrina was saying made sense—especially in regard to Ali. These days, everything Aria thought she'd known about Ali was wrong. Aria would never have imagined Ali was having a secret affair with her best friend's sister's boyfriend, though it certainly explained her cagey, bizarre actions before she disappeared. In those last few months, there were stretches when Ali wasn't around for weekends at a time. She'd say she had to go out of town with her parents—surely that was code for time alone with Ian. Or once, when Aria had biked over to Ali's house to surprise her, she'd found Ali sitting on one of the big boulders in her backyard, whispering into her cell phone. "I'll see you this weekend, okay?" Ali was saying. "We can talk about it then." When Aria called out her name, Ali whirled around, startled. "Who are you talking to?" Aria had asked innocently. Ali turned her phone over fast, narrowing her eyes. She considered her words for a while, and then said, "So, that girl your dad was kissing? I bet she's a wild, desperate college girl who throws herself at guys. I mean, she'd have to be pretty ballsy to hook up with her teacher." Aria had turned away, mortified. Ali had been with her the day she'd discovered Byron kissing

Meredith, and she wouldn't let it go. Aria was on her bike and halfway home before she realized Ali had never answered her question.

"So this is what I want us to do," Sabrina said loudly, interrupting Aria's memories. "Find the person nearest to you, and hold hands. Try to imagine what your neighbor looks like just by the way their hands feel. Then we'll turn the lights on so you can sketch each other's portraits based on what you see in your mind."

Aria fumbled in the blue-black darkness. Someone grabbed her hand, feeling her wrist bones and the mounds in her palm.

"What sort of face do you see when you touch this person?" Sabrina called.

Aria shut her eyes, trying to think. The hand was small and a bit cold and dry. A face began to form in her mind. First the pronounced cheekbones, then the bright blue eyes. Long, blond hair, pink, bow-shaped lips.

Aria tightened her stomach. She was thinking of *Ali.*

"Turn away from your partner now," Sabrina instructed. "Get your sketch pads out, and I'm going to turn on the lights. Do not look at your partners. I want you to sketch exactly what you saw in your brain, and we'll see how close you are to the real thing."

The bright overhead lights hurt Aria's eyes as she shakily opened her sketch pad. She tentatively brushed the charcoal across her paper, but as hard as she tried, she couldn't stop from drawing Ali's face. When she stepped back, she felt a huge lump in her throat. There was a whisper of a smile across Ali's lips and a devious sparkle in her eye.

"Very nice," said Sabrina—who looked exactly like her voice, with long, knotty brown hair; big boobs; a fleshy stomach; and puny, birdlike legs. She moved on to Aria's partner. "That's *beautiful*," she murmured. Aria felt a pinch of annoyance. Why wasn't her drawing beautiful? Did someone draw better than she did? Impossible.

"Time's up," Sabrina called. "Turn around and show your partners the results."

Aria slowly turned, her eyes greedily assessing her partner's allegedly *beautiful* sketch. And actually . . . it *was* beautiful. The drawing looked nothing like Aria, but it still was a much better rendering of a person than Aria could have done. Aria's eyes floated up her partner's body. The girl wore a fitted pink Nanette Lepore top. Her hair was dark and wild, spilling down her shoulders. She had creamy, blemish-free skin. Then, Aria saw the familiar turned-up button nose. And the giant Gucci sunglasses. There was a sleeping dog in a blue canvas vest at the girl's feet. Aria's entire body turned to ice.

"I can't see what you drew of me," her partner said in a soft, sweet voice. She pointed to her Seeing Eye dog in explanation. "But I'm sure it's great."

Aria's tongue felt leaden in her mouth. Her partner was Jenna Cavanaugh.

11

WELCOME BACK . . . SORT OF

After what seemed like days of spinning through the stars, Hanna suddenly found herself thrust into the light again. Once more, she was sitting on Ali's back porch. Once more, she could feel herself busting out of her Brandy Melville T-shirt and Good American jeans.

"We get to have our sleepover in Melissa's barn!" Spencer was saying.

"Nice." Ali grinned. Hanna recoiled. Maybe she was stuck revisiting this day over and over again, sort of like that guy in that old movie *Groundhog Day*. Maybe Hanna would have to keep reliving this one day until she got it right and convinced Ali that she was in grave danger. But . . . the last time Hanna had been in this memory, Ali had loomed close by, telling Hanna that she was okay. But she *wasn't* okay. *Nothing was okay.*

"Ali," Hanna urged. "What do you mean, you're okay?"

Ali wasn't paying attention. She watched Melissa as she strode through the Hastingses' bordering yard, her graduation gown slung over her arm. "Hey, Melissa!" Ali cooed. "Excited to go to Prague?"

"Who cares about her?" Hanna shouted. "Answer my question!"

"Is Hanna . . . *talking*?" a far-off voice gasped. Hanna cocked her head. That didn't sound like any of her old friends.

Across the yard, Melissa put her hand on her hip. "Of course I'm excited."

"Is *Ian* going?" Ali asked.

Hanna grabbed the sides of Ali's face. "Ian doesn't matter," she said forcefully. "Just listen to me, Ali!"

"Who's Ian?" The far-off voice sounded like it was coming from the other end of a very long tunnel. Mona Vanderwaal's voice. Hanna looked around Ali's backyard, but didn't see Mona anywhere.

Ali turned to Hanna, heaving an exasperated sigh. "Give it a rest, Hanna."

"But you're in danger," Hanna sputtered.

"Things aren't always what they seem," Ali whispered.

"What do you mean?" Hanna urged desperately. When she reached out for Ali, her hand went right through Ali's arm, like Ali was just an image projected onto a screen.

"What does *who* mean?" Mona's voice called.

Hanna's eyes popped open. A bright, painful light

practically blinded her. She was lying on her back on an uncomfortable mattress. Several figures stood around her—Mona, Lucas Beattie, her mother, and her father.

Her *father*? Hanna tried to frown, but her face muscles were in excruciating pain.

"Hanna." Mona's chin wobbled. "Oh my God. You're . . . *awake.*"

"Are you okay, honey?" her mother asked. "Can you talk?"

Hanna glanced down at her arms. At least they were thin and not ham hocks. Then, she saw the IV tube sticking out of the crook in her elbow and the clunky cast on her arm. "What's going on?" she croaked, looking around. The scene in front of her eyes seemed staged. Where she'd just been—on Ali's back porch, with her old best friends—seemed far more real. "Where's Ali?" she asked.

Hanna's parents exchanged uneasy looks. "Ali's dead," Hanna's mother said quietly.

"Go easy on her." A white-haired, hawk-nosed man in a white coat swept around a curtain to the foot of Hanna's bed. "Hanna? My name's Dr. Geist. How do you feel?"

"Where the hell am I?" Hanna demanded, her voice rising with panic.

Hanna's father took her hand. "You had an accident. We were really worried."

Hanna looked fitfully at the faces around her, then at the various contraptions that fed into different parts of her body. In addition to the IV drip, there was a machine that measured her heartbeat and a tube that sent oxygen into her nose. Her body felt hot, then cold, and her skin prickled with fear and confusion. "Accident?" she whispered.

"A car hit you," Hanna's mother said. "At Rosewood Day. Can you remember?"

Her hospital sheets felt sticky, like someone had drizzled nacho cheese all over them. Hanna searched her memory, but nothing about an accident was there. The last thing she remembered, before sitting in Ali's backyard, was receiving the champagne-colored slip dress for Mona's birthday party. That had been Friday night, the day before Mona's celebration. Hanna turned to Mona, who looked both distraught and relieved. Her eyes had huge, kind of ugly purple circles under them, too, as if she hadn't slept in days. "I didn't miss your party, did I?"

Lucas made a sniffing noise. Mona's shoulders tensed. "No . . ."

"The accident happened afterward," Lucas said. "You don't remember?"

Hanna tried to pull the oxygen tube out of her nose—no one looked attractive with something dangling from a nostril—and found that it had been taped down. She closed her eyes and grappled for something, *anything*, to explain all this. But the only thing she saw was Ali's face looming over her and whispering *something* before dissipating into black nothingness.

"No," Hanna whispered. "I don't remember any of that at all."

12

ON THE LAM

Late Monday evening, Emily sat on a faded blue bar stool at the counter of the M&J diner across from the Greyhound station in Akron, Ohio. She hadn't eaten anything all day and contemplated ordering a piece of nasty-looking cherry pie to go with her metallic-tasting coffee. Next to her, an old man slowly slurped a spoonful of tapioca pudding, and a bowling pin–shaped man and his knitting needle–shaped friend were shoveling down greasy burgers and fries. The jukebox was playing some twangy country song, and the hostess leaned heavily against the register, polishing dust off the Ohio-shaped magnets that were on sale for ninety-nine cents.

"Where you headed?" a voice asked.

Emily looked into the eyes of the diner's fry cook, a sturdy man who looked like he did a lot of bow hunting when he wasn't making grilled cheese. Emily searched for a name tag, but he wasn't wearing one. His red ball cap had a big, singular letter *A* stitched in the center. She licked her lips, shivering a little. "How do you know I'm headed somewhere?"

He gave her a knowing look. "You're not from here. And Greyhound's across the street. And you have a big duffel bag. Clever, aren't I?"

Emily sighed, staring into her cup of coffee. It had taken her less than twenty minutes to power walk the mile from Helene's to the mini mart down the road, even with her heavy duffel in tow. Once there, she'd found a ride to the bus station, and had bought a ticket for the first bus out of Iowa. Unfortunately it had been going to Akron, a place where Emily knew absolutely no one. Worse, the bus smelled like someone had bad gas, and the guy sitting next to her had his AirPods cranked up to maximum volume while he sang along to some death metal band with lots of screaming that she detested. Then, weirdly, when the bus pulled into the Akron station, Emily had discovered a crab scuttling around under her seat. A crab, even though they were nowhere near an ocean. When she'd stumbled into the terminal and noticed that the big departures board said there was a 10 p.m. bus to Philadelphia, an ache had welled up inside her. She'd never missed Pennsylvania as much as she did now.

Emily shut her eyes, finding it hard to believe that she was really, truly running away. There were many times she'd imagined running away before—Ali used to say she'd go with her. Hawaii was one of their top five choices. So was Paris. Ali said they could assume different identities. When Emily protested, saying that sounded difficult, Ali shrugged and said, "Nah. Becoming someone else is probably really easy." Wherever they chose, they promised to spend tons of uninterrupted time together, and Emily had always secretly hoped that maybe, just maybe, Ali would have realized she loved Emily as much as Emily loved her. But in the end, Emily always felt bad and said, "Ali, you have no reason to run away. Your life is perfect here." And Ali would shrug in response, saying Emily was right, her life *was* pretty perfect.

Until someone killed her.

The fry cook turned up the volume on the tiny TV sitting next to the eight-slice toaster and an open package of Wonder Bread. When Emily looked up, she saw a CNN reporter standing in front of the familiar Rosewood Memorial Hospital. Emily knew it well—she passed it every morning on her drive to Rosewood Day.

"We have reports that Hanna Marin, seventeen-year-old resident of Rosewood and friend to Alison DiLaurentis, the girl whose body mysteriously turned up in her old backyard about a month ago, has just awakened from the coma she'd been in since Saturday night's tragic accident," the reporter said into her microphone.

Emily's coffee cup clattered against her saucer. *Coma?* Hanna's parents swam onto the screen, saying that, yes, Hanna was awake and seemed okay. There were no leads as to who had hit Hanna, or why.

Emily covered her mouth with her hand, which smelled like the fake-leather Greyhound bus seat. She whipped her phone out of her jean jacket pocket and turned it on. She'd been trying to conserve the battery because she'd accidentally left her charger behind in Iowa. Her fingers shook as she dialed Aria's number. It went to voice mail. "Aria, it's Emily," she said after the beep. "I just found out about Hanna, and . . ."

She trailed off, her eyes returning to the screen. There, in the upper right-hand corner, was her *own* face, staring back at her from the photo she'd had taken for last year's yearbook. "In other Rosewood news, another one of Ms. DiLaurentis's friends, Emily Fields, has gone missing," the anchor said. "She was visiting relatives in Iowa this week, but vanished from the property this morning."

The fry cook turned from flipping a grilled cheese and glanced at the screen. A look of disbelief crossed his face. He looked at Emily, then back at the screen again. His metal spatula fell to the floor with a hollow clatter.

Emily hit end without finishing her message to Aria. On the TV screen, her parents were standing in front of Emily's blue-shingled house. Her father wore his best plaid polo shirt, and her mom had a cashmere sweater cardigan draped over her shoulders. Carolyn stood off to the side, holding Emily's swim team portrait for the camera. Emily was too stunned to be embarrassed that a picture of her in a high-cut Speedo tank suit was on national television.

"We're very worried," Emily's mother said. "We want

Emily to know that we love her and just want her to come home."

Tears bloomed at the corners of Emily's eyes. Words couldn't describe what it felt like to hear her mother say those three little words: *We love her.* She slid off the stool, pushing her arms into her jacket sleeves.

The word PHILADELPHIA was plastered on top of a red, blue, and silver Greyhound bus across the street. The big 7-Up clock over the diner's counter said 9:53. *Please don't let the 10 p.m. bus be sold out,* Emily prayed.

She glanced at the scribble-covered bill next to her coffee. "I'll be back," she said to the cook, grabbing her bags. "I just have to get a bus ticket."

The fry cook still looked like a tornado had picked him up and dropped him onto a different planet. "Don't worry about it," he said faintly. "Coffee's on the house."

"Thanks!" The sleigh bells on the diner's door jingled together as Emily left. She ran across the empty highway and skidded into the bus station, thanking the various forces of the universe that had prevented a line from forming at the ticket window. Finally, she had a destination: home.

13

ONLY LOSERS GET HIT BY CARS

Tuesday morning, when she *should* have been strolling into her Pilates II class at Body Tonic gym, Hanna was instead lying flat on her back as two fat female nurses cleaned her off with a sponge. After they left, her physician, Dr. Geist, strode into the room and flipped on the light.

"Turn it off!" Hanna demanded sharply, quickly covering her face.

Dr. Geist left it on. Hanna had put in a request for a different doctor—if she was spending all this time here, couldn't she at least have an MD who was a little bit hotter?—but it seemed like nobody in this hospital was listening.

Hanna slid halfway under the covers and peeked into her Chanel compact. Yep, her monster face was still there, complete with the stitches on her chin, the two black eyes, the fat, purplish bottom lip, and the enormous bruises on her collarbone—it was going to be ages before she could wear low-cut tops again. She sighed and snapped the compact closed. She couldn't wait to go to Bill Beach to fix all the damage.

Dr. Geist inspected Hanna's vital signs on a computer that looked like it had been built in the sixties. "You're recovering very well. Now that the swelling's gone down, we don't see any residual brain injury. Your internal organs look fairly good. It's a miracle."

"Ha," Hanna grumbled.

"It *is* a miracle," Hanna's father butted in, walking in to stand behind Dr. Geist. "We were sick with worry, Hanna. It makes me sick that someone did this to you. And that they're still out there."

Hanna sneaked a peek at him. Her dad wore a charcoal-gray suit and sleek black shiny loafers. In the twelve hours since she'd awakened, he'd been incredibly patient, succumbing to Hanna's every whim . . . and Hanna had lots of whims. First, she demanded that they move her into her own private room—the last thing she needed was to hear the old lady on the other side of the curtain in intensive care talk about her bowel habits and imminent hip replacement. Next, Hanna had made her dad bring her iPad so she could stream Netflix and get caught up with Instagram gossip. The hospital rent-a-TVs only got six lame-ass network channels. She'd begged her dad to make the nurses give her more painkillers, and she'd deemed the mattress on the hospital bed completely uncomfortable, forcing him to go out to the

Tempur-Pedic store an hour ago to get her a space-age foam topper. From the looks of the mammoth Tempur-Pedic plastic bag he was holding, it appeared that his trip had been successful.

Dr. Geist dropped Hanna's clipboard back into the slot at the foot of her bed. "We should be able to let you out in a few more days. Any questions?"

"Yes," Hanna said, her voice still croaky from the ventilator they'd had her on since her accident. She pointed to the IV in her arm. "How many calories is this thing giving me?" By the way her hip bones felt, it seemed as if she'd lost weight while being in the hospital—*bonus!*—but she just wanted to make sure.

Dr. Geist looked at her crazily, probably wishing *he* could switch patients too. "It's antibiotics and stuff to hydrate you," Hanna's father quickly interjected. He patted Hanna's arm. "It's all going to make you feel much better." As he and her dad left the room, Dr. Geist snapped off the light again.

Hanna glowered for a moment at the empty doorway, then fell back onto her bed. The only thing that could make her feel better right now was a six-hour massage by some hot, shirtless Italian male model. And, oh yeah, a brand-new face.

She was completely weirded out that this had happened to her. She kept wondering if, after falling asleep again, she'd wake up in her own bed with its six-hundred-thread-count pima cotton sheets, beautiful as before, ready for a day of shopping with Mona. Who gets hit by a car? She wasn't even in the hospital for something cool, like a high-stakes kidnapping or some kind of experimental treatment that made your skin look amazing.

But something that scared her far more—and something that she didn't want to think about—was that the whole night was a huge, gaping hole in Hanna's memory. She couldn't even remember Mona's party.

Just then, two figures in familiar blue blazers appeared at the door. When they saw Hanna was awake and decent, Aria and Spencer rushed in quickly, their faces pinched with worry. "We tried to see you last night," Spencer said, "but the nurses wouldn't let us in."

Hanna noticed that Aria was sneaking a peek at Hanna's greenish bruises, a grossed-out look on her face. *"What?"* Hanna snapped, smoothing out her long, auburn hair, which she'd just spritzed with Bumble and bumble Surf Spray. "You should try to be a little more Florence Nightingale, Aria. Sean's really into that."

It still rankled Hanna that her ex, Sean Ackard, had broken up with *her* to be with Aria. Today, Aria's hair hung in chunks around her face, and she wore a red-and-white checkered tent dress under her Rosewood Day blazer. She looked like a cross between Strawberry Shortcake and a tablecloth. Besides, didn't she know that if she got caught without the plaid pleated skirt part of the school's uniform, Appleton would just send her home and make her change?

"Sean and I broke up," Aria mumbled.

Hanna raised a curious eyebrow. "Oh *really*? And why is that?"

Aria sat down in the little orange plastic chair next to Hanna's bed. "That doesn't matter right now. What matters is . . . this. You." Her eyes welled with tears. "I wish we would've gotten to the playground sooner. I keep thinking about it. We could've stopped that car, somehow. We could've pulled you out of the way."

Hanna stared at her, her throat constricting. "You were *there*?"

Aria nodded, then glanced at Spencer. "We were all there. Emily too. You wanted to meet us."

Hanna's heart quickened. "I did?"

Aria leaned closer. Her breath smelled like Orbit Mint Mojito gum, a flavor Hanna hated. "You said you knew who A was."

"*What?*" Hanna whispered.

"You don't *remember*?" Spencer shrieked. "Hanna, that's who hit you!" She whipped out her phone and brought up a text. "Look!"

Hanna stared at the screen. She knew too much. —A

"A sent us this right after you were hit by the car," Spencer whispered.

Hanna blinked hard, stunned. Her mind was like a big, deep Gucci purse, and when Hanna rooted around in the bottom, she couldn't come up with the memory she needed. "A tried to *kill* me?" Her stomach began to churn. All day, she'd had this awful feeling, deep down, that this hadn't been an accident. But she'd tried to quell it, telling herself that was nonsense.

"Maybe A had spoken to you?" Spencer tried. "Or maybe you saw A doing something. Can you think? We're afraid that if you don't remember who A is, A might . . ." She trailed off, gulping.

". . . strike again," Aria whispered.

Hanna shivered spastically, breaking out in a cold, horrified sweat. "Th-the last thing I remember was the night before Mona's party," she stammered. "The next thing I know, we're all sitting in Ali's backyard. We're in seventh grade again. It's the day before Ali disappeared, and we're talking about how we're going to have the sleepover in the barn. Remember that?"

Spencer squinted. "Uh . . . sure. I guess."

"I kept trying to warn Ali that she was going to die the next day," Hanna explained, her voice rising. "But Ali wouldn't pay attention to me. And then she looked at me and said I should stop making a big deal out of it. She said she was fine."

Spencer and Aria exchanged a glance. "Hanna, it was a dream," Aria said softly.

"Well, *yeah*, obviously." Hanna rolled her eyes. "I'm just saying. It was like Ali was right *there*." She pointed at a pink GET WELL SOON balloon at the end of the bed. It had a round face and accordion-style arms and legs, and it could walk on its own.

Before either of Hanna's old friends could respond, a loud voice interrupted them. "Where's the sexiest patient in this hospital?"

Mona stood in the doorway, her arms outstretched. She, too, wore her Rosewood Day blazer and skirt along with an amazing pair of Marc Jacobs boots Hanna had never seen. Mona glanced at Aria and Spencer suspiciously, then dumped a pile of *Vogue, Elle, People,* and *Us Weekly* magazines on the nightstand. "*Pour vous,* Hanna. Just in case you get bored of social media. And we *need* to fill you in on the latest fight on Beauty TikTok."

"I *so* love you," Hanna cried, quickly trying to switch gears. She couldn't dwell on this A thing. She just *couldn't.* She was relieved that she hadn't been hallucinating yesterday when she woke up and saw Mona standing over her bed. Things with Mona had been rocky last week, but Hanna's last memory was receiving a court dress for Mona's birthday party in the mail. It was obviously an olive branch, but it was weird that she couldn't remember their makeup conversation—usually, when Hanna and Mona made up, they gave each other gifts, like a new phone case or a pair of Coach kidskin gloves.

Spencer looked at Mona. "Well, now that Hanna's awake, I guess we don't have to do that thing on Friday."

Hanna perked up. "What thing?"

Mona perched on Hanna's bed. "We were going to have a little vigil for you at the Rosewood Country Club," she admitted. "Everyone at school was invited."

Hanna put her IV-rigged hand to her mouth, touched. "You guys were going to do that . . . for me?" She caught Mona's eye. It seemed unusual that Mona would be planning a party with Spencer—Mona had a lot of issues with Hanna's old friends—but Mona actually looked excited. Hanna's heart lifted.

"Since the club's already booked . . . maybe we could have a welcome-back party instead?" Hanna suggested in a small, tentative voice. She crossed her other hand's fingers under her sheets for luck, hoping Mona wouldn't think it was a stupid idea.

Mona pursed her perfectly lined lips. "I can't say no to a party. Especially a party for you, Han."

Hanna's insides sparkled. This was the best news she'd gotten all day—even better than when the nurses had permitted her to use the bathroom unattended. She wanted to leap up and give Mona an enormous, thankful, I'm-so-happy-we're-friends-again hug, but she was attached to too many tubes. "Especially since I can't remember your birthday party," Hanna pointed out, pouting. "Was it awesome?"

Mona lowered her eyes, picking a fuzz ball off her sweater.

"It's cool," Hanna said quickly. "You can tell me it rocked. I can handle it." She thought for a moment. "And I have a fantastic idea. Since it's kind of close to Halloween, and since I don't look my absolute best right now . . ." She waved her hands around her face. "Let's make it a masquerade!"

"*Perfect,*" Mona gushed. "Oh, Han, it'll be amazing!"

She grabbed Mona's hands and they started squealing together. Aria and Spencer stood there awkwardly, left out. But Hanna wasn't about to squeal with them, too. This was something only BFFs did, and there was only one of those in Hanna's world.

14

INTERROGATION, WITH A SIDE
OF SPYING

Tuesday afternoon, after a quick yearbook meeting and an hour of field hockey drills, Spencer pulled up to her blue slate circular driveway. There was a Rosewood PD squad car sitting in her driveway next to her mother's battleship-gray Range Rover.

Spencer's heart catapulted into her throat, as it had been doing a lot the past few days. Had it been a huge mistake to confess her guilt about Ali to Melissa? What if Melissa only said that Spencer didn't have the killer instinct to throw her off track? What if she'd called up Wilden and told him that Spencer had done it?

Spencer thought of that night again. Her sister had had such an eerie smile on her face when she said Spencer couldn't have murdered Ali. The words she'd chosen were odd, too—she'd said it took a very *unique* person to kill. Why hadn't she said *crazy* or *heartless*? *Unique* made it sound special. Spencer had been so freaked out, she'd avoided Melissa ever since, feeling awkward and uncertain in her presence.

As Spencer slipped inside her front door and hung her Burberry trench coat in the hall closet, she noticed that Melissa and Ian were sitting very rigidly on the Hastingses' living room couch, as if they were being berated in the principal's office. Officer Wilden sat across from them, on the leather club chair. "H-Hi," Spencer sputtered, surprised.

"Oh, Spencer." Wilden gave Spencer a nod. "I'm just talking to your sister and Ian for a moment, if you'll excuse us."

Spencer took a big step back. "Wh-What are you talking about?"

"Just a few questions about the night Alison DiLaurentis went missing," Wilden said, his eyes on his notepad. "I'm trying to get everyone's perspective."

The room was silent except for the sound of the ionizer Spencer's mother had bought after her allergist told her that dust mites gave women wrinkles. Spencer backed out of the room slowly.

"There's a letter for you on the hall table," Melissa called out just as Spencer rounded the corner. "Mom left it for you."

There was indeed a stack of mail on the hall table, next to a hive-shaped terra-cotta vase that had allegedly been a gift to Spencer's great-grandmother from Howard Hughes. Spencer's letter was right on top,

in an already-opened creamy envelope with her name
handwritten across the front. Inside was an invitation on
heavy cream card stock. Gold, scrolling script read, *The
Golden Orchid committee invites you to a finalists' breakfast
and interview at Daniel Restaurant in New York City on
Friday, October 15.*

There was a pink Post-it note affixed to the corner.
Her mother had written, *Spencer, we already cleared this with
your teachers. We have rooms reserved at the W for Thursday
night.*

Spencer pressed the paper to her face. It smelled a
little like Polo cologne, or maybe that was Wilden. Her
parents were actually *encouraging* her to compete, knowing what they knew? It seemed so surreal. And *wrong.*

Or . . . was it? She ran her finger along the invite's
embossed letters. Spencer had longed to win a Golden
Orchid since third grade, and perhaps her parents recognized that. And if she hadn't been so freaked out about
Ali and A, she definitely would have been able to write
her own Golden Orchid–worthy essay. So why not really
go for it? She thought about what Melissa had said—her
parents would reward her handsomely for winning. She
needed a reward right now.

The living room's grandfather clock bonged six times.
Spencer guessed that Wilden was waiting to make sure
she'd gone upstairs before he began his discussion. She
stomped loudly up the first few stairs, then stopped halfway and marched in place to make it sound like she'd

climbed the rest of the way up. She had a perfect view of Ian and Melissa through the banister spindles, but no one could see her.

"Okay." Wilden cleared his throat. "So, back to Alison DiLaurentis."

Melissa wrinkled her nose. "I'm still not sure what this has to do with us. You'd be better off talking to my sister."

Spencer squeezed her eyes shut. *Here it comes.*

"Just bear with me," Wilden said slowly. "You two *do* want to help me find Alison's killer, don't you?"

"Of course," Melissa said haughtily, her face turning red.

"Good," Wilden said. As he pulled out a black spiral-bound notebook, Spencer slowly let out her breath.

"So," Wilden continued. "You guys were in the barn with Alison and her friends shortly before she disappeared, right?"

Melissa nodded. "They walked in on us. Spencer had asked our parents to use the barn for her sleepover. She thought I was going to Prague that night, but I was actually going the next day. We left, though. We let them have the barn." She smiled proudly, as if she'd been oh-so-charitable.

"Okay . . ." Wilden scribbled in his notepad. "And you didn't see anything strange in your yard that night? Anyone lurking around, nothing like that?"

"Nothing," Melissa said quietly. Again, Spencer felt grateful but also confused. Why wasn't heart-of-ice

Melissa ratting her out?

"And where did you go after that?" Wilden asked.

Melissa and Ian looked surprised. "We went to Melissa's den. Right in there." Ian pointed down the hall. "We were just . . . hanging out. Watching TV. I don't know."

"And you were together the whole night?"

Ian glanced at Melissa. "I mean, it was over four years ago, so it's kind of hard to remember, but yeah, I'm pretty sure."

"Melissa?" Wilden asked.

Melissa flicked a tassel on one of the couch pillows. For a shimmering second, Spencer saw a look of terror cross her face. In a blink, it was gone. "We were together."

"Okay." Wilden looked back and forth at them, as if something bothered him. "And . . . Ian. Was there something going on with you and Alison?"

Ian's face went slack. He cleared his throat. "Ali had a crush on me. I flirted with her a little, that's all."

Spencer rolled her jaw around, surprised. Ian, lying . . . to a cop? She peeked at her sister, but Melissa was staring straight ahead, a small smirk on her face. *I kind of knew Ian and Ali were together,* she'd said.

Spencer thought about the memory Hanna had brought up at the hospital earlier about the four of them going over to Ali's house the day before she went missing. The details of the day were foggy, but Spencer remembered that they'd seen Melissa walking back to the Hastingses' barn. Ali had yelled out to her, asking if Melissa was worried that Ian might find another girl-friend while Melissa was in Prague. Spencer had smacked Ali for the remark, warning her to shut up. Since she'd admitted to Ali and only Ali that she'd kissed Ian, Ali had been threatening to tell Melissa what Spencer had done if Spencer didn't confess to it herself. So Spencer thought Ali's comments were meant to mess with her, not Melissa.

That *was* what Ali was doing, wasn't it? She wasn't so sure anymore.

After that, Melissa had shrugged, muttered under her breath, and stormed toward the Hastingses' barn. On her way, though, Spencer remembered her sister pausing to look at the hole the workers were digging in Ali's backyard. It was as if she were trying to commit its dimensions to memory.

Spencer clapped a hand over her mouth. She'd received a text from A last week when she was sitting in front of her vanity mirror. It had said, *Ali's murderer is right in front of you,* and right after Spencer read it, Melissa had appeared in her doorway to announce that the *Philadelphia Sentinel* reporter was downstairs. Melissa had been as much in front of Spencer as her own reflec-tion had.

As Wilden shook hands with Ian and Melissa and rose to leave, Spencer scampered quietly the rest of the way up the stairs, her mind spinning. The day before she went missing, Ali had said, "You know what, guys? I think this is going to be the summer of Ali." She had seemed so certain of it, so confident that everything would work out the way she wanted. But although Ali could boss the four of them into doing everything she said, no one, absolutely *no one*, played those kinds of games with Spencer's sister. Because in the end, Melissa. Always. Won.

15

GUESS WHO'S BA-A-ACK?

Early Wednesday morning, Emily's mother silently steered the minivan out of the Philadelphia Greyhound bus station parking lot, down Route 76 in the middle of morning rush hour, past the Schuylkill River's charming row houses, and straight to Rosewood Memorial Hospital. Even though Emily was badly in need of a shower after her grueling, ten-hour bus trip, she really wanted to see how Hanna was doing.

By the time they reached the hospital, Emily began to worry that she'd made a grave mistake. She'd called her parents before getting on the bus to Philadelphia at 10 p.m. last night, saying she'd seen them on TV, that she was okay, and that she was coming home. Her parents had *sounded* happy . . . but then her cell phone's battery had died, so she didn't really know for sure. Since Emily had gotten in the car, all her mom had said to her was,

"Are you okay?" After Emily said yes, her mom told her that Hanna had woken up, and then she went mute.

Her mother pulled under the awning of the hospital's main entrance and put the car into park. She let out a long, whinnying sigh, resting her head briefly against the steering wheel. "It scares me to death, driving in Philly."

Emily stared at her mom, with her stiff gray hair, emerald-green cardigan, and prized pearl necklace that she wore every single day, kind of like Marge on *The Simpsons*. Emily suddenly realized that she had never seen her mother drive anywhere remotely near Philadelphia. And her mom had always been terrified about merging, even if no cars were coming. "Thanks for picking me up," she said in a small voice.

Mrs. Fields studied Emily carefully, her lips wobbling. "We were so worried about you. The idea that we might have lost you forever really made us rethink some things. That wasn't right, sending you to Helene's the way we did. Emily, we might not accept the decisions you've made for . . . for your life, but we're going to try and live with it as best we can. That's what Brené Brown says. Your father and I have been reading her books."

Outside the car, a young couple wheeled a Silver Cross pram to their Porsche Cayenne. Two attractive, twenty-something Black doctors shoved each other jokingly. Emily breathed in the honeysuckle air and noticed a Wawa market across the street. She was definitely in Rosewood. She hadn't crash-landed in some other girl's life.

"Okay," Emily croaked. Her whole body felt itchy, especially her palms. "Well . . . thank you. That makes me really happy."

Mrs. Fields reached into her purse and took out a plastic Barnes & Noble bag. She handed it to Emily. "This is for you."

Inside was a Blu-ray of *Finding Dory*. Emily looked up, confused.

"Ellen DeGeneres is the voice of the funny fish," Emily's mother explained in a slightly *uh-duh* voice. "We thought you might like her." Emily suddenly got it. Ellen DeGeneres was a fish—a lesbian swimmer, just like Emily.

"Thanks," she said, clutching the Blu-ray to her chest, oddly touched.

She tumbled out of the car and walked through the hospital's automatic front door in a daze. As she passed by the check-in, the coffee bar, and the high-end gift shop, her mother's words slowly sank in. Her family had *accepted her*? She wondered if she should call Maya and tell her she was back. But what would she say? *I'm home! My parents are cool now! We can date now!* It seemed so . . . cheesy.

Hanna's room was on the fifth floor. When Emily pushed open the door, Aria and Spencer were already sitting next to her bed, their hands wrapped around Venti Starbucks coffees. A row of ragged black stitches stood out on Hanna's chin, and she wore a hulking cast on her arm. There was an enormous bouquet of flowers next to her bed, and the whole room smelled like rosemary aromatherapy oil. "Hey, Hanna," Emily said, shutting the door softly. "How are you?"

Hanna sighed, almost annoyed. "Are you here to ask me about A too?"

Emily looked at Aria, then at Spencer, who was picking nervously at her coffee cup's cardboard sleeve. It was strange to see Aria and Spencer together—didn't Aria suspect that Spencer had killed Ali? She raised an eyebrow at Aria, indicating as much, but Aria shook her head, mouthing, *I'll explain later.*

Emily looked back at Hanna. "Well, I wanted to see how you were, but yeah . . ." she started.

"Save it," Hanna said haughtily, winding a tendril of hair around her finger. "I don't remember what happened. So we might as well talk about something else." Her voice wobbled with distress.

Emily stepped back. She looked beseechingly at Aria, her eyes saying, *She really doesn't remember?* Aria shook her head no.

"Hanna, if we don't keep asking, you're never going to remember," Spencer urged. "Did you get a text? A note? Maybe A put something in your pocket?"

Hanna glowered at Spencer, her lips smushed closed.

"You found out sometime during or after Mona's party," Aria encouraged. "Does it have something to do with that?"

"Maybe A said something incriminating," Spencer said. "Or maybe you saw the person behind the wheel of the SUV that hit you?"

"Would you just stop?" Tears brimmed at the corners of Hanna's eyes. "The doctor said pushing me like this isn't good for my recovery." After a pause, she ran her hands along her soft cashmere blanket and took a deep breath. "If you guys could go back to the time before Ali died, do you think you could prevent it from happening?"

Emily looked around. Her friends seemed as stunned by the question as she was. "Well, sure," Aria murmured quietly.

"Of course," Emily said.

"And you'd still want to?" Hanna goaded. "Would we really want Ali around? Now that we know Ali kept the secret about Toby from us and had been seeing Ian behind our backs? Now that we've grown up a little and realized that Ali was basically a bitch?"

"Of course I'd want her here," Emily said sharply. But when she looked around, her friends were staring at the floor, saying nothing.

"Well, we certainly didn't want her dead," Spencer finally mumbled. Aria nodded and scratched at her purple nail polish.

Hanna had wrapped a Hermès scarf around part of her cast in what Emily imagined was an attempt to make it look prettier. The rest of the cast, Emily noticed, was filled with signatures. Everyone from Rosewood had signed already—there was a sweeping signature from Noel Kahn; a tidy one from Spencer's sister, Melissa; a spiky one from Mr. Jennings, Hanna's math teacher. Someone

134 ◆ SARA SHEPARD

had signed the cast only with the word KISSES!, the dot in the exclamation point a smiley face. Emily ran her fingers over the word, as if it were Braille.

After a few more minutes of not saying much at all, Aria, Emily, and Spencer gloomily filed out of the room. They were silent until they reached the elevator bank. "What brought on all that stuff she was saying about Ali?" Emily whispered.

"Hanna had a dream about Ali while she was in the coma." Spencer shrugged and punched the down button for the elevator.

"We have to get Hanna to remember," Aria whispered. "She *knows* who A is."

It was barely 8 a.m. when they emerged into the parking lot. As an ambulance raced past them, Spencer's cell phone began to play Vivaldi's *Four Seasons*. She checked her pocket, irritated. "Who could be calling me this early in the morning?"

Then Aria's cell phone buzzed too. And Emily's.

A cold wind swept over all the girls. The hospital-logo flags that hung from the main awning billowed in the breeze. "No," Spencer gasped.

Emily peeked at the text.

Miss me, bitches? Stop digging for answers, or I'll have to erase your memories too. Kisses! —A

Kisses! Emily read, just like on Hanna's cast.

16

A NEW VICTIM

That Wednesday afternoon, Spencer waited on Rosewood Country Club's outdoor patio to begin planning Hanna's welcome-back masquerade with Mona Vanderwaal. She absentmindedly flipped through the AP Econ essay that had been nominated for a Golden Orchid. When she'd stolen the essay from Melissa's arsenal of old high school papers, Spencer hadn't understood half of it . . . and she still didn't. But since the Golden Orchid judges were going to grill her at Friday's breakfast, she'd decided to learn it word for word. How hard could it be? She memorized entire monologues for drama club all the time. Plus, she was hoping it would get her mind off A.

She closed her eyes and mouthed the first few paragraphs perfectly. Then she imagined the outfit she'd wear for her Golden Orchid interview—definitely something Calvin or Chanel, maybe with some clear-framed, academic-looking glasses. Maybe she'd even bring in the article the *Philadelphia Sentinel* had done about her and leave it sticking just slightly out of her bag. Then the interviewers would see it and think, *My, she's already been on the front page of a major newspaper!*

"Hey." Mona stood above her in a pretty olive-green dress and tall black boots. She had an oversize dark purple bag slung over her right shoulder, and she carried a Jamba Juice smoothie in her hand. "Am I too early?"

"Nope, you're perfect." Spencer moved her books off the seat across from her and stuffed Melissa's essay into her purse. Her hand grazed against her cell phone. She fought against the masochistic urge to pull it out and look at A's message again. *Stop digging for answers.* After everything that had happened, after three days of radio silence, A was still after them. Spencer was dying to talk to Wilden about it, but she was terrified about what A might do if she did.

"You okay?" Mona sat down and stared at Spencer worriedly.

"Sure." Spencer rattled the straw in her empty Diet Coke glass, trying to push A from her mind. She gestured to her books. "I just have this interview for an essay competition on Friday. It's in New York. So I'm sort of freaking out."

Mona smiled. "That's right, that Golden Orchid thing? You've been all over the announcements."

Spencer ducked her head faux-bashfully. She loved

hearing her name on the morning announcements, except when she had to read them herself—then it just seemed boastful. She inspected Mona carefully. Mona had really done a fantastic job transforming from Razor scooter–loving dork to fabulous diva, but Spencer had never really gotten past seeing Mona as one of the many girls Ali liked to tease. This was possibly the first time she'd ever spoken to Mona one-on-one.

Mona cocked her head. "I saw your sister outside your house when I left for school this morning. She said your picture was in Sunday's paper."

"*Melissa* told you that?" Spencer's eyes widened, feeling a glimmer of uneasiness. She recalled the fearful look that had crossed Melissa's face yesterday when Wilden asked her where she'd been the night Ali vanished. What was Melissa so afraid of? What was Melissa hiding?

Mona blinked, lost. "Yeah. Why? Is it not true?"

Spencer shook her head slowly. "No, it's true. I'm just surprised Melissa said something nice about me, is all."

"What do you mean?" Mona asked.

"We're not the best of friends." Spencer glanced furtively around the country club patio, filled with a horrible feeling that Melissa was here, *listening*. "Anyway," she said. "About the party. I just talked to the club manager, and they're all ready for Friday."

"Perfect." Mona pulled out a stack of cards and slid them across the table. "These are the invites I came up with.

They're in the shape of a mask, see? But then there's foil on the front, so when you look into it, you see yourself."

Spencer looked at her slightly fuzzy reflection in the invite. Her skin was clear and glowing and her newly touched-up buttery highlights brightened her face.

Mona flipped through her Gucci wallet diary, consulting her notes. "I also think, to make Hanna feel *really* special, we should bring her into the room in a grand princess–style entrance. I'm thinking four hot, shirtless guys could carry her in on a canopied pedestal. Or something like that. I've arranged for a bunch of models to come over to Hanna's tomorrow so she can choose them for herself."

"That's *awesome*." Spencer folded her hands over her Kate Spade diary. "Hanna's lucky to have you as a friend."

Mona looked ruefully out at the golf course and let out a long sigh. "The way things have been between us lately, it's a miracle that Hanna doesn't hate me."

"What are you talking about?" Spencer had heard something about Mona and Hanna getting in a fight at Mona's birthday party, but she'd been so busy and distracted, she hadn't really paid attention to the rumors.

Mona sighed and tucked a strand of white-blond hair behind her ear. "Hanna and I haven't been on the best of terms," she admitted. "It's just that, she'd been acting so *weird*. We used to do everything together, but suddenly she started keeping all these secrets, blowing off plans we made, and acting like she hated me." Mona's eyes welled with tears.

A lump formed in Spencer's throat. She knew just how that felt. Before she disappeared, Ali had done the same thing to her.

"She was spending a lot of time with you guys—and that made me a little jealous." Mona traced her pointer finger around the perimeter of an empty bread plate on the table. "Truthfully, I was stunned when Hanna wanted to be friends with me in eighth grade. She was part of Ali's clique, and you guys were *legend*. I always thought our friendship was too good to be true. Maybe I still kind of feel that way from time to time."

Spencer stared at her. It was incredible how similar Mona and Hanna's friendship was to Spencer and Ali's—Spencer had been astonished when Ali chose her to be part of her inner circle, too. "Well, Hanna's been hanging out with us because we've been dealing with some . . . issues," she said. "I'm sure she'd rather be with you."

Mona bit her lip. "I was terrible to her. I thought she was trying to ditch me, so I just . . . went on the defensive. But when she got hit by the car . . . and when I realized she might die . . . it was awful. She's been my best friend for years." She covered her face with her hands. "I just want to forget about all of it. I just want things to be *normal* again."

The charms dangling off Mona's Tiffany bracelet

tinkled together prettily. Her mouth puckered, as if she were about to start sobbing. Spencer suddenly felt guilty about the way they used to tease Mona. Ali had taunted her about her vampire tan, and even her height—Ali always said Mona was short enough to be a sixth grader. Ali also claimed that Mona had cellulite on her gut— she'd seen Mona changing in the country club locker room and had nearly thrown up it was so ugly. Spencer didn't believe her, so once, when Ali was spending the night at Spencer's, they sneaked over to Mona's house down the street and spied on Mona as she was dancing to videos on YouTube in the den. "I hope her shirt flutters up," Ali whispered. "Then you'll see her in all her nastiness."

Mona's shirt stayed put. She'd continued to dance around crazily, the way Spencer danced when she thought no one was watching. Then Ali knocked on the window. Mona's face reddened and she fled out of the room.

"I'm sure everything will be fine between you and Hanna," Spencer said gently, touching Mona's thin arm. "And the last thing you should do is blame yourself."

"I hope so." Mona gave Spencer a vulnerable smile. "Thanks for listening."

The waitress interrupted them, setting the leather booklet containing Spencer's bill on the table. Spencer opened it up and signed her two Diet Cokes to her father's account. She was surprised that her watch said it was almost five. She stood up, feeling a twinge of sadness, not wanting the conversation to end. When had she last talked to anyone about anything *real*? "I'm late for rehearsal." She let out a long, stressed sigh.

Mona inspected her for a moment, then glanced across the room. "Actually, you might not want to leave quite yet." She nodded toward the double French doors, color returning to her face. "That guy over there just checked you out."

Spencer glanced over her shoulder. Two college-age guys in Lacoste polos sat at a corner table, nursing Bombay Sapphires and sodas. "Which one?" Spencer murmured.

"Mr. Hugo Boss model." Mona pointed to a dark-haired guy with a chiseled jaw. A devious look came over her face. "Want to make him lose his mind?"

"How?" Spencer asked.

"Flash him," Mona whispered, nudging her chin at Spencer's skirt.

Spencer demurely covered her lap. "They'll kick us out!"

"No, they won't." Mona smirked. "I bet it'll make you feel better about all your Golden Orchid stress. It's like an instant spa treatment."

Spencer considered it for a moment. "I'll do it if you do it."

Mona nodded, standing up. "On three."

Spencer stood too. Mona cleared her throat to get

their attention. Both boys' heads swiveled over. "One . . . two . . ." Mona counted.

"Three!" Spencer cried. They pulled up their skirts fast. Spencer revealed green silk Eres boy shorts, and Mona showed off sexy, lacy black panties—definitely not the kind of thing worn by a girl who loves Razor scooters. They only held up their skirts for a moment, but it was enough. The dark-haired guy in the corner sputtered up a swallow of beer. Hugo Boss Model looked like he was going to faint. Spencer and Mona let their skirts drop and doubled over with laughter.

"Holy shit." Mona giggled, her chest heaving. "That was awesome."

Spencer's heart continued to rocket in her chest. Both of the guys were still staring, slack-jawed. "Do you think anyone else saw?" she whispered.

"Who the hell cares? Like they'd really kick *us* out of here."

Spencer's cheeks warmed, flattered that Mona considered her as traffic-stopping as she was. "Now I'm *really* late," she murmured. "But it was worth it."

"Of course it was." Mona blew her a kiss. "Promise me we'll do this again?"

Spencer nodded and blew her a kiss back, then breezed through the main dining room. She felt better than she had in days. With Mona's help, she'd managed to forget about A, the Golden Orchid, and Melissa for three whole minutes.

But as she walked through the parking lot, she felt a hand on her arm. "Wait."

When Spencer turned around, she found Mona nervously spinning her diamond necklace around her neck. Her expression had morphed from one of gleeful naughtiness to something much more guarded and uncertain.

"I know you're super-late," Mona blurted out, "and I don't want to bother you, but something's happening to me, and I really need to talk to someone about it. I know we don't know each other well, but I can't talk to Hanna—she's got enough problems. And everyone else would spread it around the school."

Spencer perched on the edge of a large ceramic planter, concerned. "What is it?"

Mona looked around cautiously, as if to make sure there were no Ralph Lauren–clad golfers nearby. "I've been getting these . . . text messages," she whispered.

Spencer lost hearing for a moment. *"What did you say?"*

"Text messages," Mona repeated. "I've only gotten two, but they're not really signed, so I don't know who they're from. They say these . . . these *horrible* things about me." Mona bit her lip. "I'm kind of scared."

A sparrow fluttered past and landed on a barren crab apple tree. A lawn mower rumbled to life in the distance. Spencer gaped at Mona. "Are they from . . .

A?" she whispered.

Mona went so pale, even her freckles vanished. "H-How did you know that?"

"Because." Spencer breathed in. *This wasn't happening. This* couldn't *be happening.* "Hanna and I—and Aria and Emily—we've all been getting them too."

17

CATS CAN FIGHT NICE, CAN'T THEY?

Wednesday afternoon, just as Hanna flopped over in her hospital bed—apparently, lying too still caused bedsores, which sounded even nastier than acne—she heard a knock at her door. She almost didn't want to answer it. She was a little sick of all her nosy visitors, especially Spencer, Aria, and Emily.

"Let's get ready to par-*tay*!" someone yelled. Four boys swept inside: Noel Kahn; Mason Byers; Aria's younger brother, Mike; and, surprise of all surprises, Sean Ackard, Hanna's—and Aria's, it seemed—ex-boyfriend.

"Hey, boys." Hanna lifted the oatmeal-colored cashmere blanket Mona had brought her from home over the bottom half of her face, revealing only her eyes. Seconds later, Lucas Beattie arrived, carrying a big bouquet of flowers.

Noel glanced at Lucas, then rolled his eyes. "Overcompensating for something?"

"Huh?" Lucas's face was nearly swallowed up by the bouquet.

Hanna didn't get why Lucas was always visiting her. Sure, they'd been friends for like a *minute* last week, when Lucas took her up in his dad's hot-air balloon and let her vent about all of her troubles. Hanna knew how much he liked her—he'd pretty much reached in, pulled out his heart, and handed it to her during their balloon ride together, but after she'd received Mona's court dress in the mail, Hanna clearly remembered sending Lucas a nasty text confirming that she was out of his league. She considered reminding him of that now, only . . . Lucas had been pretty useful. He'd gone to Sephora to buy Hanna a whole bunch of new makeup, read gossip blogs to her line by line, and cajoled the doctors into allowing him to douse the room with Bliss essential oils, just as Hanna had asked him to. She kind of liked having him around. If she weren't so popular and fabulous, he'd probably make a great boyfriend. He was definitely cute enough—way cuter than Sean, even.

Hanna glanced at Sean now. He was sitting stiffly in a plastic visitor's chair, peeking at Hanna's various get-well cards. Visiting Hanna in the hospital was *so* him. She wanted to ask him why he and Aria had broken up, but all of a sudden, she realized that she didn't care.

Noel looked at Hanna curiously. "What's with the veil?"

"The doctors told me to do this." Hanna pulled the

blanket tight around her nose. "To, like, keep away germs. And besides, you get to focus on my beautiful eyes."

"So, what was it like being in a coma?" Noel perched on the side of Hanna's bed, squeezing a stuffed turtle that her aunt and uncle had given her yesterday. "Was it, like, a really long acid trip?"

"And are they giving you medicinal marijuana now?" Mike asked hopefully, his blue eyes glinting. "I bet the hospital stash *rocks*."

"Nah, I bet they're giving her painkillers." Mason's parents were doctors, so he always busted out his medical knowledge. "Hospital patients have such a sweet setup."

"Are the nurses hot?" Mike burbled. "Do they strip for you?"

"Are you naked under there?" Noel asked. "Give us a peek!"

"Guys!" Lucas said in a horrified voice. The boys looked at him and rolled their eyes—except for Sean, who looked almost as uncomfortable as Lucas did. Sean was probably still in Virginity Club, Hanna thought with a smirk.

"It's fine," Hanna chirped. "I can handle it." It was actually refreshing to have the boys here, making inappropriate comments. Everyone else who visited had been so damn serious. As the boys gathered around to sign Hanna's cast, Hanna remembered something and sat up. "You guys are coming to my welcome-back party on Friday, right? Spencer and Mona are planning it, so I'm sure it's going to rock."

"Wouldn't miss it." Noel glanced at Mason and Mike, who were looking out the window, chatting about what limbs they'd break if they jumped from Hanna's fifth-floor balcony. "What's up with you and Mona, anyway?" Noel asked.

"Nothing." Hanna flinched. "Why?"

Noel capped the pen. "You guys had quite a catfight at her party. *Mrow!*"

"We did?" Hanna asked blankly. Lucas coughed uncomfortably.

"Noel, it was so not *mrow!*" Mona breezed into the room. She blew air-kisses at Noel, Mason, and Mike, shot a frosty smile at Sean, and dropped an enormous binder at the bottom of Hanna's bed. She ignored Lucas completely. "It was just a little BFF bitchiness."

Noel shrugged. He joined the other boys at the window and proceeded to get into a noogie fight with Mason.

Mona rolled her eyes. "So listen, Han, I was just talking to Spencer, and we made a must-have party list. I want to run the details by you." She opened her Tiffany-blue binder. "You, of course, have the final say before I talk to the venue." She licked her finger and turned a page. "Okay. Bisque or ivory napkins?"

Hanna tried to focus, but Noel's words were still fresh in Hanna's mind. *Mrow?* "What were we fighting about?" Hanna blurted out.

Mona paused, lowering her list to her lap. "Seriously,

Han, nothing. You remember we were fighting the week before? About the skywriter? Naomi and Riley?"

Hanna nodded. Mona had asked Naomi Zeigler and Riley Wolfe, their biggest rivals, to be part of her Sweet Seventeen party court. Hanna suspected it was in retaliation to Hanna blowing off their Frenniversary celebration.

"Well, you were totally right," Mona went on. "Those two are enormous bitches. I don't want us to hang out with them anymore. I'm sorry I let them in the inner circle for a little bit, Han."

"It's okay," Hanna said in a small voice, feeling a tiny lift.

"So, anyway." Mona pulled out two magazine cutouts. One was a longish, white, pleated bubble dress with a silk rosette on the back, and the other was a wild-print dress that hit high on the thigh. "Phillip Lim gathered gown or flirty Alice and Olivia minidress?"

"Alice and Olivia," Hanna answered. "It's boatneck and short, so it'll show lots of leg but detract from my collarbone and face." She pulled the sheet up to her eyes again.

"Speaking of that," Mona chirped, "look what I got for you!"

She reached into her butter-colored Cynthia Rowley tote and pulled out a delicate porcelain mask. It was in the shape of a pretty girl's face, with prominent cheekbones, pretty, pouty lips, and a nose that would definitely be on a plastic surgeon's most-requested list. It was so beautiful and intricate, it looked *almost* real.

"These exact masks were used in last year's Dior haute couture show," Mona breathed. "My mom knows someone at Dior's PR company in New York, and we had someone drive it down from New York City this morning."

"Oh my God." Hanna reached out and touched the edge of the mask. It felt like a mix between baby-soft skin and satin.

Mona held the mask up to Hanna's face, which was still half-covered by the blanket. "It will cover all your bruises. You'll be the most gorgeous girl at your party."

"Hanna's already gorgeous," Lucas piped up, whirling around from all the medical machines. "Even without a mask."

Mona's nose wrinkled as if Lucas had just told her he was going to take her temperature in her butt. "Oh, Lucas," she said frostily. "I didn't see you standing there."

"I've been here the whole time," Lucas pointed out tersely.

The two of them glowered at each other. Hanna noticed something almost apprehensive about Mona's expression. But in a blink, it was gone.

Mona placed Hanna's mask against her vase of flowers, positioning it so that it was staring at her. "This is going to be *the* party of the year, Han. I can't wait."

With that, Mona blew her a kiss and danced out of the room. Noel, Mason, Sean, and Mike followed, telling Hanna they'd be back tomorrow and she'd *better* share some of her medicinal marijuana with them. Only Lucas remained, leaning against the far wall next to a soothing Monet-esque poster of a field of dandelions. There was a disturbed expression on his face.

"So that cop, Wilden? He asked me some questions about the hit-and-run while we were waiting for you to wake up from your coma a couple days ago," Lucas said quietly, sitting down on the orange chair next to Hanna's bed. "Like, if I'd seen you the night it happened. If you were acting weird or worried. It kind of sounded like he thought the hit-and-run wasn't an accident."

Lucas swallowed hard and raised his eyes to Hanna. "You don't think it was the same person who was sending you those weird text messages, do you?"

Hanna shot up. She'd forgotten that she'd told Lucas about A when they'd gone up in the hot-air balloon together. Her heart started to pound. "Tell me you didn't say anything about that to Wilden."

"Of course not," Lucas assured her. "It's just . . . I'm worried about you. It's so scary that someone *hit* you, is all."

"Don't worry about it," Hanna interrupted, crossing her arms over her chest. "And please, *please* don't say a word to Wilden about it. Okay?"

"Okay," Lucas said. "Sure."

"Good," Hanna barked. She took a long sip from the glass of water that was next to her bed. Whenever she dared to consider the truth—that A had *hit her*—her mind closed off, refusing to let her ponder it any further.

"So. Isn't it nice that Mona's throwing a party for me?" Hanna asked pointedly, wanting to change the subject. "She's been such a wonderful friend. Everyone's saying so."

Lucas fiddled with the buttons on his Nike watch. "I'm not sure if you should trust her," he mumbled.

Hanna wrinkled her brow. "What are you talking about?"

Lucas hesitated for a few long seconds.

"Come on," Hanna said, annoyed. "What?"

Lucas reached over and tugged Hanna's sheet down, exposing her face. He took her cheeks in his hands and kissed her. Lucas's mouth was soft and warm and fit perfectly with hers. Tingles scampered up Hanna's spine.

When Lucas broke away, they stared at each other for seven long beeps on Hanna's EKG machine, breathing hard. Hanna was pretty sure the look on her face was one of pure astonishment.

"Do you remember?" Lucas asked, his eyes wide.

Hanna frowned. "Remember . . . what?"

Lucas stared at her for a long time, his eyes flickering back and forth. And then he turned away. "I–I should go," Lucas mumbled awkwardly, and pushed out of the room.

Hanna stared after him, her bruised lips still sparking from his kiss. What had just happened?

18

NOW, INTRODUCING, FOR THE FIRST TIME EVER IN ROSEWOOD, JESSICA MONTGOMERY

That same afternoon, Aria stood outside the Hollis art building, staring at a group of kids doing capoeira on the lawn. Aria had never understood capoeira. She went through a capoeira phase and tried to learn the interesting martial art. But she wasn't really acrobatic enough.

She felt a cold, thin hand on her shoulder. "Are you on campus for your art class?" a voice whispered in Aria's ear.

Aria stiffened. "Meredith." Today, Meredith wore a green pin-striped blazer and ripped jeans, and had an army-green knapsack slung over her shoulder. The way she was staring at Aria, Aria felt like a little ant beneath a Meredith-shaped magnifying glass.

"You're taking Mindless Art, right?" Meredith said. When Aria nodded dumbly, Meredith looked at her watch. "You'd better get up there. It starts in five minutes."

Aria felt trapped. She'd been considering bagging

this class completely—the last thing she wanted to do was spend two hours with Jenna Cavanaugh. Just seeing her the other day had brought back all sorts of uncomfortable memories. But Aria knew Meredith would relay everything to Byron, and Byron would give her a lecture on how it wasn't very nice to throw Meredith's charitable gift away. Aria pulled her pink cardigan around her shoulders. "Are you going to walk me up?" she snapped.

Meredith looked surprised. "Actually . . . I can't. I have to go do something. Something . . . important."

Aria rolled her eyes. She wasn't being serious, but Meredith was looking back and forth shiftily, as if concealing a big secret. A horrible thought occurred to Aria: What if she was doing something *wedding* related? Even though Aria really, really didn't want to imagine Meredith and her father standing at the front of a church altar, repeating their vows, the horrible image popped into her head anyway.

Without saying goodbye, Aria walked over to the building and took the stairs two at a time. Upstairs, Sabrina was about to start her lecture, instructing all the artists to find workstations. It was like a big game of musical chairs, and when the dust settled, Aria still didn't have a seat. There was only one art table left . . . next to the girl with the white cane and the big golden retriever guide dog. Naturally.

It felt like Jenna's eyes were following her as Aria's

thin-soled Chinese slippers slapped against the wood floor toward the empty workstation. Jenna's dog panted amiably at Aria as she passed. Today, Jenna wore a low-cut black blouse with a tiny bit of a lacy black bra peeking through. If Mike were here, he would probably adore Jenna because he could stare at her boobs without her ever knowing. When Aria sat down, Jenna cocked her head closer to her. "What's your name?"

"It's . . . Jessica," Aria blurted, before she could stop herself. She glanced at Sabrina at the front of the room; half the time, art teachers for the continuing ed classes didn't bother to learn people's names, and hopefully Meredith hadn't told Sabrina to look out for her in class.

"I'm Jenna." She stuck out her hand, and Aria shook it. Afterward, Aria turned away quickly, wondering how on earth she would get through the rest of the class. A new Jenna memory had come to mind that morning when Aria was eating breakfast in Meredith's freak show of a kitchen, probably brought on by the looming dwarves on top of Meredith's refrigerator. Ali, Aria, and the others used to call Jenna Snow, after Snow White in the Disney movie. Once, when their class went to the Longwood Orchards for apple-picking, Ali had suggested they give Jenna an apple they'd dunked in the orchard's filthy women's toilet, just like the wicked witch gave Snow White a poisoned apple in the movie.

Ali suggested that Aria give Jenna the apple—she

always made the others do her dirty work. "This apple is special," Aria had said to Jenna, holding the fruit outstretched, listening as Ali snickered behind her. "The farmer told me it was from the sweetest tree. And I wanted to give it to you." Jenna's face had been so surprised and touched. As soon as she took a big, juicy bite, though, Ali crowed, "You ate an apple that's been peed on! Toilet breath!" Jenna had stopped mid-chew, letting the apple chunk fall out of her mouth.

Aria shook the memory from her head and noticed a bunch of oil paintings stacked at the edge of Jenna's workstation. They were portraits of people, all done in vibrant colors and energetic strokes. "Did you paint those?" she asked Jenna.

"The stuff on my desk?" Jenna asked, laying her hands on her lap. "Yeah. I was talking to Sabrina about my work, and she wanted to see them. I might be in one of her gallery shows."

Aria balled up her fists. Could this day get *any* worse? How the hell had Jenna gotten a gallery show? How on earth did Jenna even know how to paint if she couldn't see?

At the front of the room, Sabrina told the students to pick up a pouch of flour, strips of newspaper, and an empty bucket. Jenna tried to retrieve the things herself, but in the end, Sabrina carried them back for her. Aria noticed how all of the students were looking at Jenna out of the corners of their eyes, afraid that if they looked too pointedly, someone would chastise them for staring.

When they all returned to their desks, Sabrina cleared her throat. "Okay. Last time, we talked about seeing things by touch. We're going to do something similar today by making masks of one another's faces. We all wear masks in our own ways, don't we? We all pretend. What you might find, when you look at a mold of your face, is that you don't really look the way you thought you did at all."

"I've done this before," Jenna whispered in Aria's ear. "It's fun. Do you want to work together? I'll show you how to do it."

Aria wanted to dive out the classroom window. But she found herself nodding, and then, realizing Jenna couldn't *see* she was nodding, she said, "Sure."

"I'll do you first." As Jenna turned, something in her jeans pocket beeped. She pulled out a phone and hit a button.

"Siri, read me the text." Jenna turned toward Aria. "Hopefully it's nothing personal," she said in a teasing voice.

Luckily, Siri recited that Jenna's mother was telling her that she would pick her up after class. Then Jenna slid her phone back into her pocket.

Aria and Jenna cut up strips of newspaper. "So, where do you go to school?" Jenna asked.

"Um, Rosewood High," Aria said, naming the local public school.

"That's cool," Jenna said. "Is this your first art class?"

Aria stiffened. She had taken art classes before she'd even learned to read, but she had to swallow her pride. She wasn't Aria—she was *Jessica*. Whoever Jessica was. "Um, yeah," she said, quickly conjuring up a character. "It's a big jump for me—I'm usually more into sports, like field hockey."

Jenna poured water into her bowl. "What position do you play?"

"Um, all of them," Aria mumbled. Once, Ali had tried to teach her field hockey, but she'd stopped the lesson about five minutes in because she said Aria ran like a pregnant gorilla. Aria wondered why on earth she'd conjured up a Typical Rosewood Girl—the exact type of girl she tried her hardest *not* to be—as her alter ego.

"Well, it's nice that you're trying something new," Jenna murmured, mixing the flour and water together. "The only time the field hockey–playing girls at my old school tried something new was when they took a chance on some emerging designer they read about in *Vogue*." She snorted sarcastically. "I wonder if our schools ever played each other," Jenna said.

"I doubt it. We, um, usually don't play schools in the city." Aria thought of the school Jenna's parents sent her to in Philly.

Jenna straightened. "How did you know I went to school in Philly?"

Aria pinched the inside of her palm. What was she

going to say next, that Aria had given her a toilet-poisoned apple in sixth grade? That she'd kind of been involved in her stepbrother's death a couple weeks back? That she'd blinded her and ruined her life? "Just a guess."

"Well, I meant my old school before that. It's around here, actually. Rosewood Day? Do you know it?"

"I've heard of it," Aria mumbled.

"I'm going back there next year." Jenna dunked a strip of paper into the flour-and-water mixture. "But I don't know how I feel about it. Everyone at that school is so perfect. If you aren't into the right kinds of things, you're nothing." She shook her head. "Sorry. I'm sure you have no idea what I'm talking about."

"No! I totally agree!" Aria protested. She couldn't have put it more succinctly herself. A nagging feeling prodded at her. Jenna was beautiful—tall, graceful, cool, and artistic. *Really* artistic, in fact—if she really did go to Rosewood Day, Aria probably wouldn't be the school's best artist anymore. Who knew what Jenna could've been if her accident hadn't happened. Suddenly, the desire to tell Jenna who Aria really was and how sorry she felt about what they'd done was so nauseatingly overpowering, it took all of Aria's strength to keep her mouth shut.

Jenna came close to her. She smelled like cupcake icing. "Hold still," Jenna instructed Aria as she located Aria's head and laid the goopy strips over her face. They were wet and cool now, but soon they would harden over her face's contours.

"So, do you think you'll use your mask for anything?" Jenna asked. "Halloween?"

"My friend is having a masquerade," Aria said, then immediately wondered if she was again giving up too much information. "I'll probably wear it there."

"That's great," Jenna cooed. "I'm going to take mine with me to Venice. My parents are taking me there next month, and I hear it's the mask capital of the world."

"I love Venice!" Aria squeaked. "I've been there with my family four times!"

"Wow." Jenna layered newspaper strips over Aria's forehead. "Four times? Your family must like to travel together."

"Well, they *used* to," Aria said, trying to keep her face still for Jenna.

"What do you mean, used to?" Jenna began to cover Aria's cheeks.

Aria twitched—the strips were beginning to harden and get itchy. She could tell Jenna this, right? It wasn't like Jenna knew anything about her family. "Well, my parents are . . . I don't know. Getting divorced, I guess. My dad has a new girlfriend, this young girl who teaches art classes at Hollis. And I'm living with them right now. She hates me."

"And do you hate her?" Jenna asked.

"Totally," Aria said. "She's running my dad's life. She makes him take vitamins and do yoga. And she's convinced she has the stomach flu, but she seems fine to me." Aria bit down hard on the inside of her cheek. She wished Meredith's supposed stomach flu would just kill her already. Then she wouldn't have to spend the next few months trying to figure out ways to stop Meredith and Byron from getting married.

"Well, at least she cares about him." Jenna paused, then smiled halfway. "I can feel you frowning, but all families have issues. Mine certainly does."

Aria tried not to make any more facial movements that would give anything away.

"But maybe you should give this girlfriend a chance," Jenna went on. "At least she's artistic, right?"

Aria's stomach dropped. She couldn't control the muscles around her mouth. "How did you know she's artistic?"

Jenna stopped. Some of the floury goop on her hands plopped to the scuffed wood floor. "You just said it, right?"

Aria felt dizzy. *Had* she? Jenna squished more newspaper strips to Aria's cheeks. As she moved from Aria's cheeks to chin to forehead to nose, Aria realized something. If Jenna could feel her frowning, she could probably tell other things about her face, too. She might be able to *feel* what Aria looked like. Just then, when she looked up, a startled, uncomfortable look settled on Jenna's face, as if she'd figured it all out, too.

The room felt sticky and hot. "I have to . . ." Aria fumbled around her workstation, nearly tipping over her large unused bucket of water.

"Where are you going?" Jenna called.

All Aria needed was to get out of here for a few minutes. But as she stumbled toward the door, the mask tightening and suctioning to her face, Aria's phone let out a bleep. She reached into her bag for it, careful not to get flour all over the screen. She had one new text message.

Sucks to be in the dark, huh? Imagine how the blind must feel! If you tell ANYONE what I did, I'll put you in the dark for good. Mwah! —A

Aria glanced back at Jenna. She was sitting at her workstation, fiddling with her cell phone, oblivious to the flour all over her fingers. Another beep from her own phone startled her. She glanced down at the screen again. Another text had come in.

P.S. Your stepmommy-to-be has a secret identity, just like you! Want an eyeful? Go to Hooters tomorrow. —A

19

WANDERING MINDS WANT TO KNOW

Thursday morning, as Emily emerged from one of the bathroom stalls in the gym locker room dressed in her regulation Rosewood Day white T-shirt, hoodie, and royal blue gym shorts, an announcement blared over the PA system.

"Hey, everyone!" a chirpy, way-too-enthusiastic boy's voice called out. "This is Andrew Campbell, your class president, and I just want to remind you that Hanna Marin's welcome-back party is tomorrow night at the Rosewood Country Club! Please come out and bring your mask—it's costumes only! And also, I want everyone to wish Spencer Hastings a great big good luck—she's off to New York City tonight for her Golden Orchid finalist interview! Best wishes, Spencer!"

Several girls in the locker room groaned. There was *always* at least one announcement about Spencer. Emily found it strange, though, that Spencer hadn't mentioned the Golden Orchid trip yesterday at the hospital when they were visiting Hanna. Spencer usually overtalked about her achievements.

As Emily passed the giant cardboard cutout of Rosewood's shark mascot and emerged into the gym, she heard hooting and clapping, like she'd just walked into her own surprise party.

"Our favorite girl is back!" Mike Montgomery whooped, standing underneath the basketball hoop. It seemed like every freshman boy in Emily's mixed-grade gym class had gathered behind him. "So, you were on a sex vacation, right?"

"*What?*" Emily looked back and forth. Mike was talking kind of loudly.

"You know," Mike goaded, his elfin face a near mirror of Aria's. "To Thailand or whatever." He got a dreamy smile on his face.

Emily wrinkled her nose. "I was in Iowa."

"Oh." Mike looked confused. "Well, Iowa's hot, too. There are lots of milkmaids there, right?" He winked knowingly, as if milkmaids equaled instant porn.

Emily wanted to say something nasty, but then shrugged. She was pretty sure Mike wasn't teasing her in a mean way. The other gangly freshman boys gaped, as if Emily were Angelina Jolie, and Mike had been brave enough to ask for her email address.

Mr. Draznowsky, their gym teacher, blew his whistle. All the students sat down cross-legged on the gym floor in their squads, which was basically gym-speak for rows. Mr. Draznowsky took roll and led them through stretches, and then everyone started to file out to the tennis courts. As Emily selected a Wilson racket from the equipment bin, she heard someone behind her whisper. *"Psssst."*

Maya stood by a box of Bosu balls, Pilates magic circles, and other equipment that exercise-aholic girls used during their free periods. "Hi," she squealed, her face bright pink with pleasure.

Emily tentatively walked into Maya's arms, inhaling her familiar banana gum smell. "What are you doing here?" she gasped.

"I skipped out of Algebra III to find you," Maya whispered. She held up a wooden hall pass carved into *pi*'s squiggly shape. "When did you get back? What happened? Are you here for good?"

Emily hesitated. She'd been in Rosewood for a whole day, but yesterday had been such a blur—there was her visit to the hospital, then A's note, then classes and swimming and time spent with her parents—she hadn't had time to talk to Maya yet. Emily had noticed Maya in the halls once yesterday, but she'd ducked into an empty classroom and waited for Maya to pass. She couldn't exactly explain why. It wasn't as if she was *hiding* from Maya or anything.

"I didn't get back that long ago," she managed. "And I'm back for good. I hope."

The door to the tennis courts banged shut. Emily looked at the exit longingly. By the time she got outside, everyone in her gym class would've already found a tennis partner. She'd have to hit balls with Mr. Draznowsky, who, because he was also a health teacher, liked to give his students on-the-fly contraception lectures. Then, Emily blinked hard, as if startled out of a dream. What was her *problem*? Why did she care about stupid gym class when Maya was here?

She whipped back around. "My parents have done a one-eighty. They were so worried that something had happened to me after I left my aunt and uncle's farm, they've decided to accept me for who I am."

Maya widened her eyes. "That's awesome!" She grabbed Emily's hands. "So what happened at your aunt and uncle's? Were they mean to you?"

"Sort of." Emily shut her eyes, picturing Helene's and Allen's stern faces. Then, she imagined do-si-do'ing with Trista at the party. Trista had told Emily that if she were a dance, she'd most definitely be the Virginia reel. Maybe she should confess to Maya what happened with Trista . . . only, what *had* happened? Nothing, really. It would be better to just forget the whole thing. "It's a long story."

"You'll have to give me all the details later, now that we can actually hang out in *public*." Maya jiggled up and down, then glanced at the enormous clock on the scoreboard. "I should probably get back," she whispered. "Can we meet up tonight?"

Emily hesitated, realizing this was the first time she could say yes without sneaking around behind her parents' backs. Then she remembered. "I can't. I'm having dinner out with my family."

Maya's face fell. "Tomorrow, then? We could go to Hanna's party together."

"S-Sure," Emily stammered. "That would be great."

"And, oh! I have a huge surprise for you." Maya hopped from foot to foot. "Scott Chin, the yearbook photographer? He's in my history class, and he told me that you and I were voted this year's best couple! Isn't that fun?"

"Best *couple*?" Emily repeated. Her mouth felt gummy.

Maya took Emily's hands and swung them back and forth. "We have a photo shoot in the yearbook room tomorrow. Won't that be so cute?"

"Sure." Emily picked up the hem of her T-shirt and squeezed it in her palm.

Maya cocked her head. "You sure you're okay? You don't sound so enthused."

"No. I am. Totally." Just as Emily took a breath to go on, her cell phone vibrated in her hoodie pocket, jolting straight through to her waist. She jumped and pulled it out, her heart pounding. *One new text message*, the screen said.

When she hit read and saw the signature, her stomach turned for a different reason. She put her phone in her pocket without reading the message. "Get anything good?" Maya asked, a little nosily, Emily thought.

"Nah."

Maya tossed the *pi* hall pass from one hand to the other. She gave Emily a quick kiss on the cheek, then sauntered out of the gym, her tall, sandstone-colored Frye boots clunking heavily against the wood floor. As Maya rounded the corner into the hall, Emily pulled out her cell phone, took a deep breath, and looked at the screen again.

> Hey, Emily! I just heard the news that you're GONE! I'm really going to miss you! Where do you live in PA? If you were a famous Philadelphia historical figure, who would you be? I'd be that guy on the Quaker Oats box. . . . He counts, right?
> Maybe I could visit sometime? xxx, Trista

The gym's central heater came on with a clank. Emily turned her phone off completely. Years ago, right before Emily had kissed Ali up in the DiLaurentises' old tree house, Ali had confessed that she was secretly seeing an older guy. She'd never said what his name was, but Emily realized now that she must have been talking about Ian Thomas. Ali had grabbed Emily's hands, full of giddy emotion. "Whenever I think about him, my stomach swoops around like I'm on a roller coaster," she'd swooned. "Being in love is the best feeling in the world."

Emily zipped up her hoodie to her chin. She thought

she was in love, too, but it certainly didn't make her feel like she was on a roller coaster. Inside the fun house was more like it—with surprises at every turn, and absolutely no idea what would happen next.

20

NO SECRETS BETWEEN FRIENDS

Thursday afternoon, Hanna stared at her reflection in the downstairs powder room mirror. She dabbed a bit of foundation on the stitches in her chin and winced. Why did stitches have to *hurt* so much? And why did Dr. Geist have to sew up her face with Frankenstein black thread? Couldn't he have used a nice flesh-tone color?

She picked up her brand-new iPhone, considering. The phone had been waiting for her on the kitchen island when her father brought her home from the hospital earlier today. There was a card on the iPhone's box that said, WELCOME HOME! LOVE, MOM. Now that Hanna wasn't on the brink of death, her mother had returned to her round-the-clock hours at work, business as usual.

Hanna sighed, and then looked at the website on the back of her foundation bottle. Nikkie de Jager had a "contact me" page, but that felt like a rookie move.

Instead, she logged into Instagram and sent the brand a DM. *Hello,* she typed. *I need a makeup artist for my photo shoot. Please let me know if Nikkie is available. If not, there are lots of other famous beauty stars banging on my door. Ciao!*

To her astonishment, she got a DM back almost immediately. *Yes, please leave your information, and we will contact you directly.* Hanna almost burst out laughing. On one hand, she loved that she could still push people to do what she wanted. On the other, was she actually going to let Nikkie de Jager see her wreck of a face? What if she wanted to use her as a "before" in a makeup video? Horrors!

The doorbell rang. Hanna dabbed more foundation on her stitches and headed into the hall. That was probably Mona, coming over to help audition male models for her party. She'd told Hanna she wanted to book her the best hotties money could buy.

Hanna paused in the foyer next to her mother's giant raku ceramic pot. What had Lucas meant at the hospital yesterday, when he said that Hanna shouldn't trust Mona? And more than that, what had that kiss been about? Hanna had thought of little else since it happened. She'd expected to see Lucas at the hospital this morning, greeting her with magazines and a Starbucks latte. When he wasn't there, she'd felt . . . disappointed. And this afternoon, after her father dropped her off, Hanna had lingered on All My Children on TV for three whole minutes before changing the channel. Two characters on the soap were passionately kissing, and she'd watched them, wide-eyed, with tingles running up and down her back again, suddenly able to relate.

Not that she *liked* Lucas or anything. He wasn't in her stratosphere. And just to make sure, she'd asked Mona last night what she thought of Lucas, when Mona dropped off the coming-home-from-the-hospital outfit she'd selected from Hanna's closet—high-rise AG jeans, a cropped plaid Moschino jacket, and an ultrasoft tee. Mona had said, "Lucas *Beattie*? Huge loser, Han. Always has been."

So there you had it. No more Lucas. She would tell no one about the kiss, ever.

Hanna reached the front door, noticing the way Mona's white-blond hair glowed through the frosted panels. She nearly fell over when she opened the door and saw Spencer standing there behind Mona. And Emily and Aria were walking up the front path. Hanna wondered if she'd accidentally told all of them to visit at the same time.

"Well, this is a surprise," Hanna said nervously.

But it was Spencer who pushed around Mona and walked into Hanna's house first. "We need to talk to you," she said. Mona, Emily, and Aria followed, and the girls assembled on Hanna's toffee-colored leather couches, sitting in the exact same seats they used to sit in when they used to be friends: Spencer in the big leather chair in the corner, and Emily and Aria on the couch. Mona had taken Ali's seat, on the chaise by the window. When Hanna squinted, she could almost mistake Mona for Ali. Hanna snuck a look at Mona to see if she was pissed, but Mona looked sort of . . . okay.

Hanna sat down on the leather chair's ottoman. "Um, we need to talk about *what*?" she asked Spencer. Aria and Emily looked a little confused too.

"We got another note from A after we left your hospital room," Spencer blurted.

"*Spencer,*" Hanna hissed. Emily and Aria gaped at her too. Since when did they talk about A around other people?

"It's okay," Spencer said. "Mona knows. She's been getting notes from A too."

Hanna suddenly felt faint. She looked at Mona for confirmation, and Mona's mouth was taut and serious. "*No,*" Hanna whispered.

"You?" Aria gasped.

"How many?" Emily stammered.

"Two," Mona admitted, staring at the outline of her knobby knees through her burnt orange jersey dress. "I got them this week. When I told Spencer about it yesterday, I never would have imagined that you guys were getting them too."

"But that doesn't make sense," Aria whispered, looking around at the others. "I thought A was only sending messages to Ali's old friends."

"Maybe everything we thought was wrong," Spencer said.

Hanna's stomach spun. "Did Spencer tell you about the SUV that hit me?"

"That it was A. And that you knew who A was." Mona's face was pale.

Spencer crossed her legs. "Anyway, we got a new note. A obviously doesn't want you to remember, Hanna. If we keep pushing you on it, A's going to hurt us next."

Emily let out a small whimper.

"This is really scary," Mona whispered. She hadn't stopped jiggling her foot, something she did only when she was very tense. "We should go to the police."

"Maybe we should," Emily agreed. "They could help us. This is serious."

"No!" Aria nearly shrieked. "A will *know*. It's like . . . A can see us, at all times."

Emily clamped her mouth shut, staring down at her hands.

Mona swallowed hard. "I guess I know what you mean, Aria. Ever since I've gotten the notes, I've felt like someone has been watching me." She looked around at them, her eyes wide and scared. "Who knows? A could be watching us right now."

Hanna shivered. Aria looked around frantically, canvassing Hanna's stuffy living room. Emily peeked behind Hanna's baby grand piano, as if A might be crouching in the corner. Then Mona's phone buzzed, and everyone let out startled little yelps. When Mona pulled it out, her face paled. "Oh my God. It's another one."

Everyone gathered around Mona's phone. Her newest message was a belated birthday e-card. Below the images of happy balloons and a frosted white cake that Mona would *never* eat in real life, the message read:

Happy belated b-day, Mona! So when are you going to tell Hanna what you did? I say wait until AFTER she finally gives you your birthday present. You might lose the friendship, but at least you'll get to keep the gift! —A

Hanna's blood turned to ice. "What you *did*? What's A talking about?"

Mona's face went white. "Hanna . . . okay. We did get into a fight the night of my party. But it was just a little one. Honestly. We should just forget about it."

Hanna's heart thrummed as loud as a car engine. Her mouth instantly went dry.

"I didn't want to bring up the fight after your accident because I didn't think it mattered," Mona went on, her voice high-pitched and desperate. "I didn't want to upset you. And I felt terrible about us fighting last week, Hanna, especially when I thought I'd lost you forever. I just wanted to forget about it. I wanted to make it up to you by throwing you this amazing party, and—"

A few aching seconds passed. The heat switched on, making them all jump. Spencer cleared her throat. "You guys shouldn't fight," she said gently. "A's just trying to distract you from figuring out who's sending these awful notes in the first place."

Mona shot Spencer a grateful look. Hanna lowered her shoulders, feeling all eyes on her. The last thing she wanted to do was talk about this with the others around. She wasn't sure she wanted to talk about it at all. "Spencer's right. This *is* what A does."

The girls fell into silence, staring at the square-shaped, paper Noguchi lamp that sat on the coffee table. Spencer grabbed Mona's hand and squeezed. Emily grabbed Hanna's.

"What else have your notes been about?" Aria asked Mona quietly.

Mona ducked her head. "Just some stuff from the past."

Hanna bristled, focusing on the bluebird-shaped hair clip in Aria's hair. She had a feeling she knew just what A was taunting Mona about—the time before Hanna and Mona were friends, when Mona was dorky and uncool. What secret had A focused on most? When Mona had tagged along behind Ali, wanting to be just like her? When Mona was the butt of everyone's jokes? She and Mona never discussed the past, but sometimes Hanna felt like the painful memories loomed close behind, bubbling just below the surface of their friendship like an underground geyser.

"You don't have to tell us if you don't want to," Hanna said quickly. "A lot of our A notes have been about the past, too. There's lots of stuff we *all* want to forget."

She met her best friend's eyes, hoping Mona understood. Mona squeezed Hanna's hand. Hanna noticed that Mona was wearing the silver-and-turquoise ring Hanna had made for her in Jewelry II, even though it looked more like one of the clunky Rosewood Day class rings that only nerds wore than a pretty bauble from Tiffany. A small spot in Hanna's pounding heart warmed. A was right about one thing: Best friends shared everything. And now she and Mona could too.

The doorbell rang, three short Asian-inspired *bongs*. The girls shot up. "Who's that?" Aria whispered fearfully.

Mona stood, shaking out her long blond hair. She broke into a big smile and pranced toward Hanna's front door. "Something to make us forget about our problems."

"What, like pizza?" Emily asked.

"No, ten male models from the Philly branch of the Wilhelmina modeling agency, of course," Mona said simply.

As if it were preposterous to think it could be anyone else.

21

HOW DO YOU SOLVE A PROBLEM LIKE EMILY?

Thursday night, after leaving Hanna's, Emily skirted her way around all of the shopping bag–laden, expensive perfume–wearing King James Mall consumers. She was meeting her parents at All That Jazz!, the Broadway musical–themed restaurant next to Nordstrom. It had been Emily's favorite restaurant when she was younger, and Emily guessed that her parents assumed it still was. The restaurant looked the same as always, with a fake Broadway marquee facade, a giant *Phantom of the Opera* statue next to the hostess podium, and photos of Broadway stars all over the walls.

Emily was the first to arrive, so she slid into a seat at the long, granite-topped bar. For a while, she stared at the collectible *Little Mermaid* dolls in a glass case near the hostess stand. When she was younger, Emily wished she could switch places with Ariel the Mermaid Princess–Ariel could have Emily's human legs, and Emily would take Ariel's mermaid fins. She used to make her old friends watch the movie, up until Ali told her it was lame and babyish and she should just stop.

A familiar image on the TV screen above the bar caught her eye. There was a blond, busty reporter in the foreground, and Ali's seventh-grade school picture in the corner. "For the past year, Alison DiLaurentis's parents have been living in a small Pennsylvania town not far from Rosewood while their son, Jason, finishes up his degree at Yale University. They've all been leading quiet lives . . . until now. While Alison's murder investigation rolls on with no new leads, how is the rest of the family holding up?"

A stately, ivy-covered building flashed on the screen over a caption that read, NEW HAVEN, CONNECTI-CUT. Another blond reporter chased after a group of students. "Jason!" she called. "Do you think the police are doing enough to find your sister's killer?"

"Is this bringing your family closer together?" someone else shouted.

A boy in a Phillies ball cap turned around. Emily's eyes widened—she'd only seen Jason DiLaurentis a couple of times since Ali had gone missing. His eyes were cold and hard, and the corners of his mouth turned down.

"I don't speak to my family much," Jason said. "They're too messed up."

Emily hooked her feet under her stool. Ali's family . . . messed up? In Emily's eyes, the DiLaurentises seemed perfect. Ali's father had a good job but was able to come home on the weekends and barbecue with his kids. Mrs. DiLaurentis used to take Ali, Emily, and the others shopping and made them great oatmeal raisin cookies. Their house was spotless, and whenever Emily ate dinners at the DiLaurentises', there was always lots of laughing.

Emily thought of the memory Hanna had mentioned earlier, the one from the day before Ali went missing. After Ali had emerged on the back patio, Emily had excused herself to go to the bathroom. As she passed through the kitchen and skirted around Charlotte, Ali's Himalayan cat, she'd heard Jason whispering to someone on the stairs. He sounded angry.

"You better stop it," Jason hissed. "You know how that pisses them off."

"I'm not hurting anything," another voice whispered back.

Emily had pressed her body against the foyer wall, befuddled. The second voice sounded a little like Ali's.

"I'm just trying to help you," Jason went on, getting more and more agitated.

Just then, Mrs. DiLaurentis whirled in through the side door, running to the sink to wash dirt off her hands. "Oh, hi, Emily," she chirped. Emily stepped away from the stairs. She heard footsteps climbing to the second floor.

Emily glanced again at the TV screen. The news

anchor was now issuing an advisory to Rosewood Country Club members because the Rosewood Stalker had been spotted sneaking around the club's grounds. Emily's throat itched. It was easy to draw parallels between the Rosewood Stalker and A . . . and the country club? Hanna's party was going to be there. Emily had been very careful not to ask Hanna any questions ever since she received A's last note, but she still wondered if they *should* go to the police—this had gone far enough. And what if A had not only hit Hanna but killed Ali, too, as Aria suggested the other day? But maybe Mona was right: A was close by, watching their every move. A would know if they told.

As if on cue, her cell phone trumpeted. Emily jumped, nearly teetering off her chair. She had a new text, but thankfully, it was only from Trista. Again.

Hey, Em! What are you doing this weekend? xxx, Trista

Emily wished Rita Moreno wouldn't sing "America" so loudly, and she wished she weren't sitting so close to a picture of the cast of *Cats*—all the felines leered at her like they wanted to use her as a scratching post. She looked at her phone screen. It would be rude not to reply, right? She typed, Hi! I'm going to a masquerade party for my friend this Friday. Should be fun! —Em

Almost immediately, Trista sent back a reply. OMG! Wish I could come!

Me too, Emily texted back. See ya! She wondered what Trista really planned to do this weekend—go to another silo party? Meet another girl?

"Emily?" Two ice-cold hands curled around her shoulders. Emily whirled around, dropping her phone on the floor. Maya stood behind her. Emily's mother and father and her sister Carolyn and her boyfriend, Topher, stood behind Maya. Everyone grinned madly.

"Surprise!" Maya crowed. "Your mom called me this afternoon to ask if I wanted to come to your dinner!"

"Oh-Ohh," Emily stammered. "That's . . . great." She rescued her phone from the floor and held it between her hands, covering the screen as if Maya could see what Emily had just written. It felt like there was a hot, beaming spotlight on her. She looked at her parents, who were standing next to a big photo of the *Les Misérables* actors storming the barricades. Both of them were nervously smiling, acting the same way they had when they'd met Emily's old boyfriend, Ben.

"Our table's ready," Emily's mother said. Maya took Emily's hand and followed the rest of her family. They all slid into an enormous royal-purple banquette. An impeccably dressed waiter asked if they wanted any cocktails.

"It's so nice to finally meet you, Mr. and Mrs. Fields," Maya said once the waiter left. She grinned across the booth at Emily's parents.

Emily's mom smiled back. "It's nice to meet you too."

There was nothing but warmth in her voice. Emily's father smiled too.

Maya pointed at Carolyn's bracelet. "That is *so* pretty. Did you make it?"

Carolyn blushed. "Yeah. In Jewelry III."

Maya's burnt-umber eyes widened. "I wanted to take jewelry, but I have no sense for color. Everything on that bracelet goes so well together."

Carolyn looked down at her gold-flecked dinner plate. "It's not really that hard." Emily could tell she was flattered.

They eased into small talk, about school, the Rosewood Stalker, Hanna's hit-and-run, and then California—Carolyn wanted to know if Maya knew any kids who went to Stanford, where she'd be attending next year. Topher laughed at a story Maya told about her old neighbor in San Francisco who had had eight pet parakeets and made Maya parakeet-sit for her. Emily looked at all of them, annoyed. If Maya was so easily likable, then why hadn't they given her a chance before? What was all that talk about how Emily should stay away from Maya? Did she really have to run away for them to take her life seriously?

"Oh, I forgot to mention," Emily's father said as everyone received their dinners. "I reserved the house in Duck for Thanksgiving again."

"Oh, wonderful." Mrs. Fields beamed. "Same house?"

"Same one." Mr. Fields stabbed at a baby carrot.

"Where's Duck?" Maya asked.

Emily raked her fork through her mashed potatoes. "It's this little beach town in the Outer Banks of North Carolina. We rent a house there every Thanksgiving. The water's still warm enough to swim if you have a wet suit."

"Perhaps Maya would like to come," Mrs. Fields said, primly wiping her mouth with a napkin. "You always bring a friend, after all."

Emily gaped. She always brought a *boyfriend*, more like it—last year, she'd brought Ben. Carolyn had brought Topher.

Maya pressed her palm to her chest. "Well . . . yeah! That sounds great!"

It felt like the restaurant's faux stage-set walls were closing in around her. Emily pulled at the collar of her shirt, then stood up. Without explaining, she wound her way around a pack of waiters and waitresses dressed up as the characters from *Rent*. Fumbling into a bathroom stall, she leaned against the mosaic-tiled wall and shut her eyes.

The door to the bathroom opened. Emily saw Maya's square-toed Mary Janes under her stall door. "Emily?" Maya called softly.

Emily peeked through the crack in the metallic door. Maya had her crocheted bag slung across her chest, her lips pressed together in worry. "Are you okay?" Maya asked.

"I just felt a little faint," Emily stammered, awkwardly flushing and then walking to the sink. She stood with her back to Maya, her body rigid and tense. If Maya touched her right now, Emily was pretty sure she would explode.

Maya reached out, then recoiled, as if sensing Emily's vibe. "Isn't it so sweet your parents invited me to Duck with you? It'll be so fun!"

Emily pumped a huge pile of foamy soap into her hands. When they went to Duck, Emily and Carolyn always spent at least three hours in the ocean every day bodysurfing. Afterward, they watched marathons on the Cartoon Network, refueled, and went into the water again. She knew Maya wouldn't be into that.

Emily turned around to face her. "This is all kind of . . . weird. I mean, my parents *hated* me last week. And now they like me. They're trying to win me over, having you surprise me at dinner, and then inviting you to the Outer Banks."

Maya frowned. "And that's a *bad* thing?"

"Well, yes," Emily blurted out. "Or, no. Of course not." This was coming out all wrong. She cleared her throat and met Maya's eyes in the mirror. "Maya, if you could be any kind of candy, what kind would you be?"

Maya touched the edge of a gilded tissue box that sat in the middle of the bathroom's vanity counter. "Huh?"

"Like . . . would you be Mike and Ike? Laffy Taffy? A
Snickers bar? What?"

Maya stared at her. "Are you drunk?"

Emily studied Maya in the mirror. Maya had glowing,
honey-colored skin. Her boysenberry-flavored lip gloss
gleamed. Emily had fallen for Maya as soon as she'd laid
eyes on her, and her parents were making a huge effort
to accept Maya. What was her problem, then? Why,
whenever Emily tried to think about kissing Maya, did
she imagine kissing Trista instead?

Maya leaned back against the counter. "Emily, I think
I know what's going on."

Emily looked away quickly, trying not to blush. "No,
you don't."

Maya's eyes softened. "It's about your friend Hanna,
isn't it? Her accident? You were there, right? I heard that
the person who hit her had been stalking her."

Emily's canvas Banana Republic purse slipped out of
her hands and fell to the tiled floor with a clunk. "Where
did you hear that?" she whispered.

Maya stepped back, startled. "I . . . I don't know. I
can't remember." She squinted, confused. "You can talk
to me, Em. We can tell each other anything, right?"

Three long measures of the Gershwin song that was
twinkling out of the speakers passed. Emily thought about
the note A had sent when she and her three old friends
met with Officer Wilden last week: *If you tell ANYONE*

about me, you'll be sorry. "No one is stalking Hanna," she whispered. "It was an accident. End of story."

Maya ran her hands along the ceramic sink basin. "I think I'm going to go back to the table now. I'll . . . I'll see you out there." She backed out of the bathroom slowly. Emily listened to the main door waft shut.

The song over the speakers switched to something from *Aida.* Emily sat down at the vanity mirrors, clunking her purse in her lap. *No one said anything,* she told herself. *No one knows except for us. And no one is going to tell A.*

Suddenly, Emily noticed a folded-up note sitting in her open purse. It said EMILY on the front, in round pink letters. Emily opened it up. It was a membership form for PFLAG–Parents and Friends of Lesbians and Gays. Someone had filled in Emily's parents' information. At the bottom was familiar spiky handwriting.

Happy coming-out day, Em—your folks must be so proud! Now that the Fields are alive with the sound of love and acceptance, it would be such a shame if something happened to their little girl. So you keep quiet . . . and they'll get to keep you! —A

The bathroom door was still swinging from Maya's exit. Emily stared back at the note, her hands trembling. All at once, a familiar scent filled the air. It smelled like . . .

Emily frowned and sniffed again. Finally, she put A's note right up to her nose. When she breathed in, her insides turned to stone. Emily would recognize this smell anywhere. It was the seductive scent of Maya's banana gum.

22

IF THE W'S WALLS COULD TALK . . .

Thursday evening, after a dinner at Smith & Wollensky, an upscale Manhattan steak house Spencer's father frequented, Spencer followed her family down the W Hotel's gray-carpeted hallway. Sleek black-and-white Annie Leibovitz photographs lined the halls, and the air smelled like a mix between vanilla and fresh towels.

Her mother was on her cell phone. "No, she's sure to win," she murmured. "Why don't we just book it now?" She paused, as if the person on the other end was saying something very important. "Good. I'll talk to you tomorrow." She hung up.

Spencer tugged at the lapel of her dove-gray Armani Exchange suit—she'd worn a professional outfit to dinner to get into award-winning essayist mode. She wondered who her mom was talking to on the phone. Perhaps she was planning something amazing for Spencer if she won the Golden Orchid. A fabulous trip? A day with a

Barneys personal shopper? A meeting with the family friend who worked at the *New York Times*? Spencer had begged her parents to let her be a summer intern at the *Times,* but her mother had never allowed it.

"Nervous, Spence?" Melissa and Ian appeared behind her, pulling matching plaid suitcases. Unfortunately, Spencer's parents insisted that Melissa come along to Spencer's interview for moral support, and Melissa had brought Ian. Melissa held up a little bottle labeled MARTINI TO GO! "Do you want one of these? I could get one for you, if you need something to calm you down."

"I'm fine," Spencer snapped. Her sister's presence made Spencer feel like roaches were crawling under her bra. Whenever Spencer shut her eyes, she saw Melissa fidgeting as Wilden asked her and Ian where they'd been the night of Ali's disappearance and heard Melissa's voice saying, *It takes a very unique person to kill. And that's not you.*

Melissa paused, shaking the mini martini bottle. "Yeah, it's probably best you don't drink. You might forget the gist of your Golden Orchid essay."

"That's very true," Mrs. Hastings murmured. Spencer bristled and turned away.

Ian and Melissa's room was right next to Spencer's, and they slipped inside, giggling. As her mother reached for Spencer's room key, a pretty girl about Spencer's age swept past. Her head was down, and she was studying a cream-colored card that looked suspiciously similar to the Golden Orchid breakfast invite Spencer had tucked into her tweed Kate Spade bag.

The girl noticed Spencer staring and broke into a glimmering smile. "Hi!" she called brightly. She had the look of a CNN newscaster: poised, perky, congenial. Spencer's mouth fell open and her tongue lolled clumsily in her mouth. Before she could respond, the girl shrugged and looked away.

The single glass of wine Spencer's parents had allowed her to drink at dinner gurgled in her stomach. She turned to her mom.

"There are a lot of *really* smart applicants up for the Golden Orchid," Spencer whispered, after the girl rounded the corner. "I'm not a shoo-in or anything."

"Nonsense." Mrs. Hastings's voice was clipped. "You are going to win." She handed her a room key. "This one's yours. We got you a suite." With that, she patted Spencer's arm and continued down the hall to her own room.

Spencer bit her lip, unlocked the door to her suite, and snapped on the light. The room smelled like cinnamon and new carpet, and her king-size bed was loaded with a dozen pillows. She squared her shoulders and wheeled her bag to the dark mahogany wardrobe. Immediately, she hung up her black Armani interview suit and placed her lucky pink Wolford bra and panty set in the top drawer of the adjacent bureau. After changing into her pajamas, she went around the suite and made sure all of the chunky picture frames were straight and the enormous cerulean bed pillows were fluffed symmetrically. In the bathroom, she fixed the towels so they hung evenly on the racks. She positioned the Bliss body wash, the shampoo, and the conditioner in a diamond pattern around the sink. When she returned to her bedroom, she stared blankly at a copy of the *New York Times.* On the cover was a confident-looking Kamala Harris.

Spencer did yoga fire breaths, but she still didn't feel any better. Finally, she pulled out her five economics books and a marked-up copy of Melissa's paper and spread everything on her bed. *You are going to win,* her mother's voice rang in her ear.

After a mind-numbing hour of rehearsing parts of Melissa's paper in front of the mirror, Spencer heard a knock at the little adjoining door that led to the next suite. She sat up, confused. That door led to Melissa's room.

Another knock. Spencer slid out of bed and crept toward the door. She glanced at her cell phone, but it was impassive and blank. "Hello?" Spencer called softly.

"Spencer?" Ian called hoarsely. "Hey. I think our rooms connect. Can I come in?"

"Um," Spencer stammered. The adjoining door made a few clanking noises, then opened. Ian had changed out of his dress shirt and khakis into a T-shirt and Ksubi jeans. Spencer curled up her fingers, afraid and excited.

Ian looked around Spencer's suite. "Your room is *huge* compared to ours."

Spencer clasped her hands behind her back, trying not to beam. This was probably the first time ever she'd gotten a better room than Melissa. Ian gazed at the books splayed out on Spencer's bed, then shoved them aside and sat down. "Studying, huh?"

"Sort of." Spencer stayed glued to the table, afraid to move.

"Too bad. I thought we could take a walk or something. Melissa's sleeping, after just one of those to-go cocktails. She's such a lightweight." Ian winked.

Outside, a series of cabs honked their horns, and a neon light blinked on and off. The look on Ian's face was the same one Spencer remembered from years ago, when he'd stood in her driveway, about to kiss her. Spencer poured a glass of ice water from the pitcher on the table and took a long gulp, an idea forming in her mind. She actually had questions for Ian . . . about Melissa, about Ali, about the missing pieces of her memory, and about the dangerous, almost taboo suspicion that had been growing in her mind since Sunday.

Spencer set down her glass, her heart thumping hard. She tugged at her oversize University of Pennsylvania T-shirt so that it fell off one of her shoulders. "So, I know a secret about you," she murmured.

"About me?" Ian thumbed his chest. "What is it?"

Spencer pushed some of her books aside and sat next to Ian. When she inhaled his Kiehl's Pineapple Papaya facial scrub smell—Spencer knew the whole Kiehl's skin-care line by heart, she loved it so much—her head felt faint. "I know that you and a certain little blond girl used to be more than just friends."

Ian smiled lazily. "And would that little blond girl be . . . you?"

"No . . ." Spencer pursed her lips. "Ali."

Ian's mouth twitched. "Ali and I hooked up once or twice, that's it." He poked Spencer's bare knee. Tingles shot up Spencer's back. "I liked kissing *you* more."

Spencer leaned back, perplexed. In their last fight, Ali had told Spencer that she and Ian were *together,* and that Ian only kissed Spencer because Ali made him. Why, then, did Ian always seem so flirty with Spencer? "Did my sister know you hooked up with Ali?"

Ian scoffed. "Of course not. You know how jealous she gets."

Spencer stared out over the wide Manhattan boulevard, counting ten yellow taxis in a row. "So were you and Melissa really together the whole night Ali went missing?"

Ian leaned back on his elbows, letting out an exaggerated sigh. "You Hastings girls are something. Melissa's been talking about that night too. I think she's nervous that cop is going to find out that we were drinking, since we were underage. But so what? It was over four years ago. No one's going to bust us for it now."

"She's been . . . nervous?" Spencer whispered, her eyes widening.

Ian lowered his eyes seductively. "Why don't you forget about all that Rosewood stuff for a little while?" He brushed Spencer's hair off her forehead. "Let's just make out instead."

Desire teemed through her. Ian's face came closer and closer, blocking out Spencer's view of the buildings across the street. His hand kneaded her knee. "We shouldn't do this," she whispered. "It's not right."

"Sure it is," Ian whispered back.

And then, there was another knock on her adjoining door.

"Spencer?" Melissa's voice was thick. "Are you there?"

Spencer sprang out of bed, knocking her books and notes to the floor. "Y-Yeah."

"Do you know where Ian went?" her sister called.

When she heard Melissa turning the adjoining door's knob, Spencer frantically gestured Ian toward the front door. He leapt off the bed, straightened his clothes, and slipped out of the room, just as Melissa pushed the door open.

Her sister had shoved her black silk sleeping mask onto her forehead and wore striped Kate Spade pajama top and bottoms. She raised her nose slightly to the air, almost as if she was sniffing for Kiehl's Pineapple Papaya. "Why is your room so much *bigger* than mine?" Melissa finally said.

They both heard the mechanical sound of Ian's key

card sliding into his door. Melissa turned around, her hair swinging. "Oh, *there* you are. Where'd you go?"

"To the vending machines." Ian's voice was buttery and smooth. Melissa shut the adjoining door without even saying goodbye.

Spencer flopped back on the bed. "*So* close," she groaned loudly, although, she hoped, not loud enough for Melissa and Ian to hear.

23

BEHIND CLOSED DOORS

When Hanna opened her eyes, she was behind the wheel of her Toyota Prius. But hadn't the doctors told her she shouldn't drive with a broken arm? Shouldn't she be in bed, with her miniature Doberman, Dot, by her side?

"Hanna." A blurry figure sat next to her in the passenger seat. Hanna could only tell that it was a girl with blond hair—her vision was way too blurry to see anything else. "Hey, Hanna," the voice said again. It sounded like . . .

"Ali?" Hanna croaked.

"That's right." Ali leaned close to Hanna's face. The tips of her hair grazed Hanna's cheek. *"I'm A,"* she whispered.

"What?" Hanna cried, her eyes wide.

Ali sat up straight. "I said, *I'm okay.*" Then she opened the door and fled into the night.

Hanna's vision snapped into focus. She was sitting in the parking lot of the Hollis Planetarium. A big poster that said THE BIG BANG flapped in the wind.

Hanna shot up, panting. She was in her cavernous bedroom, snuggled under her cashmere blanket. Dot was curled up in a ball on his little Gucci dog bed. To her right was her closet, with its racks and racks of beautiful, expensive clothes. She took deep breaths, trying to get her bearings. "Jesus," she said out loud.

The doorbell rang. Hanna groaned and sat up, feeling like her head was stuffed with straw. What had she just *dreamed* about? Ali? The Big Bang? A?

The doorbell rang again. Dot was now out of his dog bed, jiggling up and down at Hanna's closed door. It was Friday morning, and when Hanna checked her bedside clock, she realized it was after ten. Her mom was long gone, if she'd even come home last night at all. Hanna had fallen asleep on the couch, and Mona had helped her upstairs to bed.

"Coming," Hanna said, pulling on her navy blue silk robe, sweeping her hair into a quick ponytail, and checking her face in the mirror. She winced. The stitches on her chin were still jagged and black. They reminded her of the crisscrossed laces on a football.

When she peeped through the panels of her front door, she saw Lucas standing on the porch. Hanna's heart immediately sped up. She checked her reflection in the hallway mirror and pushed back a few strands of hair. Feeling like a circus fat lady in her billowing silk robe, she considered running back upstairs and putting on real clothes.

Then she stopped herself, letting out a haughty laugh.

What was she *doing*? She couldn't like Lucas. He was . . .
Lucas.

Hanna wriggled her shoulders, let out a breath, and
flung open the door. "Hi," she said, trying to act bored.

"Hi," Lucas said back.

They stared at each other for what seemed like ages.
Hanna was certain Lucas could hear her heart beating.
She wanted to muzzle it. Dot danced around their legs,
but Hanna was too transfixed to reach down and shoo
him away.

"Is this a bad time?" Lucas asked cautiously.

"Um, no," Hanna said quickly. "Come in."

When she backed up, she nearly tripped over a carved
Buddha doorstop that had been in her hallway for at
least ten years. She wheeled her arms around, trying
to keep herself from falling. Suddenly, she felt Lucas's
strong arms wrap around her waist. When he pulled
Hanna upright again, they stared at each other. The corner of Lucas's mouth curled into a smile. He leaned to
her, and his mouth was on hers. Hanna melted into him.
They danced over to the couch and fell down onto the
cushions, Lucas carefully maneuvering around her sling.
After minutes of nothing but smacking and slurping
noises, Hanna rolled over, catching her breath. She let
out a whimper and covered her face in her hands.

"I'm sorry." Lucas sat back up. "Should I not have
done that?"

Hanna shook her head. She certainly couldn't tell him

that for the past two days, she'd been fantasizing that this would happen again. Or that she had an eerie feeling that she'd kissed Lucas before their kiss on Wednesday—only, how was that possible?

She pulled her hands away from her face. "I thought you said you were in the ESP club at school," she said quietly, remembering something Lucas had told her on their balloon ride. "Shouldn't you telepathically *know* if you should've done that or not?"

Lucas smirked and poked her bare knee. "Well, then, I would guess that you did want me to. And that you want me to do it again."

Hanna licked her lips, feeling as though the thousands of wild butterflies she'd seen at the Museum of Natural History a few years ago were fluttering around in her stomach. When Lucas reached out and lightly touched the inside of her elbow, where all the IVs had been, Hanna thought she was going to dissolve into goo. She ducked her head and let out a groan. "Lucas . . . I just don't know."

He sat back. "What don't you know?"

"I just . . . I mean . . . Mona . . ." She waved her hands futilely. This wasn't coming out right at all, not that she had any idea what she was trying to say.

Lucas raised an eyebrow. "What about Mona?"

Hanna picked up the stuffed dog her father had given her in the hospital. It was supposed to be Cornelius Maximilian, a character they'd made up when Hanna was younger. "We just became friends again," she said in a small eggshell of a voice, hoping that Lucas knew what that meant without her having to explain.

Lucas leaned back. "Hanna . . . I think you should watch out for Mona."

Hanna dropped Cornelius Maximilian to her lap. "What do you mean?"

"I just mean . . . I don't think she wants the best for you."

Hanna's mouth fell open. "Mona's been by my side at the hospital this whole time! And you know, if this has something to do with the fight at her party, she *told* me about it. I'm over it. It's fine."

Lucas studied Hanna carefully. "It's fine?"

"Yes," Hanna snapped.

"So . . . you're okay with what she did to you?" Lucas sounded shocked.

Hanna looked away. Yesterday, after they'd finished talking about A and interviewed the male models and the other girls had left, Hanna found a bottle of Stoli Vanil in the same cabinet where her mother hid her wedding china. She and Mona had flopped down in the den. They turned on *Emily in Paris* and played their favorite drinking game. Whenever Emily was wearing a color-clashing outfit, they drank. Whenever Emily flirted with a hot French man, they drank. They didn't talk about the note A had sent Mona—the one about their fight. Hanna was certain they'd just bickered about something stupid, like party pictures or whether Justin Timberlake was an idiot. Mona always said he was, and Hanna always said he wasn't.

Lucas blinked furiously. "She *didn't* tell you, did she?"

Hanna breathed forcefully out of her nose. "It doesn't *matter*, okay?"

"Okay," Lucas said, holding up his hands in surrender.

"Okay," Hanna stated again, squaring her shoulders. But when she closed her eyes, she saw herself in her Prius again. The Hollis Planetarium flag flapped behind her. Her eyes stung from crying. Something—maybe her phone—beeped at the bottom of her bag. Hanna tried to grab hold of the memory, but it was useless.

She could feel warmth radiating off Lucas's body, he was sitting so close. He didn't smell like cologne or fancy deodorant or other weird things boys sprayed on themselves, but just kind of like skin and toothpaste. If only they lived in a world where Hanna could have both things—Lucas *and* Mona. But she knew that if she wanted to stay who she was, that wasn't possible.

Hanna reached out and grabbed Lucas's hand. A sob welled up in her throat, for reasons she couldn't explain or even understand completely. As she moved forward to kiss him, she tried yet again to access her memory of what was surely the night of her accident. But, as usual, there was nothing there.

24

SPENCER GETS THE GUILLOTINE

Friday morning, Spencer stepped into Daniel on Sixty-Fifth Street between Madison and Park, a quiet, well-maintained block somewhere between Midtown Manhattan and the Upper East Side. It looked like she'd stepped onto the set of a period movie about Marie Antoinette. The restaurant's walls were made of carved marble, which reminded Spencer of creamy white chocolate. Luxurious dark red curtains billowed, and small, elegantly sculpted topiaries lined the entrance to the main dining room. Spencer decided that when she earned her millions, she would design her house to look exactly like this.

Her entire family was right behind her, Melissa and Ian included. "Do you have all your notes?" her mother murmured, fiddling with one of the buttons on her pink houndstooth Chanel suit—she was dressed as if *she* were going to be interviewed. Spencer nodded. Not only did she have them, she'd *alphabetized* them.

Spencer tried to quell the churning feelings in her stomach, although the smell of scrambled eggs and truffle oil wafting in from the dining room wasn't helping. There was a sign that said GOLDEN ORCHID INTERVIEW CHECK-IN over the hostess station. "Spencer Hastings," she said to a hot Zendaya look-alike who was taking names.

The girl found Spencer on the list, smiled, and handed her a laminated name tag. "You're at table six," she said, gesturing toward the dining room entrance. Spencer saw bustling waiters, giant flower arrangements, and a few adults milling about, chatting and drinking coffee. "We'll call you when we're ready," the check-in girl assured her.

Melissa and Ian examined a marble statuette near the bar. Spencer's father had migrated out to the street and was talking to someone on his cell phone. Her mom was on her cell phone, too, half-concealed behind one of Daniel's bloodred curtains. Spencer heard her say, "So we're booked? Well, fantastic. She'll love it."

I'll love what? Spencer wanted to ask. But she wondered if her mom wanted to keep it a surprise until after Spencer won.

Melissa slipped off to the bathroom, and Ian plopped down on the chaise beside Spencer. "Excited?" He grinned. "You should be. This is huge."

Spencer wished that just *once,* Ian would smell like

rotting vegetables or dog breath—it would make it much easier to be near him. "You didn't tell Melissa you were in my room last night, did you?" she whispered.

Ian's face became businesslike. "Of course not."

"And she didn't seem suspicious or anything?"

Ian put on aviator sunglasses, concealing his eyes. "Melissa isn't *that* scary, you know. She's not going to bite you."

Spencer clamped her mouth shut. These days, it seemed that Melissa wasn't *just* going to bite her—she was going to give Spencer rabies. "Just don't say anything," she growled.

"Spencer Hastings?" the girl at the desk called. "They're ready for you."

When Spencer stood up, her parents gathered around her like bees swarming a hive. "Don't forget about the time you played Eliza Doolittle in *My Fair Lady* with the raging stomach flu," Mrs. Hastings whispered.

"Don't forget to mention that I know Elon Musk," her father added.

Spencer frowned. "You do?"

Her father nodded. "We sat next to each other at Cipriani once and exchanged business cards."

Spencer breathed yoga fire breaths as covertly as she could.

Table six was a small, intimate nook at the back of the restaurant. Three adults had already gathered there, sipping coffee and picking at croissants. When they saw

Spencer, they all stood. "Welcome," a balding, baby-faced man said. "Jeffrey Love. Golden Orchid 2003. I have a seat on the New York Stock Exchange."

"Amanda Reed." A tall, wispy woman shook Spencer's hand. "Golden Orchid 2000. I'm editor in chief at *Barron's*."

"Quentin Hughes." A Black man in a beautiful Turnbull & Asser button-down nodded at her. "Nineteen-ninety. I'm a managing director at Goldman Sachs."

"Spencer Hastings." Spencer tried to sit down as daintily as possible.

"You're the one who wrote the 'Invisible Hand' essay." Amanda Reed beamed, settling back down in her chair.

"We were all very impressed with it," Quentin Hughes murmured.

Spencer folded and unfolded her white cloth napkin. Naturally, everyone at this table worked in finance. If only they could've thrown her an art historian, or a biologist, or a documentary filmmaker, someone she could talk to about something else. She tried to picture her interviewers in their underwear. She tried to picture her labradoodles, Rufus and Beatrice, humping their legs. Then she imagined telling them the truth about all this: that she didn't understand economics, that she really *hated* it, and that she'd stolen her sister's paper for fear of messing up her 4.0 average.

At first, the interviewers asked Spencer basic questions—about where she went to school, what she liked to do, and what her volunteering and leadership experiences were. Spencer breezed through the questions, the interviewers smiling, nodding, and jotting notes down in their little leather Golden Orchid notebooks. She told them about her part in *The Tempest,* how she was the yearbook editor, and how she'd organized an ecology trip to Costa Rica her sophomore year. After a few minutes, she sat back and thought, *This is okay. This is really okay.*

And then her cell phone beeped.

The interviewers looked up, their stride broken. "You were supposed to turn off your phone before you came in here," Amanda said sternly.

"I'm sorry, I thought I did." Spencer fumbled in her bag, reaching to turn the phone to silent. Then, the preview screen caught her eye. She had received a DM from someone called AAAAAA.

> AAAAAA: Helpful hint to the not-so-wise: You're not fooling anyone. The judges can see you're faker than a knockoff Vuitton.
>
> P.S. She did it, you know. And she won't think twice about doing it to you.

Spencer quickly shut off her phone, biting hard on her lip. *She did it, you know.* Was A suggesting what Spencer *thought* A was suggesting?

When she looked again at her interviewers, they seemed like completely different people—hunched and serious, ready to get down to the *real* questions. Spencer started folding the napkin again. *They don't know I'm fake,* she told herself.

Quentin folded his hands next to his plate. "Have you always been interested in economics, Miss Hastings?"

"Um, of course." Spencer's voice came out scratchy and dry. "I've always found . . . um . . . economics, money, all that, very fascinating."

"And whom do you consider to be your philosophical mentors?" Amanda asked.

Spencer's brain felt hollowed out. *Philosophical mentors?* What the hell did that mean? Only one person came to mind. "Elon Musk?"

The interviewers sat stunned for a moment. Then Quentin began to laugh. Then Jeffrey, then Amanda. They were all smiling, so Spencer smiled, too. Until Jeffrey said, "You're kidding, right?"

Spencer blinked. "Of *course* I'm kidding." The interviewers laughed again. Spencer wanted so badly to rearrange the croissants in the middle of the table into a neater pyramid. She shut her eyes, trying to focus, but all she saw was the image of a plane falling from the sky, its nose and tail in flames. "But as far as inspirations . . . well, I have so many. It's hard to name just one," she sputtered.

The interviewers didn't look particularly impressed. "After college, what's your ideal first job?" Jeffrey asked.

Spencer spoke before thinking. "Working as a reporter at the *New York Times*."

The interviewers looked confused. "A reporter in the economics section, right?" Amanda qualified.

Spencer blinked. "I don't know. Maybe?"

She hadn't felt this awkward and nervous since . . . well, ever. Her interview notes remained in a neatly stacked pile in her hands. Her mind felt like a chalkboard erased clean. A peal of laughter floated over from table ten. Spencer looked over and saw the brunette girl from the hotel smiling easily, her interviewers happily smiling back. Beyond her was a wall of windows; outside, on the street, Spencer saw a girl looking in. It was . . . Melissa. She was just standing there, staring blankly at her.

And she won't think twice about doing it to you.

"So." Amanda added more milk to her coffee. "What would you say is the most significant thing that's happened to you during your high school career?"

"Well . . ." Spencer's eyes flicked back to the window, but Melissa was gone. She took a nervous breath and tried to get a grip. Quentin's Rolex gleamed in the light of the chandelier. Someone had put on too much musky cologne. A French-looking waitress poured another round of coffee at table three. Spencer knew what the right answer was: competing in the econ math bowl in ninth grade. Summer interning on the options trading desk at the Philly branch of J. P. Morgan. Only, those weren't *her* accomplishments, they were Melissa's, this award's rightful winner. The words swelled on the tip of her tongue, but suddenly, something unexpected spilled out of her mouth instead.

"My best friend went missing in seventh grade," Spencer blurted out. "Alison DiLaurentis? You may have heard about it. For years, I had to live with the question of what happened to her, where she'd gone. This September, they found her body. She'd been murdered. I think my greatest achievement is that I've held it together. I don't know how any of us have done it, how we've gone to school and lived our lives and just kept *going*. She and I may have hated each other sometimes, but she meant everything to me."

Spencer shut her eyes, returning to the night Ali went missing, to when she had shoved Ali hard, and Ali slid backward. A horrible crack rang through the air. And suddenly, her memory opened an inch or two wider. She saw something else . . . something new. Just after she shoved Ali, she heard a small, almost girlish gasp. The gasp sounded close, as if whoever it was had been standing right behind her, breathing on her neck.

She did it, you know.

Spencer's eyes sprang open. Her judges seemed to be on pause. Quentin held a croissant an inch from his face. Amanda's head was cocked at an awkward angle. Jeffrey kept his napkin at his lips. Spencer wondered, suddenly, if she'd just voiced her newly recalled memory out loud.

"Well," Jeffrey said finally. "Thank you, Spencer."

Amanda stood, tossing her napkin on her plate. "This has been very interesting." Spencer was pretty sure that was shorthand for *You have no chance of winning.*

The other interviewers snaked away, as did most of the rest of the candidates. Quentin was the only one who remained sitting. He studied her carefully, a proud smile on his face. "You're a breath of fresh air, giving us an honest answer like that," he said in a low, confidential voice. "I've followed your friend's story for a while now. It's just awful. Do the police have any suspects?"

The air-conditioning vent far above Spencer's head showered cold air on her full force, and the image of Melissa beheading a Barbie doll popped into her mind. "They don't," she whispered.

But I might.

25

WHEN IT RAINS, IT POURS

After school on Friday, Emily wrung out her still-wet-from-swim-practice hair and walked into the yearbook room, which was plastered with snapshots of Rosewood Day's finest. There was Spencer from last year's graduation-pin ceremony, accepting the Math Student of the Year award. And there was Hanna, emceeing last year's Rosewood Day charity fashion show, when she really should've been a model herself.

Two hands clapped over Emily's eyes. "Hey there," Maya whispered in her ear. "How was swimming?" She said it teasingly, sort of like a nursery rhyme.

"Fine." Emily felt Maya's lips brush against hers, but she couldn't quite kiss back.

Scott Chin, a yearbook photographer, swept into the room. "Guys! Congratulations!" He air-kissed both of them, then reached out to turn Emily's collar out and sweep a stray curly hair out of Maya's face.

"Perfect," he said.

Scott pointed Maya and Emily toward the white backdrop on the far wall. "We're taking all the Most Likely To photos there. Personally, I would *love* to see the two of you against a rainbow background. Wouldn't that be awesome? But we have to be consistent."

Emily frowned. "Most likely to . . . what? I thought we were voted best couple."

Scott's houndstooth newsboy cap slipped over one of his eyes as he bent over the camera tripod. "No, you were voted most likely to be together at the five-year reunion."

Emily's mouth fell open. At the *five-year reunion*? Wasn't that a tad extreme?

She massaged the back of her neck, trying to calm down. But she hadn't felt calm since she found A's note in the restaurant bathroom. Not knowing what else to do with it, she'd stashed it in the front pocket of her bag. She'd been taking it out periodically through her classes, each time pressing it to her nose to smell the sweet scent of banana gum.

"Say gouda!" Scott cried, and Emily moved toward Maya and tried to smile. The flash from Scott's camera left spots in front of her eyes, and she suddenly noticed that the yearbook room smelled like burning electronics. In the next shot, Maya kissed Emily on the cheek. And in the next, Emily willed herself to kiss Maya on the lips.

"Hot!" Scott encouraged.

Scott peeked into his camera's preview windowpane.

"You're free to go," he said. Then, he paused, looking curiously at Emily. "Actually, before you do, there's something you might want to see."

He led Emily to a large drafting table and pointed to a bunch of pictures arranged in a two-page layout. *Missing You Terribly,* said the headline across the top of the mock-up. A familiar seventh-grade portrait stared at Emily—not only did she have a copy in the top drawer of her nightstand, but she'd also seen it nearly every night on the news for months now.

"The school never did a page for Alison when she went missing," Scott explained. "And now that she . . . well . . . we thought we should. We might even have a commemorative event to show off all these old Ali photos. Sort of an Ali retrospective, if you will."

Emily touched the edge of one of the photos. It was of Emily, Ali, Spencer, Aria, and Hanna at a lunch table. In the photo, they all clutched cans of La Croix, their heads thrown back in hysterical laughter.

Next to it was a photo of just Ali and Emily, walking down the hall with their books clutched to their chests. Emily towered over the petite Ali, and Ali was leaning up to her, whispering something in her ear. Emily bit down on her knuckles. Even though she'd found out lots of things about Ali, things that she wished Ali had shared with her years ago, she still missed her so much that it ached.

There was someone else in the background of the

photo that Emily hadn't noticed at first. She had long, dark hair and a familiar apple-cheeked face. Her eyes were round and green, and her lips were pink and bow-shaped. Jenna Cavanaugh.

Jenna's head was turned toward someone beside her, but Emily could only see the edge of the other girl's thin, pale arm. It was strange to see Jenna . . . sighted. Emily glanced at Maya, who had moved on to the next photo, obviously not seeing this one's significance. There was so much Emily hadn't told her.

"Is that Ali?" Maya said. She pointed to a shot of Ali and her brother, Jason, embracing on the Rosewood Day commons.

"Uh, *yeah*." Emily couldn't control the annoyance in her voice.

"Oh." Maya stood back. "It just doesn't look like her, is all."

"It looks like every *other* picture of Ali here." Emily fought the urge to roll her eyes as she glanced at the picture. Ali looked impossibly young, maybe only ten or eleven. It had been taken before they'd become friends. It was hard to believe that once upon a time, Ali had been the leader of a completely different clique—Naomi Zeigler and Riley Wolfe had been her underlings. They'd even teased Emily and the other girls from time to time, making fun of Emily's hair, which was tinged green from hours spent in chlorinated water.

Emily studied Jason's face. He seemed so delighted to be

giving Ali a bear hug. What in the world had he meant in that news interview yesterday, when he said his family was messed up?

"What's this?" Maya pointed to the photos on the next desk.

"Oh, that's Brenna's project." Scott stuck his tongue out, and Emily couldn't help but giggle. The bitter rivalry between Scott and Brenna Richardson, another yearbook photographer, was the stuff of reality TV. "But for once, I think it's a good idea. She took pictures of the insides of people's bags to show what a typical Rosewood student carries around each day. Spencer hasn't seen it yet, though, so she might not approve."

Emily leaned over the next desk. The yearbook committee had written each bag's owner's name next to each photo. Inside Noel Kahn's lacrosse duffel bag were a bacteria-laden towel, the lucky squirrel stuffed animal he always talked about, and Axe body spray. Ick. Naomi Zeigler's elephant-gray quilted tote held an iPhone, a Dolce & Gabbana glasses case, and a square object that was either a tiny camera or a jeweler's loupe. Mona Vanderwaal carried around M.A.C. lip gloss, a pack of Sniff tissues, and three different organizers. Part of a photo showing a slim arm with a frayed sleeve cuff poked out of the blue one. Andrew Campbell's backpack contained eight textbooks, a leather day planner, and the same Beats headphones Emily had. The photo showed the start of a text message he had either written or received, but Emily couldn't tell what it said.

When Emily looked up, she saw Scott fiddling with his camera, but she didn't see Maya anywhere in the room. Just then, her cell phone started vibrating. She had one new text message.

Tsk tsk, Emily! Does your girlfriend know about your weakness for blondes? I'll keep your secret . . . if you keep mine. Kisses! —A

Emily's heart hammered. Weakness for blondes? And . . . where had Maya gone?

"Emily?"

A girl stood in the yearbook doorway, wearing a gauzy pink baby-doll top, as if she were impervious to the mid-October chill. Her blond hair whipped around like she was a bikini model standing in front of a wind machine.

"Trista?" Emily blurted out.

Maya reemerged from the hallway, frowning, then smiling. "Em! Who's this?"

Emily whipped her head around at Maya. "Where were you just now?"

Maya cocked her head. "I was . . . in the hall."

"What were you doing?" Emily demanded.

Maya shot her a look that seemed to say, *What does it matter?* Emily blinked hard. She felt like she was losing her mind, suspecting Maya. She looked back at Trista, who was striding across the room.

"It's so good to see you!" Trista crowed. She gave Emily a huge hug. "I hopped a plane! Surprise!"

"Yeah," Emily croaked, her voice barely more than a whisper. Over Trista's shoulder, Emily could see Maya glaring at her. "Surprise."

26

DELIGHTFULLY TACKY,
YET UNREFINED

After school on Friday, Aria drove down Lancaster Avenue past the strip malls, Fresh Fields, A Pea in the Pod, and Home Depot. The afternoon was overcast, making the normally colorful trees that lined the road look faded and flat.

Mike sat next to her, sullenly screwing and unscrewing his Nalgene bottle cap over and over again. "I'm missing lacrosse," he grumbled. "When are you going to tell me what we're doing?"

"We're going somewhere that's going to make everything right," Aria said stiffly. "And don't worry, you're going to love it."

As she paused at a stop sign, a shimmer of pleasure ran through her. A's hint about Meredith—that she had a dirty little Hooters secret—made perfect sense. Meredith had acted so funny when Aria saw her at Hollis the other day, saying she had to be somewhere but not telling where that somewhere was. And just two nights ago, Meredith had commented that because the rent on the Hollis house was going up and she hadn't made much on her artwork lately, she might have to get a second job to make ends meet. Hooters girls probably got great tips.

Hooters. Aria clamped her mouth shut to keep from laughing. She couldn't wait to reveal this to Byron. Every time they'd driven by the place in years past, Byron had said that only puerile philistines went to Hooters, men who were more closely related to monkeys than humans. Last night, Aria had given Meredith a chance to admit her sins to Byron on her own, sidling up to her and saying, "I know what you're hiding. And you know what? I'm going to tell Byron if you don't."

Meredith had stepped back, dropping the dish towel from her hands. So she *did* feel guilty about something! Still, Meredith clearly hadn't said a word about it to Byron. Just this morning they'd peacefully crunched on bowls of Kashi GoLean at the table, getting along as happily as before. So Aria had decided to take matters into her own hands.

Even though it was midafternoon, the Hooters parking lot was nearly full. Aria noticed four cop cars lined up—the place was a notorious cop hangout, as it was right next to the police station. The Hooters owl on the sign grinned at them, and Aria could just make out girls in skintight shirts and orange mini shorts through the restaurant's tinted windows. But when she looked over to Mike, he wasn't frothing at the mouth or getting a hard-on or whatever normal boys did when they pulled up to this place. Instead, he looked annoyed. "What the hell are we doing here?" he sputtered.

"Meredith works here," Aria explained. "I wanted you to be here with me so we could confront her together."

Mike's mouth dropped open so wide, Aria could see the bright green gum lodged behind his molars. "You mean . . . Dad's . . . ?"

"That's right." Aria reached into her faux-fur bag for her phone—she wanted to take pictures of Meredith, for evidence—but it wasn't in its usual place. Aria's stomach churned. Had she lost it? She'd dropped her phone on a table after she'd gotten A's note in art class, fleeing the room and peeling off her mask in Hollis's lobby bathroom. Had she forgotten to pick it up? She made a mental note to stop by class later to look for it.

When Aria and Mike passed through the double doors, they were greeted by a blaring Rolling Stones song. Aria was overcome by the stench of hot wings. A blond, super-tan girl stood at the hostess station. "Hi!" she said happily. "Welcome to Hooters!"

Aria gave their name and the girl turned around to check on available tables, shaking her ass as she walked away. Aria nudged Mike. "Did you see the boobs on her? Gi*nor*mous!"

She couldn't believe the things that were spilling out of her mouth. Mike, however, didn't even crack a smile.

He was acting like Aria had dragged him to a poetry reading instead of hooter heaven. The hostess returned and led them to their booth. When she bent to place their silverware on the table, Aria could see right down the girl's T-shirt to her bright fuchsia bra. Mike's eyes remained fixed on the orange carpet.

After the hostess left, Aria looked around. She noticed a group of cops across the room, shoveling in enormous plates of ribs and french fries, staring alternately at a football game on TV and the waitresses that passed by their table. Among them was Officer Wilden. Aria slid down in her seat. It wasn't as if she couldn't be here—Hooters always stressed that it was a *family place*—but she didn't really feel like seeing Wilden right now, either.

Mike stared sourly at the menu as six more waitresses passed by, each one more jiggly than the last. Aria turned away—if he was going to be like that, fine. She'd search for Meredith herself.

All the girls were dressed alike, their shirts and shorts eight sizes too small and their sneakers the kind the cheerleading squad wore on game day. They all sort of had the same face, too, which would make it easy to pick out Meredith among them. Only, she didn't see a single dark-haired girl here, much less one with a spiderweb tattoo. By the time the waitress set down their enormous plate of fries, Aria finally got up the courage to ask. "Do you know if someone named Meredith Gates works here?"

The waitress blinked. "I don't recognize that name. Although sometimes the girls here go by different names. You know, stuff that's more . . ." She paused, searching for an adjective.

"Hooters-y?" Aria suggested jokily.

"Yes!" The girl smiled. When she sashayed away again, Aria snorted and poked Mike with a fry. "What do you think Meredith goes by here. Randi? Fifi? Oh! What about Caitlin? That's really perky, right?"

"Would you stop?" Mike exploded. "I don't want to hear anything about . . . about *her*, okay?"

Aria blinked, sitting back.

Mike's face flushed. "You think this is the big thing that's going to make things right? Shoving the fact that Dad is with someone else in my face *yet again*?" He stuffed a bunch of fries in his mouth and looked away. "It doesn't matter. I'm over it."

"I wanted to make everything up to you," Aria squeaked. "I wanted to make this all better."

Mike let out a guffaw. "There's nothing you can do, Aria. You've ruined my life."

"I didn't ruin anything!" Aria gasped.

Mike's ice-blue eyes narrowed. He threw his napkin on the table, stood up, and shoved his arm into his anorak sleeve. "I have to get to lacrosse."

"Wait!" Aria grabbed his belt loop. Suddenly, she felt like she was going to cry. "Don't go," Aria wailed. "Mike, please. My life is ruined too. And not just because of Dad and Meredith. Because of . . . of something else."

Mike glanced at her over his shoulder. "What are you talking about?"

"Sit back down," Aria said desperately. A long second passed. Mike grunted, then sat. Aria stared at their plate of fries, working up the courage to speak. She overheard two men discussing the Eagles' defensive tactics. A used-car-dealership commercial on the flat-screen TV above the bar featured a man in a chicken suit babbling about deals that were more cluck for your buck.

"I've been getting these threats from someone," Aria whispered. "Someone who knows *everything* about me. The person who's been threatening me even tipped off Ella about Byron and Meredith's relationship. Some of my friends have been getting messages, too, and we think the person writing them is behind Hanna's hit-and-run accident. I even got a message about Meredith working here. I don't know how this person knows all this stuff, but they just . . . do." She shrugged, trailing off.

Two more commercials passed before Mike spoke. "You have a *stalker*?"

Aria nodded miserably.

Mike blinked, confounded. He gestured to the booth of cops. "Have you told any of *them*?"

Aria shook her head. "I can't."

"Of course you can. We can tell them right now."

"I have it under control," Aria said through her teeth.

She pressed her fingers to her temples. "Maybe I shouldn't have told you."

Mike leaned forward. "Don't you remember all the freaky shit that's happened in this town? You have to tell someone."

"Why do you care?" Aria snapped, her body filling with anger. "I thought you hated me. I thought I ruined your life."

Mike's face went slack. His Adam's apple bobbed as he swallowed. When he stood up, he seemed taller than Aria remembered. Stronger, too. Maybe it was from all of the lacrosse he'd been playing, or maybe it was that he'd grown up in Iceland more than Aria realized. He snatched Aria's wrist and pulled her to her feet. "You're telling them."

Aria's lip wobbled. "But what if it's not safe?"

"What's unsafe is *not* telling," Mike urged. "And . . . and I'll keep you safe. Okay?"

Aria's heart felt like a brownie, straight out of the oven—all gooey and warm and a little melted. She smiled unsteadily, then glanced at the blinking neon sign above the Hooters' dining room. It read DELIGHTFULLY TACKY, YET UNREFINED. But the sign was broken; all the letters were dark except for *tacky*'s lowercase *A,* which flickered menacingly. When Aria shut her eyes, the *A* still remained, glowing like the sun.

She took a deep breath. "Okay," she whispered.

Just as she moved away from Mike toward the cops, the waitress returned with their check. Now Mike couldn't take his eyes off her.

"Mike!" Aria snapped, nudging him. "You're being gross."

Mike shot her a look back that seemed to say, *Sorry. I'm a teenage boy.*

Aria sighed loudly. She had a lot to teach her brother about objectifying women. At least this was the Mike she recognized, for better or worse.

27

BIZARRE LOVE TRIANGLE

Friday night, just before the limo was supposed to arrive to escort Hanna to her party, Hanna stood in her bedroom, twirling around in her brightly printed Alice + Olivia dress. She was finally a perfect size two, thanks to a diet of IV fluids and facial stitches that made it too painful to chew solid foods.

"That looks great on you," a voice called. "Except I think you're a tad too thin."

Hanna whirled around. In his black wool suit, dark purple tie, and purple-striped button-down, her father looked like George Clooney on the red carpet with Amal. "I'm *so* not too thin," she answered quickly, trying to hide her thrill. "Kate's way thinner than me."

Her father's face clouded over, perhaps at the mention of his perfect, poised, yet incredibly evil quasi-stepdaughter. "What are you doing here, anyway?" Hanna demanded.

"Your mom let me in." He walked into Hanna's room and sat down on her bed. Hanna's stomach flipped. Her dad hadn't been in her bedroom since she was twelve, right before he moved out. "She said I could change here for your big party."

"*You're* coming?" Hanna squawked.

"Am I allowed?" her father asked.

"I . . . I guess so." Spencer's parents were coming, as well as some Rosewood Day faculty and staff. "But, I mean, I thought you'd want to get back to Annapolis . . . and Kate and Isabel. You've been away from them for almost a *week*, after all." She couldn't hide the bitterness in her voice.

"Hanna . . ." her father started. Hanna turned away. She suddenly felt so angry that her dad had left her family, that he was here now, that maybe he loved Kate more than he loved her—not to mention that she had scars all over her face and that her memory about Saturday night still hadn't returned. She felt tears in her eyes, which made her even angrier.

"Come here." Her father put his strong arms around her, and when she pressed her head to his chest, she could hear his heart beating.

"You okay?" he asked her.

A horn honked outside. Hanna pulled back her bamboo blinds and saw the limo Mona had arranged waiting in her driveway, its wipers moving furiously over the windshield to keep off the rain. "I'm great," she said suddenly, the whole world tipping up again. She slid her Dior mask over her face. "I'm Hanna Marin, and I'm fabulous."

Her father handed Hanna a huge black golf umbrella. "You definitely are," he said. And for the first time ever, Hanna thought she just might believe him.

What seemed like only seconds later, Hanna was perched atop a pillow-laden platform, trying to keep the balcony's tassels from knocking off her Dior mask. Four gorgeous men had hoisted her up, and they were now beginning their slow parade into the party tent on the fifteenth green of the Rosewood Country Club.

"Presenting . . . in her big return to Rosewood . . . the fabulous Hanna Marin!" Mona screamed into a microphone. As the crowd erupted, Hanna waved her arms around excitedly. All of her guests were wearing masks, and Mona and Spencer had transformed the tent into the Salon de l'Europe at Le Casino in Monte-Carlo, Monaco. It had faux-marble walls, dramatic frescoes, and roulette and card tables. Sleek, gorgeous boys roamed the room with trays of canapés, manned the tents' two bars, and acted as croupiers at the gambling tables. Hanna had demanded that none of her party's staff be female.

The DJ switched to a new Lil Nas X song and everyone began to dance. A thin, pale hand caught Hanna's arm, and Mona dragged her through the crowd and gave her a huge hug.

"Do you love it?" Mona cried from behind her expressionless mask, which looked similar to Hanna's Dior masterpiece.

"Naturally." Hanna bumped her hip. "And I *love* the gambling tables. Does anyone win anything?"

"They win a hot night with a hot girl—you, Hanna!" Spencer cried, prancing up behind them. Mona grabbed her hand, too, and the three jiggled with glee. Spencer looked like a blond Audrey Hepburn in her black satin trapeze dress and adorable round-toe flats. When Spencer put her arm around Mona's shoulders, Hanna's heart leapt. As much as she didn't want to give A credit for anything, A's notes to Mona had made Mona accept Hanna's old friends. Yesterday, in between rounds of their *Emily in Paris* drinking game, Mona had told Hanna, "You know, Spencer's really cool. I think she could be part of our posse." Hanna had waited *years* for Mona to say something like that.

"You look great," a voice said in Hanna's ear. A boy stood behind her, dressed in fitted pin-striped pants, a white long-sleeved button-down, a matching pin-striped vest, and a long-nosed bird mask. Lucas's telltale white-blond hair peeked out from the mask's top. When he reached out and clasped her hand, Hanna's heart started racing. She held it for a second, squeezed, and let it drop before anyone could see. "This party is awesome," Lucas said.

"Thanks, it was nothing," Mona piped in. She nudged

Hanna. "Although, I don't know, Han. Do you think that hideous thing Lucas is wearing qualifies as a mask?"

Hanna glanced at Mona, wishing she could see her face. She looked over Lucas's shoulder, pretending she'd been distracted by something that was going on over at the blackjack table.

"So, Hanna, can I talk to you for a sec?" Lucas asked. "Alone?"

Mona was now chatting with one of the waiters. "Um, okay," Hanna mumbled.

Lucas led her to a secluded nook and pulled off his mask. Hanna tried to thwart the tornado of nerves rumbling inside her stomach, avoiding looking anywhere near Lucas's super-pink, super-kissable lips. "Can I take yours off, too?" he asked.

Hanna made sure they were truly alone, and that no one else would be able to see her bare, scarred face, and then she let him lift off her mask. Lucas kissed her softly on her stitches. "I missed you," he whispered.

"You only saw me a couple hours ago." Hanna giggled.

Lucas smiled crookedly. "That seems like a long time."

They kissed for a few more minutes, snuggled together on a single couch cushion, oblivious to the cacophony of party noises. Then Hanna heard her name through the tent's gauzy curtains. "Hanna?" Mona's voice called. "Han? Where are you?"

Hanna freaked. "I should go back out." She picked up Lucas's mask by its long bird beak and shoved it at him.

"And you should put this back on."

Lucas shrugged. "It's hot under that thing. I think I'll leave it off."

Hanna tied her own mask's strings tight. "It's a masquer*ade*, Lucas. If Mona sees that you've taken yours off, she'll kick you out for real."

Lucas's eyes were hard. "Do you always do everything Mona says?"

Hanna tensed. *"No."*

"Good. You shouldn't."

Hanna flicked a tassel on one of the pillows. She looked at Lucas again. "What do you want me to say, Lucas? She's my best friend."

"Has Mona told you what she did to you yet?" Lucas goaded. "I mean, at her party."

Hanna stood up, annoyed. "I told you, it doesn't matter."

He lowered his eyes. "I care about you, Hanna. I don't think she does. I don't think she cares about anyone. Don't let it drop, okay? Ask her to tell you the truth. I think you deserve to know."

Hanna stared at him long and hard. Lucas's eyes were shiny and his lip quivered a little. There was a purple welt on his neck from their earlier make-out session. She wanted to reach out and touch it with her thumb.

Without another word, she whipped the curtain open and stormed back onto the dance floor. Aria's brother, Mike, was demonstrating his best stripper pole dance to a girl from the Quaker school. Andrew Campbell and his nerdy Knowledge Bowl friends were talking about counting cards in blackjack. Hanna smiled when she saw her father chatting with her old cheerleading coach, a woman whom she and Mona had privately called The Rock, because she thought it was hilarious to use the phrase *can you smell what I'm cooking?*

She finally found Mona sitting in another one of the pillow-laden enclaves. Eric Kahn, Noel's older brother, dangled next to her, whispering in her ear. Mona noticed Hanna and sat up. "Thank *God* you got away from Loser Lucas," she groaned. "Why has he been hanging around you so much, anyway?"

Hanna scratched at her stitches underneath her mask, her heart suddenly racing. All at once, she needed to ask Mona. She needed to know for sure. "Lucas says I shouldn't trust you." She forced a laugh. "He says there's something you're not telling me, as if there would *ever* be something you wouldn't tell me." She rolled her eyes. "I mean, he's totally bullshitting me. It's so lame."

Mona crossed her legs and sighed. "I think I know what he's talking about."

Hanna swallowed hard. The room suddenly smelled too strongly of incense and freshly cut Bermuda grass. There was a burst of applause at the blackjack table; someone had won. Mona moved closer to her, talking right in Hanna's ear. "I never told you this, but Lucas and I dated the summer between seventh and eighth grade. I was his first kiss. I dumped him when you and I became friends. He called me for, like, six months afterward. I'm not sure he's ever gotten over it."

Hanna sat back, stunned. She felt like she was on one of those amusement park swings that abruptly changed directions halfway through the ride. "You and Lucas . . . dated?"

Mona lowered her eyes and pushed a stray lock of golden hair off her mask. "I'm sorry I never said anything about it before. It's just that . . . Lucas is a loser, Han. I didn't want you to think *I* was a loser too."

Hanna ran her hands through her hair, thinking about her conversation with Lucas in the hot-air balloon. She had told him *everything,* and his face had been so innocent and open. She thought about how intensely they'd kissed, and the little moaning noises he'd made when she ran her fingers up and down his neck.

"So, he was trying to be my friend and saying nasty things about you to . . . to get back at you for dumping him?" Hanna stammered.

"I think so," Mona said sadly. "*He's* the one you shouldn't trust, Hanna."

Hanna stood up. She remembered how Lucas had said she was so pretty, and how *good* that had felt. How he'd read her Instagram posts while the nurses changed her IV fluids. How, after he'd kissed her in the hospital bed, Hanna's heart rate had stayed elevated for a full half hour—she'd watched it on the heart monitor. Hanna had told Lucas about her eating issues. About Kate. About her friendship with Ali. About *A*! Why had he never told her about Mona?

Lucas was now sitting on another couch, talking to Andrew Campbell. Hanna made a beeline right for him, and Mona followed close behind, grabbing her arm. "Deal with this later. Why don't I just throw him out? You should be enjoying your big night."

Hanna waved Mona away. She poked Lucas in the back of his pin-striped vest. When Lucas turned around, he looked genuinely happy to see her, giving her a sweet, ecstatic smile.

"Mona told me the truth about you," Hanna hissed, placing her hands on her hips. "You guys used to date."

Lucas's lip twitched. He blinked hard, opened his mouth, then shut it again. "Oh."

"*That's* what this is all about, isn't it?" she demanded. "It's why you want me to hate her."

"Of course not." Lucas looked at her, his brows furrowed. "We weren't serious."

"*Right,*" Hanna scoffed.

"Hanna doesn't like boys who lie," Mona added, appearing behind Hanna.

Lucas's mouth dropped open. A bloom of redness crawled from his neck to his cheeks. "But I suppose she likes *girls* who lie, huh?"

Mona crossed her arms over her chest. "I'm not lying about anything, Lucas."

"No? So then you told Hanna what really happened at your party?"

"It doesn't *matter*," Hanna screeched.

"Of course I told her," Mona said at the same time.

Lucas looked at Hanna, his face growing more and more crimson. "She did something awful to you."

Mona inserted herself in front of him. "He's just *jealous*."

"She *humiliated* you," Lucas added. "*I* was the one who came and saved you."

"What?" Hanna squeaked in a small voice.

"Hanna." Mona grabbed Hanna's hands. "It's all a misunderstanding."

The DJ switched to a Lexi song. It was a song Hanna didn't hear often, and at first she wasn't sure when she'd heard it last. Then, all at once, she remembered. Lexi had been the special musical guest at Mona's party.

A memory suddenly caught fire in Hanna's mind. She saw herself wearing a skintight champagne-colored dress, struggling to walk into the planetarium without her outfit bursting at the seams. She saw Mona laughing at her, and then she felt her knee and elbow hitting the hard marble floor. There was a long, painful *riiiip* noise as her dress gave way, and everyone stood around her, laughing. Mona laughed the hardest of all.

Underneath her mask, Hanna's mouth dropped open and her eyes widened. *No.* It couldn't be true. Her memory was scrambled from the accident. And even if it was true, did it matter now? She looked down at her brand-new Paul & Joe bracelet, a delicate gold chain with a pretty butterfly charm clasp. Mona had bought it for her as a welcome-back-from-the-hospital present, giving it to Hanna right after A sent Mona that taunting e-card. "I don't want us ever to be mad at each other again," Mona had said as Hanna lifted the jewelry box lid.

Lucas stared at her expectantly. Mona had her hands on her hips, waiting. Hanna tied the mask's ribbon closure in a tighter knot. "You're just jealous," she said to Lucas, putting her arm around Mona. "We're best friends. Always will be."

Lucas's face crumpled. "Fine." He wheeled around and ran out the door.

"*What* a lame-ass," Mona said, sliding her arm in the crook of Hanna's elbow.

"Yeah," Hanna said, but her voice was so quiet, she doubted Mona heard.

28

POOR LITTLE DEAD GIRL

The sky was darkening on Friday night as Mrs. Fields dropped Emily and Trista off at the country club's main entrance. "Now, you know the rules," Mrs. Fields said sternly, draping her arm over Emily's seat. "No drinking. Be home by midnight. Carolyn will give you girls a ride home. Got it?"

Emily nodded. It was kind of a relief that her mom was enforcing some rules. Her parents had been so lenient since she'd come home, she was beginning to think that they both had brain tumors or had been replaced by clones.

As Emily's mom sped away, Emily straightened the black jersey dress she'd borrowed from Carolyn's closet and tried not to wobble in her red leather kitten heels. In the distance, she could see the huge, glowing party tent. An Ariana Grande song blared out of the speakers, and Emily heard Noel Kahn's unmistakable voice cry, "That's so *hot*!"

"I am so excited for tonight," Trista said, grabbing Emily's arm.

"Me too." Emily pulled her jacket closer around her, watching the skeleton wind sock twist from the country club's main entrance. "If you could be any Halloween character in the world, what would you be?" she asked. Lately, Emily had been thinking of everything in Trista-isms, trying to figure out which sort of spaghetti noodle she was most like, which Great Adventure roller coaster, which kind of deciduous Rosewood tree.

"Catwoman," Trista answered promptly. "You?"

Emily looked away. Right now, she kind of felt like a witch. After Trista surprised Emily in the yearbook room, she'd explained that since her father was a pilot with American Airlines, she got big discounts even on last-minute flights. After Emily's text yesterday, she'd decided to hop on a flight, accompany Emily to Hanna's masquerade party, and camp out on Emily's bedroom floor. Emily didn't quite know how to say, "You shouldn't have come" . . . and didn't quite want to, either.

"When's your friend meeting us?" Trista asked.

"Um, she's probably already here." Emily started across the parking lot, passing eight BMW 7 Series cars in a row.

"Cool." Trista spread ChapStick over her lips. She passed it to Emily, and their fingers lightly touched. Emily felt tingles run through her, and when she met Trista's eyes, the amorous look on Trista's face indicated she was thinking equally tingly thoughts.

Emily stopped short next to the valet stand. "Listen. I have a confession to make. Maya is sort of my girlfriend."

Trista stared at her blankly.

"And I kind of told her—and my parents—that you're my pen pal," Emily went on. "That we've been writing for a few years."

"Oh, *really*?" Trista nudged her playfully. "Why didn't you just tell her the truth?"

Emily swallowed, crushing a few dried, fallen leaves under her toe. "Well . . . I mean, if I told her what really happened . . . in Iowa . . . she might not get it."

Trista smoothed down her hair with her hands. "But nothing *did* happen. We just danced." She poked Emily in the arm. "Geez, is she *that* possessive?"

"No." Emily stared at the Halloween scarecrow display on the country club's front lawn. It was one of three scarecrows around the grounds, and yet a crow was perched on a nearby flagpole, not one bit frightened. "Not exactly."

"Is it a problem that I'm here?" Trista asked pointedly.

Trista's lips were the exact same pink as Emily's favorite tutu back when she'd taken ballet. Her pale blue shift dress pulled against her shapely chest and showed the flatness of her stomach and the roundness of her butt. She was like a ripe, juicy fruit, and Emily sort of wanted to bite her. "Of course it's not a problem you're here," Emily breathed.

"Good." Trista pulled her mask over her face. "Then I'll keep your secret."

Once they entered the tent, Maya found Emily immediately, untied her rabbit-shaped mask, and pulled Emily close for an extra-passionate kiss. Emily opened her eyes in the middle of it, and noticed that Maya was staring directly at Trista, seemingly flaunting what she and Emily were doing. "When are you going to ditch her?" Maya whispered in Emily's ear. Emily looked away, pretending she hadn't heard.

As they moved through the party tent, Trista kept grabbing Emily's arm and gasping, "It's so beautiful! Look at all the pillows!" And, "There are so many hot *guys* in Pennsylvania!" And, "So many girls here wear diamonds!" Her mouth fell open like a little kid's on her first trip to Disney World. When a crowd of kids at the bar separated them, Maya pulled off her mask.

"Was that girl raised in a hermetically sealed terrarium?" Maya's eyes bugged out. "Honestly, why does she find everything so amazing?"

Emily glanced at Trista as she leaned up against the bar. Noel Kahn had approached her and was now seductively running his hand up and down Trista's arm. "She's just excited to be here," she mumbled. "Things are pretty boring in Iowa."

Maya cocked her head and stood back. "It's quite a coincidence that you have a pen pal in the *exact same* Iowa town you were banished to last week."

"Not really," Emily croaked, staring at the shimmering disco ball in the middle of the tent. "She's from the same town as my cousins, so Rosewood Day did an exchange with her school. We started writing a couple years ago."

Maya mushed her lips together, her jaw tense. "She's awfully *pretty*. Did you pick pen pals by their pictures?"

"It wasn't, like, Match.com." Emily shrugged, trying to act oblivious.

Maya gave her a knowing look. "It would make sense if you did. You loved Alison DiLaurentis, and Trista looks a lot like her."

Emily tensed up, her eyes flicking back and forth. "No, she doesn't."

Maya looked away. "Whatever."

Emily considered her next words very carefully. "That banana gum you chew, Maya. Where do you get it?"

Maya looked confused. "My father brought me a carton from London."

"Can you get it in the States? Do you know anyone else who chews it?" Emily's heart pounded.

Maya stared at her. "Why the hell are you asking me about banana gum?" Before Emily could answer, Maya turned away. "Look, I'm going to go to the bathroom, okay? Don't go anywhere without me. We can talk when I get back."

Emily watched Maya snake through the baccarat tables, feeling like she had hot coals in her stomach. Almost immediately, Trista emerged from the crowd, holding three plastic cups. "They're spiked," she whispered excitedly, pointing to Noel, who was still standing by the bar. "That boy had a flask of something and gave me some." She looked around. "Where's Maya?"

Emily shrugged. "Off being pissy."

Trista had removed her mask, and her skin glowed in the flashing dance floor lights. With her pursed, pink lips, her wide, blue eyes, and high cheekbones, maybe she did look a little like Ali. Emily shook her head and reached for one of the cups—she would drink this first, figure out everything else later. Trista's finger ran seductively down Emily's wrist. Emily tried to keep her face impassive, even though she felt like she was about to melt.

"So, if you were a color right now, what color would you be?" Trista whispered.

Emily looked away.

"I'd be red," Trista whispered. "But . . . not a mad red. Like a deep, dark, beautiful sexy red. A lusty red."

"I think I'd be that color, too," Emily admitted.

The music thumped like a pulse. Emily took a long, needy drink, her nose tickling with the spicy flavor of rum. When Trista curled her hand around Emily's, Emily's heart jumped. They moved closer, then closer still, until their lips were nearly touching. "Maybe we shouldn't do this," Trista whispered.

But Emily moved closer anyway, her body rippling with excitement.

A hand smacked Emily on the back. "What the *hell*?"

Maya stood behind them, her nostrils flaring. Emily

took a giant step away from Trista, opening and closing her mouth like a goldfish. "I thought you were going to the bathroom" was all Emily could think to say.

Maya blinked, her face purple with fury. Then, she turned and stormed out of the tent, pushing people out of her way.

"Maya!" Emily followed her through the doors. But just before she was about to exit, she felt a hand on her arm. It was a man she didn't recognize in a police uniform. He had short spiky hair and a lanky build. His badge said SIMMONS.

"Are you Emily Fields?" the cop asked.

Emily nodded slowly, her heart suddenly quickening.

"I need to ask you a couple questions." The cop placed his hand gently on Emily's shoulder. "Have you . . . have you been getting some threatening messages?"

Emily's mouth fell open. The flickering strobe lights made her woozy. "W-why?"

"Your friend Aria Montgomery told us about them this afternoon," the cop said.

"What?" Emily shrieked.

"It'll be okay," the cop reassured her. "I just want to know what you know, all right? It's probably someone you know, someone right under your nose. If you talk to us, maybe we can figure it out together."

Emily looked out the tent's filmy opening. Maya was darting across the grass, her heels sinking into the dirt. A horrible feeling washed over Emily. She thought of how Maya had looked at her when she said, *I heard that the person who hit Hanna was stalking her.* How could Maya have known that?

"I can't talk right now," Emily whispered, a lump growing in her throat. "I have to take care of something first."

"I'll be here," the cop said, stepping aside so Emily could pass. "Take your time. I have a few other people to find anyway."

Emily could just make out Maya's shape running into the country club's main building. She sprinted after her, through two glass French doors and down a long hallway. She looked through the last door at the end of the hall, which led to the indoor pool. The window had fogged up with condensation, and Emily could just make out Maya's tiny body walking to the pool's edge, looking at her reflection.

She pushed her way in and walked around a small tiled wall separating the entryway from the pool. The pool's water was flat and dead, and the air was thick and humid. Even though Maya had surely heard Emily come in, she didn't turn around. If things had been different, Emily might jokingly have pushed her in the water, then jumped in too. She cleared her throat. "Maya, the Trista thing isn't what it looks like."

"No?" Maya peeked over her shoulder. "It looked pretty obvious to me."

"It's just . . . she's fun," Emily admitted. "She doesn't put any pressure on me."

"And I do?" Maya shrieked, whirling around. Tears streamed down her face.

Emily swallowed hard, gathering her strength. "Maya . . . have you been sending me . . . text messages? Notes? Have you been . . . spying on me?"

Maya's brow crinkled. "Why would I spy on you?"

"Well, I don't know," Emily started. "But if you are . . . the police know."

Maya slowly shook her head. "You're not making any sense."

"I won't tell if it's you," Emily pleaded. "I just want to know *why*."

Maya shrugged, then let out a little whimper of frustration. "I have no idea what you're talking about." A tear streaked down her face. She shook her head, disgusted. "I love you," she spat. "And I thought you loved me." She turned around, yanked the pool's glass door open, then slammed it shut.

The pool's overhead lights dimmed, turning the reflections coming off the pool from whitish-gold to orangish-yellow. Beads of humid sweat gathered on the top of the diving board. All of a sudden, the realization hit Emily, like the shock of diving into ice-cold water on an already cold day. Of course Maya wasn't A. A had set all this up for Maya to look suspicious, so things would be ruined between the two of them forever.

Her cell phone buzzed. Emily grabbed for it, her hands shaking.

Emmykins:

There's a girl waiting for you in the hot tub. Enjoy! —A

Emily let her phone drop to her side, her heart pounding. The hot tub was separated from the rest of the room by a partition, and it had its own door that led back out to the hall. Emily crept slowly to the hot tub. It bubbled like a cauldron, and mist rose off the water's surface. Suddenly, she noticed a flash of red in the bubbly water and jumped back in terror. Looking again, she realized it was only a doll floating facedown, its long red hair fanned out around it.

She reached in and pulled the doll out. It was an Ariel doll from *The Little Mermaid*. The doll had scaly green and purple fins, but instead of a clamshell bikini, Ariel wore a sleek racing suit that said ROSEWOOD DAY SHARKS across the boobs. There were *X*'s over her eyes, as if she'd drowned, and there was something written in thick marker across her forehead.

Tell and die. —A

Emily's hands started to shake, and she dropped the doll on the slick, tiled floor. As she stepped away from the hot tub's edge, a door slammed.

Emily shot up, her eyes wide. "Who's there?" she whispered.

Silence.

She stepped out from the hot tub partition and looked around. There was no one in the pool area. She couldn't see around the tiled wall that hid the front door, but she saw a distinct shadow on the far wall. Someone was here with her.

Emily heard a giggle and jumped. Then a hand flew out from behind the tiled wall. A blond ponytail appeared, then another pair of hands, larger and masculine, with a silver Rolex dangling from one wrist.

Noel Kahn emerged first, darting from behind the wall to one of the nearby chaises. "Come on," he whispered. Then the blonde scampered to him. It was Trista. They lay down on the chaise together and resumed kissing.

Emily was so stunned, she burst out laughing. Trista and Noel glanced at her. Trista's mouth fell open, but then she shrugged, as if to say, *Hey, you weren't around.* Emily suddenly thought of Abby's warning—*Trista Taylor tries to hump anything that moves, girl or guy.* She had a feeling Trista wouldn't be camping out on Emily's bedroom floor tonight after all.

Noel's lips spread into an easy smile. Then they went back to what they were doing, as if Emily didn't exist at all. Emily looked back at the drowned Ariel splayed out on the ground and shivered. Of course if she told anyone about A, A would make sure that Emily *really* didn't exist.

29

NO ONE CAN HEAR YOU SCREAM

Aria dashed from her dented Subaru to the Hollis art building. A storm was building on the horizon, and the rain had already begun to fall. She had finished telling the cops about A only a little while ago, and although she'd tried to call her old friends on Wilden's phone, none of them had picked up—probably because they didn't recognize his number. She was now going into the Hollis art building to see if she had left her phone here; without it, she had no concrete proof of what A was doing to her. Mike had offered to go into the building with her, but Aria had told him she'd see him later, at Hanna's party.

As Aria pushed the call button for the elevator, she pulled her Rosewood Day blazer around her—she hadn't had time to change yet. Mike's insistence that she tell Wilden about A had been a wake-up call, but had she done the right thing? Wilden had wanted to know the details of every last text, DM, email, and note that A had sent. He had asked over and over again, "Is there anyone the four of you hurt? Is there anyone who might want to harm you?"

Aria had paused and shaken her head, not wanting to answer. Who *hadn't* they hurt, back in the day, with Ali at the helm? There was one clear front-runner, though . . . Jenna.

She thought of A's notes: *I know EVERYTHING. I'm closer than you think.* She thought of Jenna asking Siri to perform various functions on her cell phone. But was Jenna truly capable of something like this? She was blind—A obviously wasn't.

The elevator doors slid open, and Aria got in. As it pulled her to the third floor, she thought about the memory Hanna had mentioned when she first woke up from her coma—the one about the afternoon before Ali went missing. Ali had been acting so strangely that day, first reading some notebook she wouldn't show the others, then appearing downstairs moments later, seeming so disoriented. Aria had lingered on Ali's porch by herself for a few minutes after the others left, knitting the last few rows of one of the cuff bracelets she planned to give to each of them as a first-full-day-of-summer present. As she went around the house to retrieve her bike, she saw Ali standing in the middle of her front yard, transfixed. Ali's eyes flickered from the DiLaurentises' curtained dining room window to the Cavanaughs' house across the street.

"Ali?" Aria had whispered. "Are you okay?"

Ali didn't move. "Sometimes," she said in an entranced voice, "I just wish she was out of my life forever."

"What?" Aria whispered. "Who?"

Ali seemed stunned, as if Aria had snuck up on her. There was a flash of something in the DiLaurentises' window—or perhaps it was just a reflection. And when Aria looked at the Cavanaughs' yard, she saw someone lurking behind the large shrub by Toby's old tree house. It reminded Aria of the figure she swore she'd seen standing in the Cavanaughs' yard the night they blinded Jenna.

The elevator let out a *ding,* and Aria jumped. Who had Ali been talking about when she said, *I just wish she was out of my life forever*? At the time, she'd thought Ali meant Spencer—they were constantly fighting. Now she wasn't sure at all. There were just so many things she hadn't known about Ali.

The hallway leading to the Mindless Art studio was dark, save for a brief moment when a zigzag of lightning came dangerously close to the window. When Aria reached the open door of her classroom, she flipped on the light and blinked in the sudden brightness. Her class's cubbies were along the back wall, and amazingly, Aria's phone was in an empty cubby, seemingly untouched. She ran to it and cradled it in her arms, letting out a sigh of relief.

Then, she noticed the masks her class had completed,

252 • SARA SHEPARD

one drying in each cubby. The alcove with Aria's name
written in Scotch tape on the bottom was empty, but
Jenna's wasn't. Someone else must have helped Jenna
make her mask, because there it was, faceup and perfectly
formed, the blank, hollowed-out eyes staring at the
cubby's ceiling. Aria lifted it slowly. Jenna had painted
her mask to look like an enchanted forest. Vines swirled
around the nose, a flower bloomed above her left eye,
and there was a gorgeous butterfly on her right cheek.
The detailed brushwork was impeccable—perhaps *too*
impeccable. It didn't seem possible for someone who
couldn't see.

A crack of thunder sounded like it was splitting open
the earth. Aria yelped, dropping the mask to the table.
When she looked to the window, she saw the silhouette
of something swinging from the window's top crank. It
looked like a tiny . . . person.

Aria stepped closer. It was a plush doll of the Wicked
Queen from *Snow White*. She wore a long black robe and
a gold crown on her head, and her frowning face was
ghostly pale. She hung from a rope around her neck, and
someone had drawn big, black *X*'s over her eyes. There
was a note pinned to the doll's long gown.

Mirror, mirror on the wall, who's the naughtiest of them all?
You told. So you're next. —A

Tree branches scraped violently against the window.

More lightning set fire to the sky. As another crack of thunder sounded, the studio's lights died. Aria shrieked.

The streetlights just outside the window had gone off, too, and somewhere, far away, Aria heard a fire alarm screaming. *Stay calm,* Aria told herself. She grabbed her phone and dialed the number for the police dispatch. Just as someone picked up, a knife-shaped bolt of lightning flickered outside the window. Aria's phone slipped from her fingers and clattered to the floor. She reached for it, then tried to dial again. But her phone no longer had service.

Lightning lit up the room again, illuminating the shapes of the desks, the cabinets, the swinging Wicked Queen from the window, and, finally, the door. Aria widened her eyes, a scream frozen in her throat. *There was someone there.*

"H-Hello?" she cried out.

With another zing of lightning, the stranger was gone. Aria bit into her knuckles, her teeth chattering. "Hello?" she called. Lightning flashed again. A girl was standing just inches from her face. Aria felt dizzy with fear. It was . . .

"Hello," the girl said.

It was Jenna.

30

THREE LITTLE WORDS CAN CHANGE EVERYTHING

Spencer sat at the roulette table, moving her shiny plastic casino chips from one palm to the other. As she placed a few chips on numbers 4, 5, 6, and 7, she felt the push of the crowd now gathered thickly behind her. It seemed like all of Rosewood was here tonight—everyone from Rosewood Day, plus the people from rival private schools who were staples at Noel Kahn's parties. There was even a cop here, wandering the perimeter. Spencer wondered why.

When the wheel stopped, the ball landed on the number 6. This was the third time in a row she'd won. "Nice job," someone said in her ear. Spencer looked around, but she couldn't locate who'd spoken to her. It sounded like her sister's voice. Only, why would Melissa be here? No other college kids had come, and before Spencer's Golden Orchid interview, Melissa had said Hanna's party sounded ridiculous.

She did it, you know. Spencer couldn't get A's text out of her head.

She scanned the tent. Someone with chin-length blond hair was slinking toward the stage, but when Spencer stood up, the person seemed to have evaporated into the crowd. She rubbed her eyes. Maybe she was going crazy.

Suddenly, Mona Vanderwaal grabbed her arm. "Hey, sweetie. You have a sec? I have a surprise."

She led Spencer through the crowd to a more secluded spot, snapped her fingers, and a waiter magically appeared, handing each of them a tall, fluted glass filled with bubbly liquid. "It's real champagne," Mona said. "I wanted to propose a toast to thank you, Spencer. For planning this fantastic party with me . . . and also for being there for me. About . . . you know. The notes."

"Of course," Spencer said faintly.

They clinked glasses and sipped. "This party is really awesome," Mona went on. "I couldn't have done it without you."

Spencer waved her hand humbly. "Nah. You put it all together. I just made a couple of calls. You're a natural at this."

"We're *both* naturals at this," Mona said, belting back her champagne. "We should start a party-planning business together."

"And we'll flash country club boys on the side," Spencer joked.

"Of course!" Mona chirped, bumping Spencer's hip.

Spencer ran her finger up and down the length of the champagne flute. She wanted to tell Mona about her newest text from A—the one about Melissa. Mona would understand. Only, the DJ switched songs to something fast with a techno beat, and before Spencer could say a word, Mona squealed and made a run for the dance floor. She glanced over her shoulder at Spencer, as if to say, *Are you coming?* Spencer shook her head.

The few sips of champagne had made her dizzy. After a couple minutes of wading through the crowd, she walked out of the tent into the clear night air. Except for the spotlights that surrounded the tent, the golf course was very dark. The man-made grassy knolls and sand traps weren't visible, and Spencer could only see the bare outlines of the trees in the distance. Their branches waved like bony fingers. Somewhere, a bunch of crickets screamed.

A doesn't know anything about Ali's killer, Spencer assured herself, looking back at the fuzzy shapes of the partygoers inside. And anyway, it made no sense—Melissa wouldn't ruin her whole future by killing someone over a guy. This was just another one of A's tactics to make Spencer believe something that wasn't true.

She sighed and headed off for the bathrooms, which were outside the tent in a bubble-shaped trailer. Spencer climbed the wheelchair ramp and pushed through the flimsy plastic door. Of the three stalls, one was occupied, and two were empty. As she flushed and wriggled her dress back into position, the bathroom's main door slammed shut. Pale silver Loeffler Randall shoes made their way over to the trailer's minuscule sink. Spencer clapped her hand over her mouth. She'd seen those shoes plenty of times before—they were Melissa's favorite pair.

"Uh, hi?" Spencer said when she stepped out of her stall. Melissa was leaning against the sink, her hands on her hips, a small smile on her face. She wore a long, narrow black dress with a slit up the side. Spencer tried to breathe calmly. "What are you doing here?"

Her sister didn't say anything, just kept staring. A droplet of water struck the sink basin, making Spencer jump.

"*What?*" Spencer sputtered. "Why are you looking at me like that?"

"Why did you lie to me again?" Melissa growled.

Spencer pressed her back against one of the stall doors. She looked back and forth for something she could use as a weapon. The only thing she could think of was her shoe's kitten heel, and she slowly slid her foot out of the toe box. "Lie?"

"Ian told me he was in your hotel room last night," Melissa whispered, her nostrils flaring in and out. "I told you he wasn't good at keeping a secret."

Spencer's eyes widened. "We didn't do anything. I swear."

Melissa took a step toward her. Spencer covered her face with one hand and pulled her shoe off her foot with the other. *"Please,"* she begged, holding out her shoe like a shield.

Melissa hovered just inches from her face. "After all you admitted to me at the beach, I thought we had an understanding. But I guess not." She whirled around and stormed out of the bathroom. Spencer heard her clonk down the ramp and stamp across the grass.

Spencer leaned over the sink and rested her forehead on the mirror's cool surface. Suddenly, a toilet flushed. After a pause, the third stall door swung open. Mona Vander-waal strode out. There was a horrified look on her face.

"Was that your *sister?*" Mona whispered.

"Yeah," Spencer sputtered, turning around.

Mona grabbed Spencer's wrists. "What's going on? Are you okay?"

"I think so." Spencer stood back up. "I just need a second alone is all."

"Of course." Mona's eyes widened. "I'll be outside if you need me."

Spencer smiled gratefully at Mona's back. After a pause, she heard the door swoosh closed. Spencer faced the mirror and smoothed down her hair. Her hands shook wildly as she reached for her sequined clutch, hoping there was a tube of aspirin inside. Her hands bumped against her wallet, her lip gloss, her poker chips . . . and then something else, something square and glossy. Spencer pulled it out slowly.

It was a photograph. Ali and Ian stood close together,

their arms entwined. Behind them was a round, stone building, and behind that was a line of yellow school buses. By the looks of Ali's shaggy haircut and her tropical-shade long-sleeve J. Crew polo, Spencer was pretty sure this photo had been taken during their class trip to see *Romeo and Juliet* at the People's Light playhouse a few towns away. A bunch of Rosewood Day students had gone along—Spencer, Ali, her other friends, and a slew of juniors and seniors like Ian and Melissa. Someone had written something in big, jagged letters over Ali's smiling face.

You're dead, bitch.

Spencer stared at the handwriting, immediately identifying it. Not too many people made their lowercase a's look like a curly number 2. Cursive was practically the only thing Melissa had gotten a B in, ever. Her second-grade penmanship teacher had chastised her, but making funny-looking a's was a habit Melissa had never been able to break.

Spencer let the picture slip from her hands and let out a small, pained yelp of disbelief. "Spencer?" Mona called from outside. "You okay?"

"Fine," Spencer said after a long pause. Then she looked down at the floor. The photo had landed face-down. There was more writing on the back.

Better watch your back . . . or you'll be a dead bitch too. —A

31

SOME SECRETS GO EVEN DEEPER

As Aria opened her eyes, something wet and smelly scraped its tongue up and down her face. She reached out, her hand sinking into soft, warm fur. For some reason, she was now on the art studio floor. A lightning bolt lit up the room, and she saw Jenna Cavanaugh and her dog sitting on the floor next to her.

Aria shot up, screaming.

"It's okay!" Jenna cried, catching her arm. "Don't worry! It's okay!"

Aria scuttled backward, away from Jenna, knocking her head on a nearby table leg. "Don't hurt me," she whispered. "Please."

"You're safe," Jenna reassured her. "I think you had a panic attack. I was coming here to pick up my sketchbook, but then I heard you—and when I came close, you fell." Aria could hear herself swallowing hard in the darkness. "A woman in my service-dog-training class gets panic attacks, so I know a little about them. I tried to call for help, but my cell phone wasn't working, so I just stayed with you."

A breeze blew through the room, bringing in the smell of wet, rained-on asphalt, a scent Aria usually found calming. Aria certainly *felt* like she'd just had a panic attack—she was sweaty and disoriented, and her heart was beating like mad. "How long was I out?" she croaked, smoothing out her pleated uniform skirt so that it covered her thighs.

"About a half hour," Jenna said. "You might've hit your head, too."

"Or I might've really needed the sleep," Aria joked, and then felt like she was going to cry. Jenna didn't want to hurt her. Jenna had *sat* with her, a stranger, while she'd lain like a lump on the floor. For all Aria knew, she'd drooled on Jenna's lap and talked in her sleep. She suddenly felt sick with guilt and shame.

"I have to tell you something," Aria blurted out. "My name's not Jessica. It's Aria. Aria Montgomery."

Jenna's dog sneezed. "I know," Jenna admitted.

"You . . . *do?*"

"I could just . . . tell. By your voice." Jenna sounded almost apologetic. "But why didn't you just say it was you?"

Aria closed her eyes tight and pressed her hands hard into her cheeks. Another streak of lightning illuminated the room, and Aria saw Jenna sitting cross-legged on the floor, her hands wrapped around her ankles. Aria took a huge breath, perhaps the biggest one of her life. "I didn't tell you because . . . there's something else you should know about me." She pressed her hands to the rough wood floor, gathering strength. "You should know something about the night of your accident. Something no one ever told you. I guess you don't remember much of what happened that night, but—"

"That's a lie," Jenna interrupted. "I remember everything."

Thunder rumbled in the distance. Somewhere close by, a car alarm went off, starting a cycle of harsh, piercingly loud buzzes and *ee-oo*s. Aria could hardly breathe. "What do you mean?" she whispered, stunned.

"I remember everything," Jenna repeated. She traced the sole of her shoe with a finger. "Alison and I set it up together."

Every muscle in Aria's body went limp. "*What?*"

"My stepbrother used to set off fireworks from his tree house roof all the time," Jenna explained, frowning. "My parents kept warning him that it was dangerous—he might mess up, send a firework right into our house, and cause a fire. They said the next time he set one off, they were going to send him to boarding school. And that was final.

"So Ali agreed to steal fireworks out of Toby's stash and make it look like Toby had launched it off the tree house roof. I wanted her to do it that night because my parents were home, and they were already mad at Toby for something anyway. I wanted him out of my life as soon as possible." Her voice caught. "He . . . he wasn't a good stepbrother."

Aria clenched and unclenched her fist. "Oh my God." She tried to comprehend everything Jenna was telling her.

"Only . . . things went wrong," Jenna explained, her voice teetering. "I was with Toby in his tree house that night. And just before it happened, he looked down and said angrily, 'There's someone on our lawn.' I looked down, too, pretending to be surprised . . . and then there was a flash of light, and then . . . this horrible pain. My eyes . . . my face . . . it felt like they just melted away. I think I passed out. Afterward, Ali told me that she'd forced Toby to take the blame."

"That's right." Aria's voice was barely more than a whisper.

"Ali thought fast." Jenna shifted her weight, making the floor beneath her creak. "I'm glad she did. I didn't want her to get in trouble. And it kind of worked out the way I wanted. Toby left. He was out of my life."

Aria slowly rolled her jaw around. *But . . . you're blind!* she wanted to scream. *Was it really worth* that? Her head hurt, trying to process everything Jenna had just told her. Her whole world felt smashed open. It felt like someone had proclaimed that animals could talk, and dogs and spiders now ruled the world. Then something else hit her: Ali had set things up like it was a prank *they* pulled on Toby, but Ali and Jenna had been the ones who planned it out . . . *together*. Not only had Ali set up Toby, she'd set up her friends, too. Aria felt sick.

"So you and Ali were . . . friends." Aria's voice was faint with disbelief.

"Not exactly," Jenna said. "Not until this . . . not until I told her about what Toby was doing. I knew Ali would understand. She had sibling problems, too."

A flash of light streaked across Jenna's face, revealing a calm, matter-of-fact expression. Before Aria could ask what Jenna meant, Jenna added, "There's something else you should know. There was someone else there that night. Someone else saw."

Aria gasped. The image of that night scissored through her head. The firework burst inside the tree house, lighting up the surrounding yard. Aria always thought she'd seen a dark figure crouching near the Cavanaughs' side porch—but Ali insisted, over and over again, that she'd imagined the whole thing.

Aria wanted to smack her forehead. It was so obvious who'd seen. How could she have not realized till now?

I'm still here, bitches. And I know everything. —A.

"Do you know who it was?" Aria whispered, her heart hammering fast.

Jenna turned sharply away. "I can't tell."

"Jenna!" Aria shrieked. "Please! You have to! I need to know!"

All of a sudden, the power snapped back on. The room flooded with light so bright, it hurt Aria's eyes. The fluorescent bulbs hummed. Aria saw a streak of blood on her hands and felt a cut on her forehead. The contents of her bag had spilled out onto the floor, and Jenna's dog had eaten half of one of Aria's Balance bars.

Jenna had taken her sunglasses off. Her eyes stared out blankly at nothing, and there were wrinkled, puckered burn scars on the bridge of her nose and the bottom of her forehead. Aria winced and looked away.

"Please, Jenna, you don't understand," Aria said quietly. "Something horrible is happening. You have to tell me who else was there!"

Jenna stood up, grabbing hold of her dog's back for balance. "I've said too much already," she croaked, her voice shaky. "I should go."

"Jenna, please!" Aria pleaded. *Who else was there?*"

Jenna paused, sliding her sunglasses back on. "I'm sorry," she whispered, pulling on her dog's harness. She tapped her cane once, twice, three times, fumbling clumsily for the door. And then she was gone.

32

HELL HATH NO FURY . . .

After Emily caught Trista hooking up with Noel, she ran out of the pool room, searching frantically for Spencer or Hanna. She needed to tell them that Aria had told the police about A . . . and show them the doll she'd just found. As she rounded the craps table for the second time, Emily felt a cold hand on her shoulder and yelped. Spencer and Mona stood behind her. Spencer was clutching a small, square photograph tightly in her hands. "Emily, we need to talk."

"I need to talk to you, too," Emily gasped.

Spencer wordlessly pulled her across the dance floor. Mason Byers was in the middle, making a jackass out of himself. Hanna was talking to her father and Mrs. Cho, her photography teacher. Hanna looked up as Spencer, Mona, and Emily approached, her face clouding over. "Do you have a sec?" Spencer asked.

They found an empty booth and piled in. Without a

word, Spencer reached into her beaded purse and pulled out a photograph of Ali and Ian Thomas. Someone had drawn an *X* over Ali's face and had written, *You're dead, bitch,* in spiky letters at the bottom.

Emily clapped a hand over her mouth. Something was very familiar about the photograph. Where had she seen it before?

"I found this in my purse when I was in the bathroom." Spencer turned the photo over. *Better watch your back . . . or you'll be a dead bitch too.* Emily recognized the spiky handwriting immediately. She'd seen it scrawled on a PFLAG application just the other day.

"It was in your bag?" Hanna gasped. "So does that mean A is *here*?"

"A's definitely here," Emily said, looking around. The male model cocktail waiters swirled. A bunch of girls in minidresses flounced by, whispering that Noel Kahn had smuggled in alcohol. "I just got a . . . a message, sort of, saying so," Emily went on. "And . . . you guys. *Aria* told the cops about A. Some cop came up to me saying he wanted to ask me questions. I think A knows about that too."

"Oh my God," Mona whispered, her eyes wide. She looked from one girl to the other. "That's bad, right?"

"It could be *really* bad," Emily said. Someone elbowed her in the back of the head, and she rubbed her skull, annoyed. This party wasn't exactly the right venue to be talking about this.

Spencer ran her hands along the velvet couch cushion. "Okay. Let's not panic. The cops are here, right? So we're safe. We'll just find them and stick by them. But this . . ." She tapped the big *X* over Ali's face, then *You're dead, bitch.* "I know who wrote this part of it." She looked around at them, taking a deep breath. "Melissa."

"Your sister?" Hanna squeaked.

Spencer nodded gravely, the party's strobe lights flickering against her face. "I think . . . I think Melissa killed Ali. It makes sense. She knew that Ali and Ian were together. And she couldn't take it."

"Rewind." Mona put down her can of Red Bull. "Alison and . . . Ian Thomas? They were together?" She stuck out her tongue, disgusted. "Ew. Did you guys know?"

"We only figured it out a few days ago," Emily mumbled. She wrapped her coat around her body. Suddenly, she was freezing.

Hanna examined Melissa's signature on her cast against the writing on the photo. "The writing *is* similar."

Mona stared at Spencer fearfully. "And she was acting so weird in the bathroom just now."

"Is she still here?" Hanna craned her neck to look around the room. Behind them, a waiter dropped a tray of glasses. A crowd of kids clapped.

"I've looked all over for her," Spencer said. "I couldn't find her anywhere."

"So what are you going to do?" Emily asked, her heart pounding faster and faster.

"I'm going to tell Wilden about Melissa," Spencer said matter-of-factly.

"But, Spencer," Emily argued. "A knows what we're doing. And A knows Aria told. What if this is just some sort of big mind game?"

"She's right," Mona agreed, crossing her legs. "It could be a trap."

Spencer shook her head. "It's Melissa. I'm sure of it. I have to turn her in. We have to do it for Ali." She reached into her sequined bag and found her phone. "I'll call the station. Wilden's probably there." She dialed and pressed her phone to her ear.

Behind them, the DJ shouted out, "Is everyone having a good time tonight?!" The crowd on the dance floor screamed, "Yeah!"

Emily shut her eyes. *Melissa.* Ever since the police had deemed Ali's death a murder, Emily hadn't been able to stop herself from imagining just how the murderer had done it. She'd envisioned Toby Cavanaugh grabbing Ali from behind, hitting her on the head, and throwing her into the DiLaurentises' half-dug gazebo hole. She'd tried to picture Spencer doing the same thing to Ali, distraught over Ali's relationship with Ian Thomas. Now she saw Melissa Hastings grabbing Ali's waist and dragging her toward the hole. Only . . . Melissa was so thin Emily couldn't quite believe she'd had the strength to coerce Ali into doing what she wanted. Perhaps she'd had a weapon, like a kitchen knife or a box cutter. Emily winced, imagining a box cutter at Ali's delicate throat.

"Wilden's not answering." Spencer threw her phone back into her bag. "I'm just going to go down to the station." She paused, smacking herself on the forehead. "*Shit.* My parents drove me here. We came straight from New York. I don't have a car."

"I'll take you." Mona leapt up.

Emily stood up. "I'll go too."

"We'll all go," Hanna said.

Spencer shook her head. "Hanna, this is *your* party. You should stay."

"Seriously," Mona said.

Hanna adjusted her sling. "This party's been great, but this is more important."

Mona bit the edge of her lip awkwardly. "I think you should stay for a little while longer."

Hanna raised an eyebrow. "Why?"

Mona rocked back and forth on her heels. "We got Justin Timberlake to come."

Hanna clutched her chest as if Mona had shot her. *"What?"*

"He was my dad's client when he was just starting out, so he owed him a favor. Only, he's kind of late. I'm sure he'll be here soon, but I wouldn't want you to miss him." She smiled sheepishly.

"Whoa." Spencer widened her eyes. "Seriously? You didn't even tell *me* that."

"And you *hate* him, Mon," Hanna breathed.

Mona shrugged. "Well, it's not my party, is it? It's yours. He's going to call you up to the stage to dance with him, Han. I wouldn't want you to miss it."

Hanna had liked Justin Timberlake as long as Emily had known her. Whenever Hanna used to talk about how Justin should be with *her* instead of Jessica Biel, Ali would always cackle and say, "Well, with you, he'd sort of get *two* Jessicas for the price of one—you're twice her size!" Hanna would turn away, hurt, until Ali insisted that she shouldn't be so sensitive.

"I'll stay with you, Hanna," Emily said, grabbing Hanna's arm. "We'll stay for Justin. We'll stick really close together, next to that cop over there. Okay?"

"I don't know," Hanna said uncertainly, even though Emily could tell she wanted to stay. "Maybe we should go."

"*Stay,*" Spencer urged. "Meet us there. You'll be okay here. A can't hurt you with a cop nearby. Just don't go to the bathroom or anywhere else alone."

Mona took Spencer's arm, and they slid through the crowd toward the tent's main opening. Emily shot Hanna a brave smile, her stomach churning. "Don't leave me," Hanna said in a small, terrified voice.

"I won't," Emily assured her. She took Hanna's hand and squeezed hard, but she couldn't help scanning the crowd nervously. Spencer had said she'd run into Melissa in the bathroom. That meant Ali's murderer was here with them *right now*.

33

THE MOMENT OF CLARITY

Standing up onstage with the *real* Justin Timberlake—not a wax figure at Madame Tussauds—was going to be surreal. It would be Justin's real mouth giving Hanna a big smile, Justin's real eyes canvassing Hanna's body as she danced around, and Justin's real hands as he gave her a round of applause for having the strength to pull through such a devastating accident.

Unfortunately, Justin hadn't shown up yet. Hanna and Emily peeked out one of the tent's openings, keeping their eyes peeled for a convoy of limos. "This is going to be so exciting," Emily murmured.

"Yeah," Hanna said. But she wondered if she'd even be able to enjoy it. She felt like there was something really, really wrong. Something inside her wanted to break through, like a moth struggling inside a cocoon.

Suddenly, Aria emerged from the crowd. Her dark

hair was tangled and there was a bruise on her cheek. She still wore her Rosewood Day blazer and pleated skirt, and looked very out of place among the other dressed-up people at the party. "You guys," she said breathlessly. "I need to talk to you."

"And we need to talk to *you*," Emily shrieked. "You told Wilden about A!"

Aria's eyelid twitched. "I . . . I did. Yes. I thought it was the right thing to do."

"It *wasn't*," Hanna snapped, her body filling with rage. "A knows, Aria. A's after us. What the hell is wrong with you?"

"I know A knows," Aria said, seeming distracted. "I have to tell you guys something else. Where's Spencer?"

"Spencer went to the police station," Emily said. The disco lights came back on, turning her face from pink to blue. "We tried to call you, but you didn't pick up."

Aria sank down into a nearby couch, looking a little shaken and confused. She picked up a carafe of sparkling water and poured herself a huge glass. "Did she go to the police station because of . . . A? The cops want to ask all of us more questions."

"She didn't," Hanna said. "She went because she knows who killed Ali."

Aria's eyes were glassy. She seemed to be ignoring what Hanna just said altogether. "Something really weird just happened to me." She drained her water glass. "I just

had a long conversation with Jenna Cavanaugh. And . . .
she knows about that night."

"What were you doing talking to Jenna?" Hanna
barked. Then the rest of what Aria had said finally regis-
tered, the same way, her physics teacher had explained,
it takes radio waves years to reach outer space. Hanna's
mouth fell open, and all the blood drained from her
head. *What did you just say?*

Aria pressed her hands to her forehead. "I've been taking these art classes, and Jenna's in my class too. Tonight,
I went up to the art studio and . . . and Jenna was there.
I had this horrible fear that she was A . . . and that she
was going to hurt me. I had a panic attack . . . but when I
woke up, Jenna was still with me. She had *helped* me. I felt
terrible, and I just started to blurt out what we did. Only,
before I could really say anything, Jenna interrupted. She
said that she remembered everything about that night,
after all." Aria looked at Hanna and Emily. "She and Ali
set up the whole thing together."

There was a long pause. Hanna could feel her pulse
at her temples. "That's not possible," Emily finally said,
abruptly standing up. "It *can't* be."

"It can't be," Hanna echoed weakly. What was Aria
saying?

Aria pushed a stray strand of hair behind her ears.
"Jenna said that she came to Ali with the plan to hurt
Toby. She wanted him gone—I'm sure because he was . . .

you know. Touching her. Ali said she'd help. Only, things went wrong. But Jenna kept the secret anyway—she said that things worked out the way she wanted. Her brother was gone. But . . . she also said that someone else was there that night. Besides Ali, and besides us. Someone else saw."

Emily gaped. *"No."*

"Who?" Hanna demanded, feeling her knees go weak.

Aria shook her head. "She wouldn't tell me."

A long pause followed. A bass line from a Post Malone song throbbed in the background. Hanna looked around the party, amazed at how blissfully unaware everyone was. Mike Montgomery was grinding against some girl from the Quaker school; the adults were all hovering around the bar, getting drunk; and a bunch of girls in her grade were whispering cattily about how pudgy everyone else looked in their dresses. Hanna almost wanted to tell everyone to go home, that the universe had tipped upside down and right now, having fun was out of the question.

"Why did Jenna go to *Ali,* of all people?" Emily sounded out. "Ali hated her."

Aria ran her fingers through her hair, which was wet from the rain. "She said that Ali would understand. That Ali had sibling problems, too."

Hanna frowned, confused. *"Sibling* problems? You mean like Jason?"

"I . . . I guess," Aria mused. "Maybe Jason was doing what Toby did."

Hanna wrinkled her nose, recalling Ali's handsome-but-sullen older brother. "Jason *was* always kind of . . . weird."

"You guys, *no*." Emily's hands fell to her lap. "Jason was moody, but he wasn't a molester. He and Ali always seemed really happy around each other."

"Toby and Jenna seemed happy around each other, too," Aria reminded her.

"I heard, like, one in four boys is abusive to his sister," Hanna seconded.

"That's ridiculous," Emily snorted. "Don't believe everything you hear."

Hanna froze. She whipped her head around to Emily. "What did you just say?"

Emily's lip trembled. "I said . . . don't believe everything you hear."

The words fanned out in sonarlike concentric circles. Hanna heard them again and again, banging back and forth inside her head.

The foundations of her brain started to crumble. *Don't believe everything you hear.* She had seen those words before. It was her last text. From A. From the night she couldn't remember.

Hanna must have made some sort of noise because Aria turned. "Hanna . . . what?"

Memories began to flood back to her, like a line of dominoes falling down one after another. Hanna saw herself wobbling into Mona's party in the court dress, freaked because it didn't fit. Mona had laughed in her face and called her a whale. It wasn't Mona who had sent her that dress, Hanna realized—A had.

She saw herself taking a step back, her ankle buckling, and collapsing to the ground. The devastating *riiippppp* of seams. The sounds of laughter above her, Mona's loudest of all. And then, Hanna saw herself much later, sitting alone in her Toyota Prius in the Hollis Planetarium parking lot, wearing a sweatshirt and gym shorts, her eyes puffy from crying. She heard her phone chime and she saw herself reaching for her phone. Oops, guess it wasn't lipo! the text said. Don't believe everything you hear! —A

Except the text wasn't from A. It had been from a regular cell phone number—a number Hanna knew well.

Hanna let out a muffled shriek. The faces looking down at her blurred and shimmered, as if they were holograms. "Hanna . . . what is it?" Emily shrieked.

"Oh. My. God," Hanna whispered, her head reeling. "It's . . . Mona."

Emily frowned. "What's Mona?"

Hanna pulled off her mask. The air felt cool and liberating. Her scar pulsed, as if it was a separate entity from her chin. She didn't even look around to see how many people were staring at her bruised, ugly face, because right now, it didn't matter. "I remember what I was going to tell you guys that night, when I wanted to meet you at Rosewood Day," Hanna said, tears brimming in her eyes. "A is Mona."

Emily and Aria stared at her so blankly that Hanna wondered if they'd even heard her. Finally, Aria said, "Are you *sure*?"

Hanna nodded.

"But Mona's with . . . Spencer," Emily said slowly.

"I know," Hanna whispered. She tossed her mask on the couch and stood up. "We have to find her. Now."

34

I'LL GET YOU, MY PRETTIES . . .

It had taken Spencer and Mona almost ten minutes to cross the country club lawn to the parking lot, climb into Mona's enormous taxicab-yellow Hummer, and roar out of the parking lot. Spencer glanced at Hanna's receding party tent. It was lit up like a birthday cake, and the vibrations from the music were almost visible.

"That was a really awesome thing you did, setting up Justin Timberlake for Hanna," Spencer murmured.

"Hanna's my best friend," Mona answered. "She's been through a lot. I wanted to make it really special."

"She used to talk about Justin all the time when we were younger," Spencer went on, gazing out the window as an old farmhouse, which used to belong to one of the DuPonts but was now a restaurant, flew past. A few people who had finished dinner were standing out on the porch, happily chatting. "I didn't know she still liked him so much."

Mona smiled halfway. "I know lots of things about Hanna. Sometimes I think I know Hanna better than Hanna knows herself." She glanced at Spencer briefly. "You have to do good things for people you care about, you know?"

Spencer nodded faintly, biting at her cuticles. Mona slowed for a stop sign and rooted around in her purse, pulling out a pack of gum. The car immediately smelled like artificial bananas. "Want a piece?" she asked Spencer, unwrapping a stick and pushing it into her mouth. "I'm obsessed with this stuff. Apparently you can only get it in Europe, but this girl in my history class gave me a whole pack." She chewed thoughtfully. Spencer waved the open pack away. She wasn't much in a gum-chewing mood right now.

As Mona passed the Fairview Riding Academy, Spencer smacked her thighs hard. "I can't do this," she wailed. "We should turn around, Mona. I can't turn Melissa in."

Mona glanced at her, then turned into the riding academy's parking lot. They pulled into the accessible parking space and Mona shifted the Hummer into park. "Okay . . ."

"She's my *sister*." Spencer stared blankly forward. It was pitch-black out, and the air smelled like hay. She heard a whinnying in the distance. "If Melissa did it, shouldn't I be trying to protect her?"

Mona reached into her clutch and pulled out another

stick of gum. She offered one to Spencer, but Spencer shook her head. Mona popped the piece into her mouth, and the smell of banana filled the car.

"What did Melissa mean in the bathroom?" Mona asked quietly. "She said, after what you told her at the beach, she thought you guys had an understanding. What did you tell her?"

Spencer dug her nails into the heels of her hands. "This memory had come back to me about the night Ali went missing," she admitted. "Ali and I had this fight . . . and I shoved her. Her head smacked against the stone wall. But I'd blocked it out for years." She glanced at Mona, gauging her reaction, but Mona's face was blank. "I blurted it out to Melissa the other day. I had to tell *someone*."

"Whoa," Mona whispered, glancing at Spencer carefully. "You think *you* did it?"

Spencer pressed her palms into her forehead. "I was definitely mad at her."

Mona twisted in her seat, tossing her piece of gum out the window. "A put that photo of Ali and Ian in your purse, right? What if A fed Melissa some sort of clue, too, convincing *her* to tell on *you*? Melissa could be going to the cops right now."

Spencer's eyes widened. She remembered what Melissa said about them no longer having an "understanding." "Shit," she whispered. "Do you think?"

"I don't know." Mona grabbed Spencer's hand. "I

think you're doing the right thing. But if you want me to turn around and go back to the party, I will."

Spencer ran her fingers against the rough beads on her clutch. *Was* it the right thing? She wished she hadn't been the one to discover Melissa was the killer. She wished someone else could've found out instead. Then, she thought about how she'd torn around the country club tent, looking frantically for Melissa. Where had she gone? What was she doing right now?

"You're right," she whispered in a dry voice. "This is the right thing."

Mona nodded, then shifted gears again and backed out of the riding school lot.

When they were farther down the road, Spencer's phone beeped. Spencer unzipped her bag. "Maybe that's Wilden," she murmured. Only, it was a text from Emily.

Hanna remembered. Mona is A! Reply if you get this.

Spencer's phone slipped from her hands to her lap. She read the text again. And again. The words might as well have been written in Arabic—Spencer couldn't process them at all. Are you sure? she texted back. Yes, Emily wrote. Get out of there. NOW.

Spencer stared at a billboard for Wawa coffee, a stone sign for a housing development, then an enormous, triangular-shaped church. She tried to breathe as steadily as possible, counting from one to one hundred by fives, hoping it would calm her down. Mona was watching the road carefully and dutifully. Her halter dress didn't quite fit her in the chest. She had a scar on her right shoulder, probably from the chicken pox. It didn't seem possible that she could have done this.

"So was it Wilden?" Mona chirped.

"Um, no." Spencer's voice came out squawky and muffled, like she was talking through a can. "It was . . . it was my mom."

Mona nodded slightly, keeping the same speed. Spencer's phone lit up again. Another text had come in. Then another, then another, then another. Spencer, what's going on? Spencer, please text us back. Spencer, you're in DANGER. Please tell us if you're okay.

Mona smiled, her canine teeth glowing in the dim light shining off the Hummer's dashboard console. "You're certainly popular. What's going on?"

Spencer tried to laugh. "Um, nothing."

Mona glanced at Spencer's phone screen. "Emily, huh? Did Justin show up?"

"Um . . ." Spencer swallowed audibly, her throat catching.

Mona's smile evaporated. "Why won't you tell me what's going on?"

"N-Nothing's going on," Spencer stammered.

Mona scoffed, tossing a lock of hair behind her shoulders. Her pale skin glowed in the darkness. "What, is it a secret? Am I not good enough to know or something?"

"Of course not," Spencer squeaked. "It's just . . . I . . ."

They rolled to a red light. Spencer looked back and forth, then slowly pressed the Hummer's unlock button. As she curled her fingers around the door handle, Mona grabbed her other wrist.

"What are you *doing*?" Mona's eyes glowed in the traffic light's red glare. Her head swiveled from Spencer's phone back to Spencer's panicked face. Spencer could see the realization flooding over Mona—it was like watching black and white turn to color in *The Wizard of Oz.* Mona's expression went from confusion to shock to . . . glee. She pressed the car door's lock button again. When the light turned green, she gunned the engine and made a stomach-churning left through the intersection and veered off onto a bumpy, two-lane country road.

Spencer watched as the odometer climbed from fifty to sixty to seventy. She clutched her door handle tightly. "Where are we going?" she asked in a small, terrified voice.

Mona glanced at Spencer sideways, a sinister smile pasted on her face. "You were never one for patience." She winked and blew Spencer a kiss. "But this time you'll just have to wait and see."

35

THE CHASE IS ON

Since Hanna had arrived at the party in a limo and Emily's mother had driven her, their only vehicle option was Aria's clunky, unpredictable Subaru. Aria led the others through the parking lot, her green suede flats slapping against the pavement. She manually unlocked the door and threw herself into the driver's seat. Hanna sat in the front passenger seat, and Emily pushed aside all of Aria's books, empty coffee cups, spare clothes, skeins of yarn, and a pair of stacked-heel boots, and climbed into the back. Aria had her cell phone wedged between her chin and her shoulder—she'd called Wilden to see if Spencer and Mona had shown up at the police station. But after the eighth unanswered ring, she hung up in frustration.

"Wilden isn't at his desk," she said. "And he's not answering his cell, either." They were quiet for a moment, all lost in their own thoughts. *How could Mona be A?* Aria thought. *How could Mona know so much about us?* Aria went over everything Mona had done to her—threatened her with that Wicked Queen doll, sent Sean the pictures that got Ezra arrested, sent Ella the letter that splintered her family apart. Mona had hit Hanna with a car, outed Emily to the school, and made them think that Spencer had killed Ali. Mona had had a hand in Toby Cavanaugh's death . . . and maybe Ali's, too.

Hanna was staring straight ahead, her eyes wide and unblinking, as if she was possessed. Aria touched her hand. "Are you *sure* about this?"

Hanna nodded fitfully. "Yes." Her face was pale and her lips looked dry.

"Do you think it was a good idea that we texted Spencer?" Emily asked, checking her phone for the billionth time. "She hasn't written back again."

"Maybe they're in the police station now," Aria answered, trying to stay calm. "Maybe Spencer turned off her phone. And maybe that's why Wilden isn't answering."

Aria looked at Hanna. There was a big, glistening tear rolling down her cheek, past her bruises and her stitches. "It's my fault if Spencer is hurt," Hanna whispered. "I should have remembered sooner."

"It's absolutely not your fault," Aria said sternly. "You can't *control* when you remember things." She placed a hand on Hanna's arm, but Hanna wrenched it away, using her hands to cover her face. Aria had no idea how to console her. What must that feel like, to realize that your best friend was also your worst enemy? Hanna's best friend had tried to *kill* her.

Suddenly, Emily gasped too. "That picture," she whispered.

"What picture?" Aria asked, starting the car and speeding out of the lot.

"That . . . that picture Spencer showed us of Ali and Ian. The one with the writing on it? I *knew* I'd seen it before. Now I know where." Emily let out a laugh of disbelief. "I was in the yearbook room a couple days ago. And there were these pictures of the insides of people's bags. That's where I saw that picture." She raised her eyes, looking around at the others. "In *Mona's* bag. But I only saw Ali's arm. The pink sleeve was frayed and had a tiny rip."

The police station was only a mile or so away, right next to Hooters. It was amazing that Aria and Mike had been there just hours before. When they pulled into the lot, all three of them leaned forward over the dash. "*Shit.*" There were eight squad cars in the parking lot, and that was it. "They're not here!"

"Calm down." Aria turned off the car's headlights. They all jumped out quickly, sprinting for the police station entrance. The fluorescent light inside was greenish and harsh. Several cops stopped and stared at them, their mouths hanging open. The little green waiting benches were all empty except for a few random pamphlets about what you should do if you were the victim of a car theft.

Wilden appeared from around a corner, his cell phone in one hand, a mug of coffee in another. When he saw Hanna and Emily in their party dresses with their masks dangling from their wrists, and Aria in her Rosewood Day uniform with a big bruise on her head, he squinted in confusion. "Hi, girls," he said slowly. "What's going on?"

"You have to help us," Aria said. "Spencer is in trouble."

Wilden stepped forward, gesturing for them to sit on the benches. "How so?"

"The texts we've been getting," Aria explained. "What I was telling you about earlier today. We know who they're from."

Wilden stood up, alarmed. "You *do*?"

"It's Mona Vanderwaal," Hanna said, her voice breaking into a sob. "That's what I remembered. It's my best frickin' *friend*."

"Mona . . . Vanderwaal?" Wilden's eyes traveled from one girl to another. "The girl who planned your party?"

"Spencer Hastings is in the car with Mona now," Emily said. "They were supposed to be coming here— Spencer had something to tell you. But then I sent her a text, warning her about Mona . . . and now we don't know where they are. Spencer's phone is shut off."

"Have you tried to reach Mona?" Wilden asked.

Hanna stared at the linoleum floor. Off in the police bullpen, a phone rang, and then another. "I did. She didn't pick up either."

Suddenly, Wilden's cell phone lit up in his hand. Aria

caught a glimpse of the number on the screen. "That's Spencer!" she cried.

Wilden answered but didn't say hello. He pressed the speakerphone button, then looked around at the girls, a finger to his lips. *Shhh,* he mouthed.

Aria and her old best friends crowded around the little phone. At first, there was only white noise. Then they heard Spencer's voice. It sounded far away. "I always thought Swedesford Road was so pretty," she said. "So many trees, especially in this secluded part of town."

Aria and Emily exchanged a confused glance. And then, Aria understood—she'd seen this once in a TV show she'd watched with her brother. Mona *must* have figured it out—and Spencer must have managed to secretly call Wilden to give him clues about where Mona was taking her.

"So . . . why are we turning down Brainard Road?" Spencer asked very loudly and brightly. "This isn't the way to the police station."

"*Duh,* Spencer," they heard Mona say back.

Wilden flipped open his pad and wrote down *Brainard Road.* A few other cops had gathered around them. Emily quietly explained what was going on, and one of the cops brought out a large, foldout map of Rosewood, highlighting the intersection of Swedesford and Brainard with a yellow marker.

"Are we going to the stream?" Spencer's voice rang out again.

"Maybe," Mona singsonged.

Aria's eyes widened. The Morrell Stream was more of a gushing river.

"I just love the stream," Spencer said loudly.

Then there was a gasp and a shriek. They heard a few bumping noises, a squeal of tires, the dissonant tone of a bunch of phone buttons being pressed at once . . . and then nothing. Wilden's cell phone screen blinked. *Call ended.*

Aria sneaked a look at the others. Hanna had her head buried in her hands. Emily looked like she was going to faint. Wilden stood up, put his phone back in its holster, and pulled his car keys out of his pocket. "We'll try all the stream entrances in that area." He pointed to a big burly cop sitting behind a desk. "See if you can do a GPS trace on this phone call." Then he turned and headed for his car.

"Wait," Aria said, running after him. Wilden turned. "We're coming."

Wilden's shoulders dropped. "This isn't–"

"We're *coming*," Hanna said behind Aria, her voice strong and steely.

Wilden raised one shoulder and sighed. He gestured to the back of the squad car. "Fine. Get in."

36

AN OFFER SPENCER CAN'T REFUSE

Mona grabbed Spencer's phone out of her hands, hit end, and tossed it out the window, all without changing the Hummer's speed. She then made an abrupt U-turn, backtracked down bumpy, narrow Brainard Road, and got on the highway heading south. They drove for about five miles and got off the exit near the Bill Beach burn clinic. More horse farms and housing developments flew past, and the road devolved into woods. It wasn't until they swept by the old, dilapidated Quaker church that Spencer realized where they were really going—the Floating Man Quarry.

Spencer used to play in the big lake at the base of Floating Man Quarry. Kids used to cliff-dive off the upper rocks, but last year, during a drought-filled summer, a public-school boy had dived off the rocks and died, making Floating Man's name seem eerie and prophetic. These days, there were rumors that the boy's ghost lived at the quarry's perimeter, guarding the lake. Spencer had even heard whispers that the Rosewood Stalker had his lair here. She glanced at Mona, feeling a shiver run up her spine. She had a feeling the Rosewood Stalker was driving this Hummer.

Spencer had her fingernails pressed so deeply into the center armrest that she was certain they would leave permanent marks. Calling Wilden and giving her location had been her only plan, and now she was completely trapped.

Mona glanced at Spencer out of the corner of her eye. "So, I guess Hanna remembered, huh?"

Spencer's nod was barely perceptible.

"She shouldn't have remembered," Mona chanted. "She knew remembering would put all of you in danger. Just like Aria shouldn't have told the cops. I sent her to Hooters as a test to see if she'd really listen to my warnings—the Hooters is so close to the police station, after all. The cops are always there—so it would be tempting to tell them everything. And obviously, she did." Mona threw her hands up in the air. "Why do you girls continue to do such stupid things?"

Spencer shut her eyes, wishing she could just pass out from fear.

Mona sighed dramatically. "Then again, you've been doing stupid things for years, haven't you? Starting with good old Jenna Cavanaugh." She winked.

Spencer's mouth dropped open. Mona . . . *knew*?

Of course she knew. She was A.

Mona stole a quick glance at Spencer's horrified face and made a faux-surprised face in return. Then Mona pulled down the side zipper of her halter dress, revealing a black silky bra and a good portion of her stomach. There was a huge, wrinkled laceration circling the bottom of her rib cage. Spencer stared at it for a few seconds until she had to look away.

"I was there the night you hurt Jenna," Mona whispered, her voice rough-edged. "Jenna and I were friends, which you might have known if you hadn't been so effing self-absorbed. I went over to Jenna's to surprise her that night. I saw Ali . . . I saw everything . . . and I even got a little souvenir from it." She stroked her burn scars. "I tried to tell people it was Ali, but no one believed me. Toby took the blame so fast, my parents thought I was blaming Ali because I was *jealous* of her." Mona shook her head, her blond hair swinging back and forth. She popped another piece of gum in her mouth and chewed furiously. "I even tried to talk to Jenna about it, but Jenna refused to listen. She kept saying, 'You're wrong. It was my stepbrother.'" Mona mimicked Jenna's voice at a higher octave.

"Jenna and I weren't friends after that," Mona went on. "But every time I'm in front of my mirror at home and look at my otherwise perfect self, I'm reminded of what you bitches did. I know what I saw. And I. Will. Never. Forget."

Her mouth dripped into an eerie smile. "This summer, I found a way to get you bitches back. I found Ali's diary among all that crap the new people were throwing away. I knew it was Ali's instantly—and she wrote tons of secrets about all of *you*. Really damaging ones, actually. It's like she wanted the diary to fall into enemy hands."

A flash came to Spencer—the day before Ali went missing, discovering Ali in her bedroom, hungrily reading a notebook, an amused, greedy smile on her face. "Why didn't the cops find her diary when she went missing?" she sputtered.

Mona pulled the car under a thicket of trees and stopped. There was only darkness ahead of them, but Spencer could hear rushing water and smell moss and wet grass.

"Who the hell knows? But I'm glad they didn't and I did." Mona rezipped her dress, then turned to face Spencer, her eyes bright. "Ali wrote down every horrible thing you guys did. How you guys tortured Jenna Cavanaugh, that Emily kissed her in her tree house, that *you*, Spencer, kissed your sister's boyfriend. It made it so easy for me to just . . . I don't know, *become* her. All it took was for me to get a second phone with a blocked number. And I really had you going that it was Ali contacting you at first, didn't I?" Mona grabbed Spencer's hand and laughed.

Spencer recoiled from her touch. "I can't believe it was you the whole time."

"I know, right? It must have been so annoying not knowing!" Mona clapped happily. "It was *so fun* watching you guys go crazy . . . and then Ali's body showed up and you *really* went crazy. Sending *myself* notes, though, was pure brilliance. . . ." She reached around and patted her left shoulder blade. "I had to do a lot of running around, anticipating your moves before even *you* knew what they'd be. But the whole thing was so elegantly done, almost like a couture dress, don't you think?"

Mona's eyes canvassed Spencer for a reaction. Then, slowly, she reached out and punched Spencer jokily on the arm. "You look so freaked right now. Like I'm going to hurt you or something. It doesn't have to be this way, though."

"Be . . . what way?" Spencer whispered.

"I mean, at first, I hated you, Spencer. You most of all. You were always closest to Ali, and you had *everything*. But then . . . we became friends. It was so fun, planning Hanna's party, spending time together. Didn't you have fun flashing those boys? Wasn't it nice, *really talking*? So I thought . . . maybe I could be a philanthropist. Like Angelina Jolie."

Spencer blinked, dumbstruck.

"I decided to help you," Mona explained. "The Golden Orchid thing—that was a fluke. But this—I honestly want to make your life better, Spencer. Because I truly, honestly *care* about you."

Spencer knitted her brow. "Wh-What are you talking about?"

"Melissa, silly!" Mona exclaimed. "Setting her up as the killer. It's so *perfect*. Isn't it what you always wanted? Your sister in jail for murder and out of your life, for good. You'll look so perfect in comparison!"

Spencer stared at her. "But . . . Melissa had a motive."

"Did she?" Mona grinned. "Or is that just what you want to believe?"

Spencer opened her mouth, but no sound came out. Mona had sent the text that read Ali's murderer is right in front of you. And the DM that read She did it, you know. Mona had planted the photo in Spencer's purse.

Mona gave Spencer a devious look. "We can turn this around. We can go back to the police station and tell Hanna it's a huge misunderstanding—that she's not remembering things properly. We can pin A on someone else, someone you don't like. How about Andrew Campbell? You've always hated him, haven't you?"

"I . . ." Spencer sputtered.

"We can put your sister in jail," Mona whispered. "And we can *both* be A. We can control everyone. You're just as conniving as Ali was, Spence. And you're prettier, smarter, and richer. *You* should've been the leader of the group, not her. I'm giving you the chance, now, to be the leader you're meant to be. Your life at home would be perfect. Your life at school would be perfect." Her lips spread into a smile. "And I know how badly you want to be perfect."

"But you hurt my friends," Spencer whispered.

"Are you sure they're your friends?" Mona's eyes

glittered. "You know who I set up as the killer before Melissa? *You*, Spencer. I fed your good friend Aria all kinds of clues that *you* did it—I heard you fighting with Ali that night she went missing, over your wall. And Aria, your BFF? She totally bought it. She was all ready to turn you in."

"Aria wouldn't do that," Spencer shrieked.

"No?" Mona raised an eyebrow. "Then why did I hear her telling Wilden exactly that in the hospital on Sunday morning, the day after Hanna's accident?" She put *accident* in air quotes. "She wasted no time, Spence. Lucky for you, Wilden didn't buy it. Now, why would you call someone who did *that* to you your friend?"

Spencer took a few deep breaths, not knowing what to believe. A thought spiraled into her head. "Wait . . . if Melissa didn't kill Ali, then *you* did."

Mona leaned back in her seat, the leather crinkling underneath her. "No." She shook her head. "I do know who *did*, though. Ali wrote about it on the last page of her diary—poor widdle girl, the last thing she ever wrote before she died." Mona stuck out her lip in a pout. "She said, *Ian and I are having a supersecret meeting tonight.*" Mona did a fake Ali voice, too, but the voice sounded more like a diabolical doll in a horror movie. *"And I gave him an ultimatum. I told him that he better break up with Melissa before she goes to Prague—or I'd tell her and everyone else about us."* Mona sighed, sounding bored. "It's pretty obvious what happened—she pushed Ian to his breaking point. And he killed her."

The wind picked up the edges of Mona's hair. "I modeled myself after Ali—she was *the* perfect bitch. No one was safe from her blackmail. And if you want, no one will be safe from yours, either."

Spencer shook her head slowly. "But . . . but you hit Hanna with your car."

Mona shrugged. "Had to do it. She knew too much."

"I'm . . . I'm sorry," Spencer whispered. "There's no way I want to . . . to *be* A with you. To rule the school with you. Or whatever it is you're offering. That's nuts."

Mona's disappointed expression morphed into something darker. She knitted her eyebrows together. "Fine. Have it your way, then."

Mona's voice felt like a knife cutting into Spencer's skin. The crickets chirped hysterically. The rushing water beneath sounded like blood gushing through a vein. In one swift movement, Mona burst forward and wrapped her hands around Spencer's neck. Spencer screamed and jerked back, flailing to hit the unlock button again. She kicked Mona's chest. As Mona squealed and recoiled, Spencer yanked at the door handle and shoved it open, tumbling out of the car to the spiny grass. Immediately, she pushed herself up and sprinted into the darkness. She felt the grass under her feet, then gravel, then dirt, then mud. The noise of the water grew louder and louder. Spencer could tell she was nearing the quarry's rocky edge. Mona's footsteps rang out behind her, and Spencer felt Mona's arms wrap around her waist. She fell heavily to the ground. Mona climbed on top of her and wrapped her hands around her neck. Spencer kicked and struggled and choked. Mona giggled, as if this were all a game.

"I thought we were friends, Spencer." Mona grimaced, trying to keep Spencer still.

Spencer struggled to breathe. "I guess not!" she screamed. Using all her might, Spencer pressed her legs onto Mona's body, throwing her backward. Mona landed on her butt a few feet away, her bright yellow gum spewing out of her mouth. Spencer scrambled quickly to her feet. Mona got up, too, her eyes flashing and her teeth clenched. Time seemed to spread out as Mona advanced on her, her mouth a triangle of fury. Spencer shut her eyes and just . . . reacted. She grabbed Mona around her legs. Mona's feet went out from under her, and she started to fall. Spencer felt her arms pressing against Mona's stomach, pushing as hard as she could. She saw the whites of Mona's eyes as they widened, and heard Mona's screams in her ears. Mona fell backward, and in a blink, she disappeared.

Spencer didn't realize it at first, but she was falling, too. Then she hit the ground. She heard a scream echo through the gulch, and thought for a moment that it was her own. Her head hit the ground with a crack . . . and her eyes fluttered shut.

37

SEEING IS BELIEVING

Hanna crammed into the back of Wilden's squad car next to Aria and Emily. It was where criminals—not that Rosewood had many—typically sat. Even though she could barely see Wilden through the metal grates connected to the front seat, she could tell by his tone of CB radio voice that he was as worried and tense as she was.

"Has anyone found anything yet?" he said into the walkie-talkie. They were idling at a stop sign as Wilden decided which way to go next. They had just driven around the main mouth of Morrell Stream, but they'd only found a couple of public-school kids lying on the grass getting stoned. There weren't signs of Mona's Hummer anywhere.

"Nothing," said the voice on the CB radio.

Aria grabbed Hanna's hand and squeezed hard. Emily quietly sobbed into her collar. "Maybe she meant another stream," Hanna volunteered. "Maybe she meant the stream at the Marwyn Trail." And while she was at it, maybe Spencer and Mona were just hanging out and talking. Maybe Hanna had it wrong, maybe Mona wasn't A.

Another voice crackled through the CB radio. "We got a call about a disturbance at Floating Man Quarry."

Hanna dug her nails into Aria's hand. Emily gasped. "On it," Wilden said.

"Floating Man . . . Quarry?" Hanna repeated. But Floating Man was a happy place—not long after their makeovers, Hanna and Mona had met boys from Drury Academy there. They'd performed a swimsuit fashion show for them along the rocks, reasoning that it was much more alluring to *tease* a boy than to actually make out with him. Right after that, they'd painted *HM + MV= BBBBBFF* on the roof of Mona's garage, swearing they would be close forever.

So was that all a lie? Had Mona planned this from the beginning? Had Mona been waiting for the day she could hit Hanna with her car? Hanna felt an overwhelming urge to ask Wilden to pull over so she could throw up.

When they arrived at the Floating Man Quarry's entrance, Mona's bright yellow Hummer glowed like the beacon on top of a lighthouse. Hanna grabbed the door handle, even though the car was still moving. The door lurched open, and she tumbled out. Hanna started running toward the Hummer, her ankles twisting on the uneven gravel.

"Hanna, no!" Wilden cried. "It's not safe!"

Hanna heard Wilden stop his car, then more doors slammed. Leaves crunched behind her. As she reached the car, she noticed someone curled up in a ball near the front left tire. Hanna saw a flash of blond hair, and her heart lifted. *Mona.*

Only, it was Spencer. Dirt and tears streaked her face and hands, and there were gashes up and down her arms. Her silky dress was torn and she wasn't wearing any shoes. "Hanna!" Spencer cried raggedly, reaching out for her.

"Are you okay?" Hanna gasped, crouching down and touching Spencer's shoulder. She felt cold and wet.

Spencer could barely get the words out, she was sobbing so hard. "I'm so sorry, Hanna. I'm so sorry."

"Why?" Hanna asked, clutching Spencer's hands.

"Because . . ." Spencer gestured to the edge of the quarry. "I think she fell."

Almost instantly, an ambulance screamed behind them, followed by another police car. The rescue team and more cops surrounded Spencer.

Hanna backed away numbly as the paramedics began to ask Spencer if she could move everything, what hurt, and what happened. "Mona was threatening me," Spencer said over and over. "She was strangling me. I tried to run away from her, but we fought. And then she . . ." She gestured again toward the quarry's edge.

Mona was threatening me. Hanna's knees buckled. This was *real.*

The cops had fanned out around the quarry with German shepherds, flashlights, and guns. Within minutes, one of them yelled, "We got something!"

Hanna leapt to her feet and sprinted over to the cop. Wilden, who was closer, caught her from behind. "Hanna," he said into her ear. "No. You shouldn't."

"But I have to see!" Hanna screamed.

Wilden wrapped his arms around her. "Just stay here, okay? Just stay with me."

Hanna watched as a team of cops disappeared over the lip of the quarry, down toward the rushing water. "We need a stretcher!" one of them screamed. More EMS workers emerged with supplies. Wilden kept petting Hanna's hair, using part of his body to shield her from what was happening. But Hanna could *hear* it. She heard them saying that Mona was caught between two rocks. And that it looked like Mona's neck was broken. And that they needed to be very, very careful pulling her out. She heard their grunts of encouragement as they lifted Mona to the surface, loaded her onto a stretcher, and tucked her into the ambulance. As they passed, Hanna saw a shock of Mona's white-blond hair. She twisted free of Wilden and started to run.

"Hanna!" Wilden screamed. "No!"

But Hanna didn't run toward the ambulance. She ran to the other side of Mona's Hummer, crouched down, and threw up. She wiped her palms on the grass and curled up into a tiny ball. The ambulance doors shut and the engine roared, but they didn't turn on the siren. Hanna wondered if that was because Mona was already dead.

She sobbed until it felt like there were no more tears left in her body. Drained, she rolled over on her back. Something hard and square pressed into her thigh. Hanna sat up and wrapped her hands around it. It was a tan suede phone case, one Hanna didn't recognize. She brought it to her face and breathed in. It smelled like Jean Patou Joy, which had been Mona's favorite perfume for years.

Only, the phone nestled inside wasn't the limited-edition Chanel iPhone case Mona had begged her father to bring back from Paris, nor did it have *MV* embossed in Swarovski crystals on the back. This phone was a plain and generic Android, giving nothing away.

Hanna's heart sank, realizing what this second phone signified. All she needed to do to prove to herself that Mona had really done this to them was turn the phone on and look. The scent of the quarry's raspberry bushes drifted past her nose, and she suddenly felt like she was back three years ago, she in her Missoni string bikini and Mona in her one-piece Calvin tank. They had made their fashion show a game—if the Drury boys looked only mildly amused, they lost. If the boys salivated like starved dogs, they would buy each other a spa treatment. Afterward, Hanna chose the jasmine seaweed scrub, and Mona had a jasmine, carrot, and sesame body buff.

Hanna heard footsteps approaching behind her. She touched her thumb to the Android phone's blank, innocent screen, then dropped it into her silk purse, stumbling to find the others. People were talking all around her, but all she could hear was a voice in her head screaming, *Mona's dead!*

THE FINAL PIECE

Spencer limped to the back of the squad car with Aria's and Wilden's help. They asked her again and again if she needed an ambulance. Spencer said she was pretty sure she didn't—nothing felt broken, and luckily, she'd fallen on the grass, knocking herself out for a moment, but not damaging anything. She dangled her legs out the squad car's back door and Wilden crouched in front of her, holding a notepad and a tape recorder. "Are you sure you want to do this right now?"

Spencer nodded forcefully.

Emily, Aria, and Hanna gathered behind Wilden as he pressed the record button. The headlights of another squad car made a halo around him, backlighting his body in red. It reminded Spencer of the way bonfires used to silhouette her friends' bodies at summer camp. If only she were really at summer camp, right now.

Wilden took a deep breath. "So. You're *sure* she told

you Ian Thomas killed Ali."

Spencer nodded. "Ali had given him an ultimatum the night she went missing. She wanted them to meet . . . and she said that if Ian didn't break up with Melissa by the time she went to Prague, Ali would tell everyone what was going on." She pushed her greasy, mud-caked hair off her face. "It's written in Ali's diary. Mona has it. I don't know where, but—"

"We're going to search Mona's house," Wilden interrupted, placing a hand on Spencer's knee. "Don't worry." He turned away and spoke into his walkie-talkie, radioing other cops to locate Ian to bring him in for questioning. Spencer listened, staring numbly at the dirt caked under her fingernails.

Her friends stood around for a long time, stunned. "God," Emily whispered. "Ian *Thomas*? That just sounds . . . crazy. But I guess it makes sense. He was so much older, and if she ever told anyone, well . . ."

Spencer pulled her arms around herself, feeling goose bumps rising on her skin. To her, Ian *didn't* make sense. Spencer believed that Ali had threatened him, and she believed that Ian might've gotten angry, but angry enough to *kill* her? It was eerie, too, that in all the time Spencer had spent with him, she hadn't suspected Ian one bit. He hadn't seemed nervous or remorseful or pensive whenever Ali's murder came up.

But perhaps she'd misinterpreted the signs—she'd missed plenty of others. She'd gotten into the car with

Mona, after all. Who knew what else was right in front of her face that she didn't see?

A beep came over Wilden's walkie-talkie. "The suspect isn't at his residence," a female cop's voice called. "What do you want us to do?"

"Shit." Wilden looked at Spencer. "Can you think where else Ian might be?"

Spencer shook her head, her brain feeling like it was plodding through a swamp. Wilden threw himself in the front seat. "I'll drive you home," he said. "Your parents are on their way home from the country club, too."

"We want to go to Spencer's with you." Aria indicated for Spencer to move over, then she, Hanna, and Emily all crammed into the backseat. "We don't want to leave her alone."

"You guys, you don't have to," Spencer said softly. "And anyway, Aria, your car." She motioned to Aria's Subaru, which looked like it was sinking into the mud.

"I can leave it overnight." Aria smirked. "Maybe I'll get lucky and someone will steal it."

Spencer folded her hands in her lap, too weak to protest. The car was silent as Wilden rolled past the Floating Man Quarry sign, then along the narrow trail that led to the main road. It was hard to believe that just an hour and a half had passed since Spencer left the party. Things were so different now.

"Mona was there the night we hurt Jenna," Spencer mumbled absently.

Aria nodded. "It's a long story, but I actually talked to Jenna tonight. Jenna knows what we did. Only, get this—she and Ali set it up together."

Spencer sat up straighter. For a moment, she couldn't breathe. *"What? Why?"*

"She said that she and Ali both had sibling issues or something," Aria explained, not sounding very confident in the answer.

"I just don't understand that," Emily whispered. "I saw Jason DiLaurentis on the news the other day. He said he doesn't even speak to his parents anymore, and that his family was really messed up. Why would he say that?"

"There's a lot you can't tell about people, looking in from the outside," Hanna murmured tearfully.

Spencer covered her face with her hands. There was so much she didn't understand, so much that didn't make sense. She knew that things should at least feel resolved now—A was really gone, Ali's killer would soon be apprehended—but she felt more lost than ever. She took her hands away, staring at the sliver of moon in the sky. "You guys," Spencer broke the silence, "there's something I need to tell you."

"Something *else*?" Hanna wailed.

"Something . . . about the night Ali went missing." Spencer slid her silver charm bracelet up and down her arm, keeping her voice to a whisper. "You know how I ran out of the barn after Ali? And how I said I didn't see where she was going? Well . . . I did see. She went right down the path. I went up to her and . . . and we fought. It was about Ian. I . . . I'd kissed Ian not long before, and Ali had told me that he only kissed me because *she* told him to. And she said that she and Ian were really in love, and she teased me for caring."

Spencer felt her friends' eyes on her. She gathered up strength to go on.

"I got so mad . . . I shoved her. She fell against the rocks. There was this awful *crack* noise." A tear wobbled out of the corner of her eye and spilled down her cheek. She hung her head. "I'm sorry, guys. I should've told you. I just . . . I didn't remember. And then when I did, I was so scared."

When she looked up, her friends were aghast. Even Wilden's head tilted toward the back, as if he were trying to listen. If they wanted to, they could throw the Ian theory out the window. They could make Wilden stop the car and make Spencer repeat exactly what she'd said. Things could go in a horrible direction from here.

Emily was the first to take Spencer's hand. Then Hanna placed hers on top of Emily's, and then Aria laid hers on top of Hanna's. It reminded Spencer of when they used to all touch the photo of the five of them that hung in Ali's foyer. "We know it wasn't you," Emily whispered.

"It was Ian. It all makes sense," Aria said forcefully, gazing into Spencer's eyes. It seemed like she believed

Spencer wholly and completely.

They reached Spencer's street, and Wilden pulled into her family's long, circular driveway. Spencer's parents weren't home yet, and the house was dark. "Do you want me to stay with you guys until your folks get home?" Wilden asked as the girls got out.

"It's okay." Spencer glanced around at the others, suddenly relieved that they were here.

Wilden backed out of the driveway and turned slowly around the cul-de-sac, first passing the DiLaurentises' old house, then the Cavanaughs', and then the Vanderwaals', the big monstrosity with the detached garage down the street. There was no one home at Mona's, obviously. Spencer shuddered.

A flash of light in the backyard caught her eye. Spencer cocked her head, her heart speeding up. She walked down the stone path that led to her backyard and curled her hands along the stone wall surrounding their property. There, past the deck, the rock-lined pool, the burbling hot tub, the expansive yard, and even the renovated barn, at the very back of the property near where Ali had fallen, Spencer saw two figures, lit only by moonlight. They reminded her of something.

The wind picked up, tiptoeing up and down Spencer's back. Even though it wasn't the right season, the air briefly smelled like honeysuckle, just as it had that horrible night four and a half years ago. All at once, her memory broke free. She saw Ali fall backward into the stone wall. A *crack* rang out through the air, as loud as church bells. When Spencer heard the girlish gasp in her ear, she turned. No one was behind her. No one was anywhere. And when she turned back, Ali was still slumped against the stone wall, but her eyes were open. And then, Ali grunted and pushed herself to her feet.

She was fine.

Ali glared at Spencer, about to speak, but something down the path distracted her. She took off fast, disappearing into a thicket of trees. In seconds, Spencer heard Ali's signature giggle. There was rustling, and then two distinct shapes. One was Ali's. Spencer couldn't tell who the other person was, but it didn't look like Melissa. It was hard to believe that, only moments after this, Ian would push Ali into the DiLaurentises' half-dug gazebo hole. Ali might've been a bitch, but she didn't deserve anything like that.

"Spencer?" Hanna said softly, her voice sounding far away. "What's wrong?"

Spencer opened her eyes and shuddered. "I didn't do it," she whispered.

The figures near the barn stepped into the light. Melissa's posture was stiff and Ian's fists clenched. The wind carried their voices to the front yard, and it sounded like they were fighting.

Spencer's nerves felt ignited. She wheeled around and looked down her street. Wilden's car was gone. Frantically, she fumbled in her pocket for her phone, but remembered—Mona had thrown it out the window.

"I got it," Hanna said, pulling out her own phone and dialing a number. She handed the phone to Spencer. *Calling WILDEN*, the screen read.

Spencer had to hold the phone with two hands, her fingers were trembling so badly. Wilden answered after two rings. "Hanna?" He sounded confused. "What is it?"

"It's Spencer," Spencer bleated. "You have to turn around. Ian's here."

39

THE ALL-NEW MONTGOMERYS,
DISTURBING AS EVER

The following afternoon, Aria sat on Meredith's living room futon, absently flicking the William Shakespeare bobblehead Ezra had given her. Byron and Meredith sat next to her, and they were all staring at Meredith's television. There was a press conference about Ali's murder on TV. *Ian Thomas arrested,* said a big banner at the bottom of the screen.

"Mr. Thomas's arraignment is set for Tuesday," a newscaster said, standing in front of the grand stone steps of the Rosewood County Courthouse. "No one in this community ever expected that a quiet, polite boy like Ian Thomas could be behind this."

Aria pulled her knees into her chest. The cops had gone to the Vanderwaal residence this morning and had found Ali's diary underneath Mona's bed. Mona had been telling Spencer the truth about the last entry—it was about how Ali had given Ian an ultimatum that he either break up with Melissa Hastings or she would tell the world about them. The news showed the police leading Ian to the station in handcuffs. When asked to make a statement, all Ian said was "I'm innocent. This is a mistake."

Byron scoffed in disbelief. He reached over and grabbed Aria's hand. Then, predictably, the news flashed to the next story—Mona's death. The screen showed the string of yellow police tape around the Floating Man Quarry, then a shot of the Vanderwaal house. A random phone icon appeared in the corner. "Miss Vanderwaal had been stalking four Rosewood Day girls for over a month now, and the threats had turned deadly," the newscaster said. "There was a scuffle between Miss Vanderwaal and an unnamed minor last night at the edge of the quarry, which is notoriously dangerous. Miss Vanderwaal slipped off the edge, breaking her neck in the fall. Police found Miss Vanderwaal's personal phone in her purse at the bottom of the quarry, but they're still looking for a second phone—the one she used to send most of the troubling messages."

Aria gave Shakespeare's head another bobble. Her head felt like an overstuffed suitcase. Too much had happened in the last day for her to process things. And her emotions were all mixed up. She felt terrible that Mona had died. She felt freaked out and weirdly wounded that Jenna's accident hadn't really been an accident—that Jenna and Ali had set it up all along. And after all this time, the killer was Ian. . . . The newscaster made a sympathetic, relieved face and said, "Finally, the whole community of Rosewood can put this horrible story behind them"—something everyone had been saying all morning. Aria burst into tears. She didn't feel resolved at all.

Byron looked over at her. "What is it?"

Aria shook her head, unable to explain. She cupped the bobblehead in her hands, letting the tears drip on top of Shakespeare's plastic head.

Byron let out a frustrated sigh. "I realize this is overwhelming. You had a stalker. And you never talked about it to us. You *should* have. We should talk about it now."

"I'm sorry." Aria shook her head. "I can't."

"But we *need* to," Byron urged. "It's important you get this out."

"Byron!" Meredith hissed sharply. "Jesus!"

"What?" Byron asked, raising his arms in surrender.

Meredith jumped up, placing herself between Aria and her father. "You and your discussions," Meredith scolded. "Hasn't Aria been through enough these last few weeks? Just give her some space!"

Byron shrugged, looking cowed. Aria's mouth fell open. She met Meredith's eyes, and Meredith smiled. There was an understanding glimmer in her eye that seemed to say, *I get what you're going through. And I know it's not easy.* Aria stared at the pink spiderweb tattoo on Meredith's wrist. She thought about how eager she had been to find out something damaging about Meredith, and here Meredith was, sticking up for her.

Byron's cell phone vibrated, scooting across the scuffed coffee table. He stared at the screen, frowning, then picked it up. "Ella?" His voice cracked.

Aria tensed. Byron's eyebrows knitted together. "Yes . . . she's here." He passed the phone to Aria. "Your mother wants to talk to you."

Meredith cleared her throat awkwardly, standing up and drifting toward the bathroom. Aria stared at the phone as if it were a piece of putrefied shark, which someone in Iceland had once dared her to eat. After all, the Vikings used to eat it. She put the phone tentatively to her ear. "Ella?"

"Aria, are you all right?" Ella's voice cried from the other end.

"I'm . . . fine," Aria said. "I don't know. I guess. I'm not hurt or anything."

There was a long silence. Aria swallowed a big lump in her throat.

"I'm so sorry, honey," Ella gushed. "I had no idea you were going through this. Why didn't you tell us someone was threatening you?"

"Because . . ." Aria wandered into her tiny bedroom off Meredith's studio and picked up Pigtunia, her pig puppet. Explaining A to Mike had been hard. But now that it was over, and Aria didn't have to worry about A's retaliation, she realized the real reason didn't matter.

"Because you guys were caught up in your own stuff."
She sank onto her lumpy twin bed, and the bedsprings
let out a mooing groan. "But . . . *I'm* sorry, Ella. For
everything. It was terrible of me not to say anything
about Byron for all that time."

Ella paused. Aria snapped on the tiny TV that sat
in the windowsill. The same press conference images
emerged on the screen. "I get why you didn't," Ella
finally said. "I should've understood that. I was just
angry, that's all." She sighed. "My relationship with your
dad hadn't been good for a long time. Iceland stalled the
inevitable—we both knew this was coming."

"Okay," Aria said softly, running her hands up and
down Pigtunia's pink fur.

Ella sighed. "I'm sorry, sweetie, and I miss you."

An enormous, egg-shaped lump formed in Aria's
throat. She stared up at the cockroaches Meredith had
painted on the ceiling. "I miss you too."

"Your room is here if you want it," her mother said.

Aria hugged Pigtunia to her chest. "Thanks," she whispered, and hung up. How long had she been waiting to
hear that? What a relief it would be to sleep in her own
bed again, with its normal mattress and soft, downy pillows. To be among all her knitting projects and books and
her brother and Ella. But what about Byron? Aria listened
to him coughing in the other room. "Do you need a
Kleenex?" Meredith called from the bathroom, sounding
concerned. She thought about the card Meredith had

made for Byron and pinned up on the fridge. It was a cartoon elephant saying, *Just stamping by to say I hope you have a great day!* It seemed the kind of thing that Byron—or Aria—would do.

Maybe Aria had been overreacting. Maybe Aria could convince Byron to buy a comfier bed for this little room. Maybe she could sleep here every once in a while.

Maybe.

Aria glanced at the TV screen. The press conference on Ian had just ended, and everyone stood to leave. As the camera swung wide, Aria noticed a blond girl with a familiar heart-shaped face. *Ali?* Aria sat up. She rubbed her eyes until they hurt. The camera panned over the crowd again, and she realized the blond woman was at least thirty. Aria was obviously hallucinating from lack of sleep.

She wandered back into the living room, Pigtunia still in her hand. Byron opened his arms and Aria slid into them. Her dad patted Pigtunia absentmindedly on the head as they sat there, watching the press conference aftermath on TV.

Meredith emerged from the bathroom, her face a bit green. Byron slid his arm from Aria's shoulders. "You still feeling sick?"

Meredith nodded. "I am." There was an anxious look on her face, as if she had a secret she needed to spill. She raised her eyes to both of them, the corners of her lips spreading into a tiny smile. "But it's okay. Because . . . I'm pregnant."

40

ALL THAT GLITTERS IS NOT A
GOLDEN ORCHID

Later that evening, after the police had finished raiding the Vanderwaal mansion, Wilden arrived at the Hastingses' house to ask Melissa a few final questions. He was sitting on their leather living room couch now, his eyes puffy and tired. Everyone looked tired, actually—except for Spencer's mother, who wore a crisp Marc Jacobs shirtdress. She and Spencer's father were standing on the far side of the room, as if their daughters were covered in bacteria.

Melissa's voice was monotone. "I didn't tell you the truth about that night," she admitted. "Ian and I had been drinking, and I fell asleep. When I woke up, he wasn't there. Then I fell asleep again and he was there when I woke."

"Why didn't you say anything about this before?" Spencer's father demanded.

Melissa shook her head. "I went to Prague that next

morning. At that point, I'm not sure anyone really knew Alison was missing. When I got back and everyone was frantic . . . well, I just never thought Ian would be capable of something like that." She picked at the hem on her pale yellow Juicy hoodie. "I suspected they'd hooked up all those years ago, but I didn't think it was serious. I didn't think Alison had given him an *ultimatum*." Like everyone else, Melissa had learned of Ian's motives. "I mean, she was in *seventh grade*."

Melissa glanced at Wilden. "When you started asking questions this week about where Ian and I were, I started to wonder if maybe I should've said something years ago. But I still didn't think it was possible. And I didn't say anything then because . . . because I thought I'd somehow get in trouble for concealing the truth. And, I mean, I couldn't have that. What would people think of me?"

Her sister's face crumpled. Spencer tried hard not to gape. She'd seen her sister cry plenty of times, but usually out of frustration, anger, rage, or a ploy to get her own way. Never out of fear or shame.

Spencer waited for her parents to rush over to console Melissa. But they sat stock-still, judgmental looks on their faces. She wondered if she and Melissa had been dealing with the exact same issues all this time. Melissa had made impressing their parents look so effortless that Spencer never realized that she agonized about it, too.

Spencer plopped down at her sister's side and threw her arms around Melissa's shoulders. "It's okay," she whispered in her ear. Melissa raised her head for a moment, noted Spencer confusedly, then set her head on Spencer's shoulder and sobbed.

Wilden handed Melissa a tissue and stood up, thanking them for their cooperation throughout this ordeal. As he was leaving, the house phone rang. Mrs. Hastings walked primly to the phone in the den and answered. Within seconds, she poked her head into the living room. "Spencer," she whispered, her face still sober but her eyes bright with excitement. "It's for you. It's Mr. Edwards."

A hot, sick feeling washed over Spencer. Mr. Edwards was the head of the Golden Orchid committee. A personal phone call from him could mean only one thing.

Spencer licked her lips, then stood. The other side of the room, where her mom was standing, seemed a mile away. She wondered what her mom's secret phone calls were about—what big gift she'd bought for Spencer because she'd been so certain Spencer would win the Golden Orchid. Even if it was the most wonderful thing in the world, Spencer wasn't sure she'd be able to enjoy it.

"Mom?" Spencer approached her mother and leaned against the antique Chippendale desk next to the phone. "Don't you think it's wrong that I cheated?"

Mrs. Hastings quickly covered the phone's mouthpiece. "Well, of course. But we discussed this." She shoved the phone to Spencer's ear. "Say hello," she hissed.

Spencer swallowed hard. "Hello?" she finally croaked into the phone.

"Miss Hastings?" a man's voice chirped. "This is Mr. Edwards, the head of the Golden Orchid committee. I know it's late, but I have some very exciting news for you. It was a tough decision, given our two hundred outstanding nominees, and I am pleased to announce that . . ."

It sounded as if Mr. Edwards were talking underwater—Spencer barely heard the rest. She glanced at her sister, sitting all alone on the couch. It had taken so much courage for Melissa to admit she'd lied. She could've said she didn't remember, and no one would've been the wiser, but instead, she'd done the right thing. Spencer thought, too, of Mona's offer to her—*I know how badly you want to be perfect.* The thing was, being perfect didn't mean anything if it wasn't real.

Spencer put her mouth back up to the phone. Mr. Edwards paused, waiting for Spencer to reply. She took a deep breath, rehearsing in her head what she would say: *Mr. Edwards, I have a confession to make.*

It was a confession no one was going to like. But she could do this. She really could.

41

PRESENTING, IN HER RETURN TO ROSEWOOD, HANNA MARIN

Tuesday morning, Hanna sat on her bed, slowly stroking Dot's muzzle and staring at herself in her handheld mirror. She'd finally found the right foundation that covered her bruises and stitches and wanted to share the good news. Her first instinct, of course, was to call Mona.

She watched in the mirror as her bottom lip twitched. It still wasn't real.

She supposed she could call her old friends, whom she'd seen a lot of the last few days. They'd taken yesterday off school and hung out in Spencer's hot tub, reading *Us Weekly* articles about Justin Timberlake, who had shown up at Hanna's party *just* after she left. He and his posse had been stuck in two hours of turnpike traffic. When the girls moved on to reading beauty and style tips, Hanna was reminded of how Lucas had read to her while she was in the hospital. She felt a pang of sadness, wondering if Lucas knew what had happened to her in the past few days. He hadn't called her. Maybe he never wanted to speak to her again.

Hanna put down the mirror. All at once, as easily as recalling a random fact, like the name of the latest Disney star who'd made a pop album, Hanna suddenly saw something else from the night of her accident. After she'd ripped her dress, Lucas had appeared over her, handing her his jacket to cover herself. He'd led her to the Hollis College Reading Room and held her as she sobbed. One thing led to another . . . and they were kissing, just as greedily as they'd kissed this past week.

Hanna sat on her bed for a long time, feeling numb. Finally, she reached for her phone and dialed Lucas's number. It went straight to voice mail. "Hey," she said when it beeped. "It's Hanna. I wanted to see if . . . if we could talk. Call me."

When she hung up, Hanna patted Dot on top of his argyle-sweatered back. "Maybe I should forget him," she whispered. "There's probably a cooler boy out there for me, don't you think?" Dot cocked his head uncertainly, like he didn't believe her.

"Hanna?" Ms. Marin's voice floated upstairs. "Can you come down?"

Hanna stood, rolling back her shoulders. Perhaps it was inappropriate to wear a bright red Erin Fetherston trapeze dress to Ian's arraignment—like wearing color to a funeral—but Hanna needed a little color pick-me-up. She snapped a gold cuff bracelet on her wrist, picked up her red Longchamp hobo bag, and shook her hair down her back. In the kitchen, her father sat at the table, doing a *Philadelphia Inquirer* crossword. Her mother sat next to him, checking her email on her laptop. Hanna gulped. She hadn't seen them sitting together like this since they were married.

"I thought you'd be back in Annapolis by now," she muttered.

Mr. Marin laid down his ballpoint pen, and Hanna's mother pushed her laptop aside. "Hanna, we wanted to talk to you about something important," her dad said.

Hanna's heart leapt. *They're getting back together. Kate and Isabel are gone.*

Her mother cleared her throat. "I've been offered a new job . . . and I've accepted." She tapped her long, red nails against the table. "Only . . . it's in Singapore."

"Singapore?" Hanna squawked, sinking into a chair.

"I don't expect you to come," her mother went on. "Plus, with the amount of traveling I'll have to do, I'm not sure you *should* come. So these are the options." She held out one hand. "You could go to boarding school. Even around here, if you like." Then, she held out the other hand. "Or you could move in with your father."

Mr. Marin was nervously twiddling his pen in his fingers. "Seeing you in the hospital . . . it really made me realize a few things," he said quietly. "I want to be close to you, Hanna. I need to be a bigger part of your life."

"I'm not moving to Annapolis," Hanna blurted out.

"You don't have to," her father said gently. "I can transfer to my firm's office here. Your mother has offered to let me move into this house, in fact."

Hanna gaped. This sounded like a reality TV show gone wrong. "Kate and Isabel are staying in Annapolis, right?"

Her father shook his head no. "It's a lot to think about. We'll give you some time to decide. I only want to transfer here if you'll live here too. Okay?"

Hanna looked around her sleek, modern kitchen, trying to picture her father and Isabel standing at the counter preparing dinner. Her father would sit in his old seat at the dinner table, Isabel in her mother's. Kate could have the chair that they normally piled with magazines and junk mail.

Hanna would miss her mom, but she wasn't around that much anyway. And Hanna had longed for her father to come back—only, she wasn't sure if she wanted it like *this*. If she allowed Kate to move in, it would be war. Kate was skinny and blond and beautiful. Kate would try to march into Rosewood Day and take over.

But Kate would be the new girl. And Hanna . . . Hanna would be the popular girl.

"Um, okay. I'll think about it." Hanna stood up from the table, scooped up her bag, and walked to the downstairs powder room. Truthfully, she felt kind of . . . pumped. Maybe this would be awesome. *She* had the advantage. Over the next few weeks, she would have to make sure that she was *the* most popular girl in school. With Mona gone, it would be easy.

Hanna felt around in her purse's silk-lined pocket. Inside, two phones were nestled side by side—hers and Mona's. She knew the cops were looking for Mona's second phone, but she couldn't hand it over yet. She had one thing to do first.

She took a deep breath, pulled out the phone in the tan suede holder, and pressed the on button. The device sprang to life. There was no greeting, no personalized wallpaper. Mona had used this phone strictly for business.

Mona had saved every text message she'd sent to them, each note with a crisp, singular letter *A*. Hanna scrolled slowly through each of hers, chewing feverishly on her bottom lip. There was the first one she'd ever received, when she was at the police station for stealing the Tiffany bracelet and necklace—Hey, Hanna, since prison food makes you fat, you know what Sean's gonna say? Not it! And there was the last text Mona had sent from this phone, which included the chilling lines And Mona? She's not your friend, either. So watch your back.

The only one of Hanna's texts that hadn't been sent from this phone was the one that said, Don't believe everything you hear. Mona had accidentally sent that text from her regular phone. Hanna shivered. She'd just gotten a new phone that night and hadn't programmed everyone's numbers in yet. Mona had messed up, and Hanna had recognized her number. If she hadn't, who knew how long this would have gone on.

Hanna squeezed Mona's Android phone, wanting to crush it flat. *Why?* she wanted to scream. She knew she should despise Mona right now—the cops had found the SUV Mona used to hit Hanna stashed in the Vanderwaals' detached garage. The car had a tarp over it, but the front fender was bashed in, and blood—Hanna's blood—was spattered on the headlights.

But Hanna couldn't hate her. She just *couldn't.* If only she could erase every good memory she had of Mona instead—their shopping sprees, their triumphant popularity coups, their Frenniversaries. Who would she consult in a wardrobe crisis? Who would she go shopping with? Who would fake-friend for her?

She pressed the bathroom's peppermint-scented guest soap to her nose, willing herself not to cry and smear all her carefully applied makeup. After she took a few cleansing, calming breaths, Hanna looked at Mona's sent-message box again. She highlighted each of the texts Mona had sent to her as A, and then hit delete all. *Are you sure you want to delete?* a screen asked. Hanna clicked yes. A garbage can lid onscreen opened and closed. If she couldn't delete their friendship, at least she could delete her secrets.

Wilden stood waiting in the foyer—he had offered to drive Hanna to the arraignment. Hanna noticed that his eyes were heavy and his mouth turned down. She wondered if he was exhausted from the weekend's activity, or if her mom had just told him about her Singapore job too. "Ready?" he asked Hanna quietly.

Hanna nodded. "But hang on." She reached into her bag and held out Mona's Android. "Present for you."

Wilden took it from her, confused. Hanna didn't bother to explain. He was a cop. He'd figure it out soon enough.

Wilden opened the squad car's passenger side and Hanna slipped in. Before they drove away, Hanna rolled back her shoulders, took a deep breath, and checked out her reflection in the visor mirror. Her dark eyes shone, her auburn hair was full of body, and the creamy foundation was still covering all of her bruises. Her face was thin, her teeth were straight, and she didn't have a single zit. The ugly, chubby seventh-grade Hanna who had haunted her reflection for weeks now was banished forever. Starting now.

She was Hanna Marin, after all. And she was fabulous.

42

DREAMS—AND NIGHTMARES—
CAN COME TRUE

Tuesday morning, Emily scratched at the back of the polka-dotted cap-sleeve dress she'd borrowed from Hanna, wishing she could've just worn pants. Next to her, Hanna was all dolled up in a red retro swing dress, and Spencer wore a sleek, savvy pin-striped suit. Aria was wearing one of her usual layered getups—a short-sleeved black bubble dress over a green thermal shirt, with thick white cable-knit tights and chic ankle boots that she said she'd bought in Spain. They all stood outside in the cold morning air in an empty lot next to the courthouse, away from the media flurry on the grand front steps.

"Are we ready?" Spencer asked, gazing around at everyone.

"Ready," Emily chanted along with the others. Slowly, Spencer stretched out a large Hefty trash bag, and the girls dropped things in, one by one. Aria threw in a *Snow White* Wicked Queen doll with *X*'s over her eyes. Hanna tossed in a crumpled-up piece of paper that said, *Feel sorry for me.* Spencer threw in the photo of Ali and Ian. They took turns pitching in all the physical things A had sent them. Their first instinct had been to burn it all, but Wilden needed it as evidence.

When it was Emily's final turn, she stared down at the last thing she held in her hands. It was the letter she had written to Ali not long after she'd kissed her in the tree house, not long before she died. In it, Emily had professed her undying love for Ali, pouring out every possible shred of emotion that existed in her body. A had written over some of the words, *Thought you might want this back. Love, A.*

"I kind of want to keep this," Emily said softly, folding up the letter. The others nodded. Emily wasn't certain that they knew what it was, but she was pretty sure they had a good idea. She let out a long, tortured sigh. All this time, a little light had been burning inside of her. She had hoped that somehow, A was Ali, and that Ali somehow wasn't dead. She knew she wasn't being rational, she knew Ali's body had been found in the DiLaurentises' backyard along with her one-of-a-kind Tiffany initial ring on her finger. Emily knew she had to let Ali go . . . but as she curled her hands around her love note, she wished she didn't have to.

"We should go in." Spencer tossed the bag in her Mercedes, and Emily followed her and the others through one of the courthouse's side doors. As they entered the wood-paneled, high-ceilinged courtroom, Emily's stomach flipped. All of Rosewood was here—her peers and teachers, her swim coach, Jenna Cavanaugh and her parents, all of Ali's old hockey friends—and they were all staring. The only person Emily didn't immediately see was Maya. In fact, she hadn't heard a word from Maya since Hanna's party on Friday night.

Emily put her head down as Wilden emerged from a group of police officers and led them to an empty bench. The air was taut with tension and smelled like various expensive colognes and perfumes. After a few more minutes, the doors slammed shut. Then the room fell into dead silence as the bailiffs brought Ian down the center aisle. Emily clasped Aria's hand. Hanna put her arm around Spencer. Ian wore an orange prison jumpsuit. His hair was uncombed and there were enormous purple circles under his eyes.

Ian walked up to the bench. The judge, a stern, balding man who wore an enormous class ring, glowered at him. "Mr. Thomas, how do you wish to plead?"

"Not guilty," Ian said in a very small voice.

A murmur went through the crowd. Emily bit down on the inside of her cheek. As she shut her eyes, she saw the horrible images again—this time with a new killer, a killer that made sense: Ian. Emily remembered seeing Ian that summer when she was Spencer's guest at the Rosewood Country Club, where Ian used to lifeguard. He'd sat atop his lifeguard stand, twirling his whistle like he didn't have a care in the world.

The judge leaned over his high perch and glared at Ian. "Because of the seriousness of this crime, and because we have deemed you a flight risk, you are to remain in jail until your pretrial hearing, Mr. Thomas." He banged his gavel and then folded his hands. Ian's head slumped down, and his attorney patted him comfortingly on the shoulder. Within seconds, he was marching out again, his hands cuffed. It was all over.

The members of the Rosewood community rose to leave. Then Emily noticed a family down front that she hadn't seen earlier. The bailiffs and cameras had blocked them. She recognized Mrs. DiLaurentis's short, chic haircut and Mr. DiLaurentis's handsome, aging leading-man looks. Jason DiLaurentis stood next to them, dressed in a crisp black suit and a dark checked tie. As the family embraced, they all looked incredibly relieved . . . and maybe the slightest bit repentant, too. Emily thought about what Jason had said on the news: *I don't talk to my family much. They're too messed up.* Maybe they all felt guilty for going so long without speaking. Or maybe Emily was just imagining things.

Everyone lingered outside the courthouse. The weather was nothing like that sublime, cloudless fall day of Ali's memorial service just weeks earlier. Today, the sky was blurred with dark clouds, making the whole world dull and shadowless. Emily felt a hand on her arm. Spencer wrapped her arms around Emily's shoulders.

"It's all over," Spencer whispered.

"I know," Emily said, hugging back.

The other girls joined in on the hug. Out of the corner of her eye, Emily saw a camera flash. She could already imagine the newspaper caption: *Alison's Friends Distraught but at Peace.* At that moment, a black Lincoln idling near the curb caught her eye. A chauffeur sat in the passenger seat, waiting. The tinted back window was rolled down the tiniest crack, and Emily saw a pair of eyes staring straight at her. Emily's mouth fell open. She'd only seen blue eyes like that one other time in her life.

"Guys," she whispered, clamping down hard on Spencer's arm.

The others broke out of their hug. "What?" Spencer asked, concerned.

Emily pointed to the sedan. The back window was now closed, and the chauffeur was shifting the car into gear. "I swear I just saw . . ." she stammered, but then paused. They'd think she was crazy—fantasizing that Ali was alive was just another way to cope with her death. Emily swallowed hard, standing up straighter. "Never mind," she said.

The girls turned away, drifting back to their own families, promising to call one another later. But Emily remained where she was, her heart pounding as the sedan pulled away from the curb. She watched as it cruised down the street, turned right at the light, and disappeared. Her blood chilled. *It couldn't have been her,* she told herself.

Could it have?

ACKNOWLEDGMENTS

First and foremost, I want to thank those I've mentioned in the dedication—the people who encouraged Spencer to kiss her sister's boyfriends, Aria to kiss her English teacher, Emily to kiss a girl (or two), and Hanna to kiss the dorky boy in school. The people who aided and abetted in Alison's murder first laughed at the phrase "Icelandic boys who ride small, chunky horses," and were excited about this project from the very beginning. I'm talking, of course, about my friends at Alloy—Lanie Davis, Josh Bank, Les Morgenstein, and Sara Shandler. Being a working writer is something of an oxymoron for most, and I am immensely appreciative for all you've done for me. I'm lucky to work with all of you, and I seriously doubt these books would be half as good without your wonderfully creative minds . . . and humor . . . and, of course, baked goods. Here's to more fabulous twists and turns in the future!

I'm grateful also to all those at Harper who champion

these books—Farrin Jacobs, for your careful reading, and Kristin Marang, for all your dedication, attention, and friendship. And a big thanks to Jennifer Rudolph Walsh at William Morris for your belief in this series' future. You are truly magical.

Love to the slew of people I mention in every book: Joel, my husband, for your ability to predict the future—strangely, it always involves tickling. To my father, Shep, because you like to impersonate French travel agents, because we thought you got lost in the desert this December, and because you once threatened to leave a restaurant because they had run out of red wine. To my sister, Ali, for creating the greatest team ever (Team Alison) and for taking pictures of Squee the stuffed lamb with a cigarette hanging out of his mouth. And to my mom, Mindy—I hope you never take a vaccine for silliness. Thank you so much for your support of all of my writing.

I also want to thank all of the Pretty Little Liars readers out there. I absolutely adore hearing from you guys, and I'm so glad you care as much about the characters as I do. Keep your amazing letters coming!

Finally, much love to my grandma, Gloria Shepard. I'm touched that you read the Pretty Little Liars series—and I'm so happy you think the books are funny! I'll try to include more jokes about nose hair in the future.

WHAT HAPPENS NEXT . . .

So after big bad Mona departed this dear world and Ian was sent away to a cold prison cell, our Pretty Little Liars were finally able to live in peace. Emily found true love at Smith College; Hanna ruled as queen bee of Rosewood Day and married a billionaire; Spencer graduated first in her class at Columbia School of Journalism and went on to be managing editor of the *New York Times*; Aria got her MFA from Rhode Island School of Design and moved to Europe with Ezra. We're talking sunsets, fat babies, and blissful happiness. Nice, huh? Oh, and none of them ever told a lie again.

Are you effing kidding me? Wake up, Sleeping Beauty. There's no happily ever after in Rosewood.

I mean, have you learned *nothing*? Once a pretty little liar, *always* a pretty little liar. Emily, Hanna, Spencer, and Aria just can't *help* but be bad. That's what I love best about them. So who am I? Well, let's just say there's a new A in town, and this time our girlies aren't getting off so easily.

See ya soon. And until then, try not to be *too* good. Life's always more fun with a few pretty little secrets.

Mwah!

—A

READ ON FOR A PREVIEW OF
PRETTY LITTLE LIARS BOOK FIVE.
FROM

Wicked

Spencer Hastings was walking with Kirsten Cullen, chattering about Youth League field hockey, when she noticed the flyer. Her mouth dropped open. "Tomorrow?"

Practically every Rosewood Day sixth grader was gathered around the bike rack, gawking at the piece of paper. Aria slid off the wall and squinted at the flyer's big block letters.

Time Capsule Starts Tomorrow, it announced. *Get ready! This is your chance to be immortalized!*

The nub of charcoal slipped from Aria's fingers. The Time Capsule game had been a school tradition since 1899, the year Rosewood Day was founded. Everyone knew the game's rules—they'd been passed down by older brothers and sisters, whispered about in DMs, and scribbled on the title pages of library books. Each year, the Rosewood Day administration cut up pieces of a Rosewood Day flag and had specially selected older students hide them in places around Rosewood. Cryptic clues leading to each piece were posted in the school lobby. Whoever found a piece was honored in an all-school assembly and got to decorate it however they wanted, and all the reunited pieces were sewn back together and buried in a time capsule behind the soccer fields. Needless to say, finding a piece of the Time Capsule flag was a *huge* deal.

"Are you going to play?" Gemma asked Emily, zipping up her Upper Main Line YMCA swimming parka to her chin.

"I guess so." Emily giggled nervously. "But do you think we have a shot? I hear they always hide the clues in the high school. I've only been in there twice."

Hanna was thinking the same thing. She hadn't even been in the high school *once*. Everything about high school intimidated her—especially the beautiful girls who went there.

The school's heavy double doors opened, and the remaining sixth graders spilled out, including a group of kids that seemed to have walked right out of a page of a J. Crew catalogue. Aria returned to the stone wall and pretended to be busy sketching. She didn't want to make eye contact with any of them again—a few days ago, Naomi Zeigler had caught her staring and cawed, "What, are you in *love* with us?" These were the sixth-grade elite, after all—or, as Aria called them, the Typical Rosewoods.

The Typical Rosewoods were such cookie cutters:

they had the exact same laughs, wore matching shades of Laura Mercier lip plumper, and carried Dooney & Bourke logo bags. If Aria squinted, she couldn't tell one Typical Rosewood from another.

Except for Alison DiLaurentis. No one mistook Alison for anyone else, ever.

And it was Alison leading the crowd down the school's stone path, her blond hair streaming behind her, her sapphire-blue eyes sparkling, her ankles steady in her three-inch platforms. Naomi Zeigler and Riley Wolfe, her two closest confidantes, followed her, hanging on her every move. People had been bowing down to Ali ever since she'd moved to Rosewood in third grade.

Ali approached Emily and the other swimmers and stopped short. Emily was afraid Ali was going to tease them—*again*—but Ali's attention was elsewhere. A sneaky smile crept over her face as she read the flyer. With a quick flip of her wrist, she tore the paper off the wall and spun around to face her friends.

"My brother's hiding one of the pieces of the flag tonight," she said, loud enough for everyone else in the commons to hear. "He already promised to tell me where it is."

Everyone began to murmur. Hanna nodded with awe—she admired Ali even more than the older cheerleaders. Spencer, on the other hand, seethed. Ali's brother wasn't supposed to *tell* her where he was hiding his Time Capsule piece. That was cheating!

The older students began to descend the high school's majestic stone steps across the commons. A tall blond junior noticed Ali and stopped. "What up, Al?"

"Nothing." Ali pursed her lips and stood up straighter. "What's up with you, *Eee*?"

Scott Chin elbowed Hanna, and Hanna blushed. With his tanned, gorgeous face, curly blond hair, and stunning, soulful hazel eyes, Ian Thomas—*Eee*—was second on Hanna's All-Time Hottie list, just under Sean Ackard, the boy she'd crushed on since they were on the same kickball team in third grade.

Ian leaned against the bike racks. "Did I hear you saying you know where a piece of the Time Capsule flag is?"

Ali's cheeks pinkened. "Why, is someone jealous?" She shot him a saucy grin.

Ian shook his head. "I'd keep it down, if I were you. Someone might try and steal your piece from you. It's part of the game, you know."

Ali laughed, as if the idea was incomprehensible, but a wrinkle formed between her eyes. Ian was right—stealing someone's piece of the flag was perfectly legal, etched in the Time Capsule Official Rule Book that Principal Appleton kept in a locked drawer of his desk. Last year, a ninth-grade goth boy had stolen a piece that was dangling out of a senior crew member's gear bag. Two years ago, an eighth-grade band girl had snuck into the school's dance studio and stolen *two* pieces from two beautiful, thin ballerinas. The Stealing Clause, as it was known, leveled the playing field even more—if you weren't smart enough to figure out the clues that would allow you to find the pieces, then maybe you were cunning enough to snag one from someone's locker.

Spencer gazed at Ali's perturbed expression, a thought slowly forming in her mind. *I should steal Ali's piece of the flag.* More than likely, everyone else in sixth grade would simply let Ali find the piece *completely unfairly*, and no one would dare to take it away from her. Spencer was tired of Ali getting everything handed to her so easily.

The same idea formed in Emily's mind. *Imagine if I stole it from Ali,* she thought, shuddering with an unidentifiable emotion. What would she say to Ali if she trapped her alone?

Could I steal it from Ali? Hanna bit an already nubby fingernail. Only . . . she'd never stolen anything in her life. If she did, would Ali invite Hanna into her circle?

How awesome would it be to steal it from Ali? Aria thought too, her hand still moving over her sketchbook. Imagine, a Typical Rosewood dethroned . . . by someone like Aria. Poor Ali would have to go searching for another piece by actually reading the clues and using her brain for once.

"I'm not worried," Ali broke the silence. "No one would dare steal it from me. Once I get the piece, it's going to be on me at all times." She gave Ian a suggestive wink, and with a flip of her skirt, she added, "The only way someone is going to get it from me is if they kill me first."

Ian leaned forward. "Well, if that's what it takes."

A muscle under Ali's eye twitched, and her skin paled. Naomi Zeigler's smile wilted. There was a chilly grimace on Ian's face, but then he flashed an irresistible *I'm just kidding* smile.

Someone coughed, making Ian and Ali look over. Ali's brother, Jason, was walking straight up to Ian from the high school steps. His mouth tight and his shoulders hunched, it seemed like Jason had overheard.

"What did you just say?" Jason stopped less than a few feet from Ian's face. A crisp wind blew a few stray golden hairs up off his forehead.

Ian rocked back and forth in his black Vans. "Nothing. We were just fooling around."

Jason's eyes darkened. "You sure about that?"

"Jason!" Ali hissed, indignant. She stepped between them. "What's up your butt?"

Jason glared at Ali, then at the Time Capsule flyer in her hand, then back at Ian. The rest of the crowd exchanged confused glances, not sure whether this was a fake fight or something more serious. Ian and Jason were the same age, and both played varsity soccer. Maybe this was a pissing contest because Ian had stolen Jason's opportunity for a goal in yesterday's game against Pritchard Prep.

When Ian didn't answer, Jason smacked his arms to

his sides. "Fine. Whatever." He wheeled around, stomped to a black, late-sixties sedan that had pulled into the bus lane, and slumped in the passenger seat. "Just go," he said to the driver as he slammed the car door. The car sputtered to life, coughed up a cloud of noxious-smelling exhaust, and squealed away from the curb. Ian shrugged and sauntered away, grinning victoriously.

Ali ran her hands through her hair. For a split second, her expression seemed a little off, like something had slipped out of her control. But it quickly passed. "Hot tub at my house?" she chirped to her posse, looping her elbow around Naomi's. Her friends followed her to the woods behind the school, a shortcut back to her house. A now-familiar piece of paper peeked out of the side pocket of Ali's yellow satchel. *Time Capsule Starts Tomorrow,* it said. *Get ready.*

Get ready, indeed.

A few short weeks later, after most of the Time Capsule pieces were found and buried, the members of Ali's inner circle changed. All of a sudden, the regulars were ousted, and others took their places. Ali had found four new BFFs—Spencer, Hanna, Emily, and Aria.

None of Ali's new friends questioned why she'd chosen *them* out of the entire sixth-grade class—they didn't want to jinx things. Now and then, they thought about pre-Ali moments and how miserable they'd been. They thought about specific moments, too, including that day Time

Capsule was announced. Once or twice they recalled what Ian had said to Ali, and how uncharacteristically worried Ali had seemed. Very little fazed her, after all.

For the most part, they shrugged off thoughts like that—it was more fun to think about their future than dwell on the past. They were now *the* girls of Rosewood Day.

But maybe they shouldn't have forgotten that day so quickly. And maybe Jason should've tried a bit harder to keep Ali safe. Because, well, we all know what happened. Just a short year and a half later, Ian made good on his promise.

He killed Ali for real.